STORMS OVER SKAILL

A NOVEL OF THE VIKINGS IN ORKNEY

H.A. DOUGLAS

Copyright Hrolf Douglasson (writing as H.A. Douglas) 2007

The right of Hrolf Douglasson (writing as H.A. Douglas) to be recognised as the author of this work has been asserted by him in accordance with the Copyright, Designs and Patents Act 1988.

All rights reserved. No part of this publication may be reproduced, stored inor introduced into a retrieval system, or transmitted, in any form or by any means (electronic, mechanical, photocopying, recording or otherwise), without the prior written permission of the author. Any person who does any unauthorised act in relation to this publication may be liable to criminal prosecution and civil claims for damages.

A CIP catalogue record for this book is available from the British Library.

This book is sold subject to the condition that it shall not, by way of trade or otherwise, be lent, resold, hired out or otherwise circulated without the author's prior consent in any form of binding or cover other than that in which it is published and without a similar condition including this condition being imposed on the subsequent purchaser.

This book is dedicated to my wife and children, who in 2004 came northwards with me to make a new home in a whole new world.

INTRODUCTION

This is a novel inspired by archaeology. Orkney occupies a rare niche within Viking-Age studies in that the main document from the period, *Orkneyinga Saga*, is often capable of having its accuracy demonstrated by material finds in the soils and shorelines of the islands. The action of this book takes place at one such site.

The remains at Skaill in Deerness were uncovered by the then resident farmer on his discovering traces of walls in the sand when he was merely attempting to remove this material in the early 1960's. Excavations led by Dr. Peter Gelling (published by Buteux) on a number of sites across the property revealed a complex site right on the edges of the land and stretching inland across the line of the modern road that passes the farmstead. The initial settlement appeared to have consisted of a couple of typically Pictish roundhouses that fell out of use but were subsequently refurbished and brought back into use; at around the same time, a little complex of square or sub-rectangular buildings were erected somewhat to the north. One of these showed traces of metalworking.

Slightly later still, another building, rectangular in form and showing wall-benches and a central hearth along its main axis, went up in the lee of a ridge between the farmland and the beach. This appeared to represent a new focus for the settlement: it was rebuilt at least twice, and eventually grew enough to be considered a proper Norse longhall. Now the Saga re-enters the picture, for one Thorkell, who was farming at Sandwick in Deerness around the year 1020 AD, saw fit to murder an Earl at his house, and this largest dwelling would certainly have been considered fit for an Earl to visit. A century or so later, the infamous Svein Asleifarsson is recorded as visiting the area to intercede in a dispute between a kinswoman and her neighbour: either of these, too, might have been living at Skaill. But these are tales for another time: this book takes us back to the period of that initial settlement, its roundhouses and its cluster of little huts and workshops. The time when the Pictish culture was still dominant throughout Orkney – although unbeknownst to the Picts, they were already on the wane. Times were changing; storms were coming.

SPRING, 902 A.D.

CHAPTER ONE

The sea came rolling in, washing the feet of the girl and the little boy who walked along its edge. Further out, mist sat atop the waves, contrasting with the bright blue of a cloudless early-summer sky above it. To their other side, above the edge of the dunes, the long grass of home could be seen waving in the wind that always seemed to be tugging at hair and clothing, whatever the time of day or the time of year. In between, on the damp boundary where the two walked, the sea threw up its flotsam and the wind sent sand down to bury it all.

The girl, whose name was Rilca and who was around fourteen or fifteen years of age, watched her small cousin as he scampered around examining anything and everything he found. She was at the very end of her childhood now, strong enough now to handle any of the tools that kept the fields free of weeds and to push the animals wherever it was needful to send them. Morgan by contrast was barely six, she thought, and was just setting out to explore the world in ways that only a child can. So Rilca watched him play among the sand and the shells and the seaweed, and did so with mixed emotions. She envied his freedom, the set of the world that allowed him to fill his days with fun and interest. Yet she also found herself thinking that he ought to be doing something more useful at the same time, such as looking for shellfish or collecting driftwood. She felt certain that her own childhood had contained an element of work since its earliest days, for all that she couldn't exactly remember having any such responsibilities. But everyone had to work, didn't they? So her aunt Olwen and her uncle Drosten kept saying, usually when they needed her to do something for them. Such as keeping an eye on Morgan. Not that she minded: it was better than the work around the farm, which was harder, went on for longer, and frequently involved dung in one way or another. But since poor old Cerwed had died last winter, she was acting as nursemaid to him more often: his own mother's back was more useful in the fields, especially now that spring was upon them.

She stared unseeing out to sea as these thoughts all tumbled through her head, her dark red hair whipping around her pale, freckled face with its high cheekbones and narrow chin; the sounds of the seabirds went unheard in her ears. Green eyes gazed at the shifting mists, but could not decide whether she would rather be out here with Morgan, or doing *real* work with her foster-parents, for all that her arms, legs and back always ached afterwards. And then, suddenly, Morgan was tugging at her woollen dress, his grey eyes wide with excitement and his strangely fair hair blowing wispy in the wind.

"Rilca, come *on!* I've found something: didn't you hear me shouting?"

She smiled down. "No, cousin, I didn't. Come on then, you show me what it is."

Morgan led her along the beach, pulling at her shawl until she was more stumbling along after the boy than walking, towards a point where the waves had carved the beginnings of a tiny cove. It would never get any larger: they never did, being just the products of fickle winds and changeable tides. But this time, the disturbance in the smooth curve of the sandy bay had lasted long enough. Pushed hard into the sand, their length still mostly covered in water, were two long, thick posts of wood.

"I bet they'll last forever on the fire!" Morgan was saying excitedly. "D'you think Father will be pleased?"

Rilca went closer, dipping her shoes in the cold spring surf, and bent to inspect the treasures. "I'm not sure we'll be burning these, little one: come see, they're carved all over." She idly ran a finger along an incised line that curved down the length of the timber, one of many that writhed and twisted and knotted around each other. "These aren't just driftwood," she pronounced after a minute. She looked out along their length, absently gnawing at her lower lip as she thought. "They're big enough to hold a house up: you and I between us couldn't lift them."

"So what do we do?"

Rilca stood up. Something about these posts did not feel at all right or comforting. "We go tell your father, Morgan, that's what we do. We let him decide what happens about them."

CHAPTER TWO

Drosten had already been in his late thirties when he had married Olwen, and it had not been long after that when Morgan had appeared, much to everyone's surprise. It was odd, he thought, how everybody kept on being amazed by the things that happened to him: there had been a similar response when they had married in the first place. Yet it had almost been inevitable that they would, if only to keep the complex forces of tribal and clan dynamics under control. She had been widowed, and then left with her dead sister's child - and a girl child at that –

for a good few years. Everybody had agreed that that was a lot of influence and stability sitting around unused, and Olwen herself had been eager enough to find another husband once the shock of Uoret's death had abated. Drosten had been the only unmarried man within the clan that lived around the shores; their eventual union had been, he reckoned, prety much inevitable. And it had been a good match: they had got on well, and those initial feelings had deepened into the respect and tolerance that older newlyweds find more comfortable than the raw, wilder passions of youth. People had expressed astonishment at that too, he recalled. It seemed to have become something of a tradition.

And now, here were more wonders and causes for amazement. He stood with Rilca and Morgan, along with a couple of his farmhands, and stared at the timbers sitting in their salty bath. One hand idly scratched a cheek, a sure sign to those that knew him of worry and uncertainty in the face of a big decision. He frowned in thought.

"Well," he said at last, "you were right, little daughter. They're not just loose branches, are they?"

As she always did, Rilca chose not to argue over the fact that she was not his blood-daughter: he had always been kind and considerate towards her, and she figured he deserved a little leeway to keep things that way. But she drew the line at returning the favour: she always had, but he didn't seem to mind.

"What do you think they might be, then?" she asked. "Have you ever seen anything like them before?"

"No, I haven't," he admitted. "But from the style of those carvings, I'd say they're not from around here." His dark eyes brightened. "If that's the case, perhaps we could burn them after all! Who's going to miss them, eh?"

He wandered out into the shallow surf, peering more closely at the patterns cut into the wood. The timber itself was swollen from its immersion in the salt water but the designs had been carved deep. Clutches of lines ran in sinuous curves, seemingly at random, filling every last space they could. There had to be some sort of meaning in all that, Rilca thought; it would have been too much work for anyone to make it all and *not* intend it to mean something. But to her eyes it was all just a jumbled mess of lines and loops...

"Oh!" she exclaimed suddenly, jumping up and back. "There's an eye!"

"What, a real one?" asked Drosten, surprised. "I think I've found traces of paint on it, too. Come on, then, show me where this eye is."

Rilca touched it hesitantly. It was only carved, a part of the design, but eyes meant animals or men, which somehow changed the whole thing from a mild curiosity to something tangible, meaningful.

"Why, so it is," murmured Drosten, coming to stand beside her. To her other side, young Morgan watched the posts from half-behind her dress, clutching the pale mauve fabric with its counter-coloured warp threads as if trying to hide. Rilca wondered if perhaps he was regretting his discovery. Well, she decided, it was a little late for that. But she thought she knew how her little cousin felt.

"Look there," Drosten was saying. "There's its breast, and a leg... and is that something else caught in its mouth?" He scratched his cheek again. "It's not like any carving I've ever seen. Not that I've seen all that much, of course, but what there is in these parts has the proper markings, the signs of land and power, and things you can see without having your eyeballs nearly twisted out in the looking!" He chuckled. "They're funny old things, and no mistake. Going to be heavy, too. I think we might need a few more of us and some good lines before we try moving 'em."

"So do we leave them here, then?" asked one of his men. Drosten shook some drops of seawater from the hem of his long robe, and hitched his cloak back over his shoulder before he answered.

"I think so, yes. We can come back in the evening, perhaps, rather than take people away from the work in the middle of the day. I've taken too many of you away from scattering that seed already, and it looks to me as if there's a while before we have any lambs out. Couple of days at any rate, I reckon." He looked again at the posts. "Hard to imagine that anyone's going to come looking for them out here, isn't it?" He reached out a hand to ruffle his son's hair. "Well found, young Morgan! And good advice you had from Rilca, too. Fine, fine children, the both of you." He smiled at them in a paternally friendly sort of way. "What else do you think you might find for us today?"

"I think mussels or spoots might be more help than these old logs," decided Morgan.

"Well come along, then," suggested Rilca as the men turned away and headed back to the house. "We know some good places for shellfish, don't we? Let's go see what we can find."

The girl and her charge turned their own backs to the logs, and headed further along the beach towards the south and into the prevailing wind, towards the cliff and a tumble of jagged rocks that pushed out into the ocean and marked the end of the easy walking along the beach. Beyond those rocks, out to the east, the black bulks of the two outer islands reared sheer and dark from the sea. Neither of them noticed the smaller dark shape in the north, far out to sea and obscured by the mist.

CHAPTER THREE

Olwen watched as her children came running back towards the cluster of little round and squared houses that made up her clan's home. Around her, the servants and farmhands went about their usual tasks; further off, the sheep bleated, the cattle lowed and the pigs squealed with joy as their next meal approached. The air was heavy with aromas of dung, seaweed, salt and burning peat around her, yet Olwen's attention remained firmly set on her returning brood. There should have been more, she reflected, but life had not turned out that way. None had survived through infancy from her first marriage to Nechton, but she had taken Rilca in after *her* mother's death, and at least now there was Morgan, the second to bear the name. Drosten had been happy about that, she remembered – and so had she, when he was born healthy and whole, and had lived long enough to get his baptism. Since then they had all thrived in this place, and she was happy enough with her life. So she waited patiently as her single offspring and her niece came hurtling towards her, and spread her arms wide to wrap them in her long shawl when they reached her side.

"They're bringing them up," panted Rilca in her excitement. "They're big, aunt, big, long, heavy posts of wood! And whether they're carved all over or not, I'm reckoning they'll burn for a long, long time!"

Olwen smiled down at her. "If they've been at sea, little one, we'll have to let them dry out first."

Morgan looked around. "Where shall we put them?"

"Well now, there's a question!" Olwen stroked her narrow, angular chin with long, thin fingers as she considered. "There's the problem that wherever we want to put them, if they're as big as you both say they are, we might have to cut them up before we can put them anywhere! Maybe we'll just lay them by the side of the house and put a shelter over them. That might be easiest of all."

"It was me that found them," announced Morgan firmly, as if staking some sort of claim on the timber. Olwen smiled down at him.

"Yes, so you said, over and over. We all know it, now." Rilca smiled wryly and her aunt winked back at her.

"Come on," said Morgan suddenly, "let's go meet them before they get here."

"We could take a jug down," suggested Rilca. Olwen disentangled herself from her children and wrapped the shawl tighter around her arms.

"Alright then: go and tell Danna to bring one out, would you? Morgan and I will start off."

She let the lad pull her along gently by the edge of her shawl, out of the slight hollow between the buildings and up towards the long grass at the top of the dunes. She could already hear the grunts and slow chants of the men as they heaved their burden homeward. What *could* Morgan have found? The only wood they ever got from the sea in these parts came in odd little branches now and again, more useful for kindling and feeding the peat than for making a fire on its own. But this find sounded altogether different. Olwen mistrusted surprises, whatever form they took, and this definitely counted as one to be wary of until they understood it properly. But Drosten was not always one for understanding. He could be impatient sometimes, although never with the children, not even Rilca, who was approaching the age where she sometimes needed a lot of patience. Well, there was no use wondering idly: the answer to a lot of her questions lay just beyond that sandy ridge.

Morgan let go of her shawl and ran down to greet his father. Olwen watched as the lad was caught in Drosten's arms and spun around; then her eyes found the timbers at the centre of all this activity. The children had been right: they were massive, the sort of thing that held up the roofs of her own home. At that comparison, something tugged at a memory, but she could not pull it out enough to examine it. Her brows furrowed in thought, but it would not come just yet. Maybe later. She carried on down the slope.

"Well," smiled her husband, "what do you say to these?"

Olwen looked long and hard at the soaked, shiny posts. There were the carvings, all twisted and looping around and around; there were holes at one end, as if pegs had been driven through them at some time. The other ends were plain, unadorned, and a little darker than the rest of the wood, although that might just be the effects of the tides on them, she supposed.

Drosten watched her face carefully. "You seen this sort of thing before?" he asked. "You have that look, as if something's familiar but you can't quite place it."

She looked over at him. "How well you know me after our years together, hmm? I'm sure the memory will come: but not yet. Rilca should be coming with a jug for you all; then we can get these up to the house. I think they'll have to lay outside, though; I can't see how we're ever going to get them into the house without cutting them up."

"They're too wet to do that; will be for a while, I'd say. So out by the wall it is, then." Drosten turned to his men. "Come on lads, just a little further. If we can get them to the ridge, we'll stop for that jug, alright?"

CHAPTER FOUR

Olwen woke in the middle of the night with images of carvings and spiralled animals intertwining in a tangle of lines that pulled the eyes out of their usual habits. She *had* seen those designs before: she knew she had. And now, in the dark of the house, when the only noises were those of the wind in the rafters and the slow cooling of the fire in its pit, she thought she could remember where.

Slowly, carefully, she slid out of her bed. Across the hearth, Drosten shifted, his gentle snoring continuing undisturbed; in their own little alcoves further away from the fireside, the children also slumbered on. The bare earth floor was warm under her feet, but she knew it would be colder outside, and so she peered in the fire's dim glow for her shoes before going any further.

The house was small compared to many, sleeping only her immediate family: the others who lived and worked these lands had a cluster of newer buildings a short way to the north, but she had been unwilling to give up the old house. She reckoned that its smallness also kept it warm and snug even through the coldest of winter nights, when the sun barely shone and the wind howled with rain and ice in its teeth. Dug into the soil so that the roof almost reached the ground outside, it presented little resistance to the gales from the sea, and its pair of more-or-less circular shapes, joined together at a single place with a little passage between them, helped deflect the storms as well. But what Olwen needed to look at lay out in the open, in the dark of the night and laid hard against the outer wall of that next room across. It had taken a lot of sweat and effort to bring them here: almost the whole farmstead had come to lend their muscle as the posts were carried, rolled, and finally manhandled up against the outer wall of the house. There had been plenty of time to look them over then, and Olwen had done so. But that had been curiosity, and caught up in the excitement of the find. Since then, though, a memory had been tugging at her.

    The sensible thing would be to wait until morning, when there would be daylight and other people around to talk it over with. But Olwen decided she could not wait for dawn, and that she did not want to discuss her thoughts and worries just yet. Better to go out and make certain first, or at least be less unsure, perhaps. The only thing she had to compare these carved pillars with was her own dreaming thoughts, after all. But they certainly weren't of local origin. They were too strange, too alien in their designs. The pillar that held the centre of her own roof up was plain and unadorned, but these newcomers looked the right sort of size to be roof-posts.

    She knew also that she would never get back to sleep, having woken so suddenly with those images in her brain. Far better to go and lay her fears to rest, and then come back to the warmth of her bed and hope to get a little more slumber.

    She slipped past her inner curtain and padded quietly across the single room. The outer door was kind enough not to screech on its whalebone socket as she pulled it open, and she was outside. The light was enough to see by: the night was clear, with thousands upon thousands of stars shining high above her. She quickly crossed the yard and stood over the newly-discovered pillars. Silently, her eyes followed the lines as they turned into snakes, birds, fish; here and there among the writhing shapes, were little men – or goblins, perhaps, grasping whatever portion of anatomy happened to be within reach as it snaked past, with whichever limb happened to be available. There was hardly any bare surface left, so intensely were these timbers decorated.

As her eye traced the shapes, her mind went back and unlocked the memory. Five years or so ago and newly widowed, she had been looking for something to believe in, looking for reason and purpose to her life. As was the custom, her husband's nephew had inherited his lands, and Olwen had chosen to return to those of her own family. But that summer had been one of distractions, of changes. There had been strangers in the land, too, and she had, for a number of reasons, spent a good many days and nights among them. She had been entertained by them, given a fair hearing, negotiated with as befitted a woman of their people... and then the world had turned again. They had turned back into strangers, of whom she had no more understanding the she had of the seals that basked on her shores. Strangers who, like those selkies, travelled oversea; had sailed westwards in long, graceful ships and came ashore to put up tents, from which they traded, bartered, bought, sold... stole, raped, pillaged, seduced, even killed on occasion. Tents with frames carved and painted in the same frenetic style as these two posts that had come washing up on her shoreline. Tents and pillars that also reflected the fierce animals carved into the prows of their ships.

Olwen took a deep couple of breaths. She tore her eyes from the posts and stared hard at the rough stonework of the wall against which she suddenly found herself leaning. She could answer the question of who these had come from, even if the where and the why of it still defied her, and the pain those memories brought was enough to leave her breathless and doubled over in deep, soul-searing remembrance. But even that one answer was perhaps one too many.

Drosten would have to be told: but perhaps he need not be told everything, at least not yet. Plans would have to be made, though, and tasks allocated, a strategy decided upon. For suddenly, this was a problem that the burning of these pillars would not remove. If anything, she suspected, such an action would make matters much, much worse.

These were pillars carved by Norsemen.

CHAPTER FIVE

In the cold dawn of the following day, a ship sat rocking in the waves a short way from the shoreline. It was long, but broader than a *drakkar:* the sort of vessel that could turn its hand to buying and selling merchandise as easily as it could to sneaking in and taking whatever its masters felt they needed. From the shelter of the top-strakes, eyes full of uncharacteristic concern and apprehension peered landwards, searching, seeking – and not finding what they were looking for.

The lady Ragna turned slightly to regard her husband with a somewhat jaundiced eye. "I said you put them over the side too early on, Einar," she chuckled, brushing a stray lock of her fine blonde hair back under its headscarf. "I'm sure there was something said about actually being able to see the land before setting them on their way."

"Oh be quiet," grumbled the object of her gentle scorn. "Arguing about it doesn't make things any better right now, does it? And I reckoned we were close enough to have seen the shoreline before that mist came down."

He turned from his ardent searching of the sand-dunes and regarded his wife, his companions, and the unruly mountain of bundles and belongings that contributed nothing helpful to the ship's sailing characteristics. "You all know that this is a serious business," he pronounced gravely. "By putting the pillars of the old house over the side, we entrusted our fortunes to the wisdom of the Gods. Where they go, we settle; it's not as if we could've stayed where we were anyway, now is it? Not with Harald's men gobbling up all the farmlands and scats they can lay their grubby hands on." He sighed. "There's no good men left in the district any more: what's the use in hanging around just to draw this new king's attention, eh? All the words I've heard about him suggest he's easier to anger than he is to please, and that he works out his rages in advance when he sees somebody that needs to be got rid of. Altogether less friendly and more ambitious than his fathir Halfdan ever was. I didn't want our heads to be the next ones in the noose."

"None of which answers our immediate problem of where those same posts have gone," pointed out Ragna.

Einar grunted. "By all accounts, I did everything properly. I said the right sort of words, I put ale over them, I heaved them over the side where the tides could catch them and bring them to shore. Then we put the sail down, shipped the oars, and drifted along after them. We rode the same currents: they ought to be around here somewhere." He pushed himself away from the rail and came to a decision. "We'll put the oars out again, and follow the coast for a bit. Perhaps the tides shift things around this close to the shore."

"More likely that you've gone and got it wrong somehow," replied Ragna darkly.

Einar chose the calculated risk of ignoring her in preference to continuing the discussion. "Jump to it!" he growled at the knot of men who shared the ship with his own family. There was little room for maneouvre: there were around twenty of them in total, and the boat only measured forty feet or so from stem to stern. At the styrbord, his brother-in-law Havard looked for instruction.

"Row slowly, boys," Einar decided, "and keep us this far from the shoreline, or as close as you can." He turned to the handful of women and children. "Some of you come to the side here, and keep a lookout for those posts, y'hear? The rest ought to stay outboard, and stop us tipping over with all this mess trying to unbalance us."

"Aye, lord," came the answer in a ragged chorus, as they picked their way over the baggage. There was no deck to speak of: in loading the ship so full, Einar had found it needful to take the planks out and leave them behind. On the four-day journey from their homeland in More, everyone had nestled in among the bundles and the bulkier items, and made their beds as best they could. Consequently they were all short on sleep, and full of aches. But Einar was their master, and they all knew that their own bad tempers lost any significance in relation to his.

The coast passed slowly, the oarsmen barely

taking the ship faster than the current. Time dragged on, but all eyes stayed at their work, scanning the rocks and coves as they gave way to a broad, sandy bay, then staring along the shore for any signs of their missing cargo. Then one of the bondswomen, Thora, pointed and said, "the sand in there looks messed up, lord..."

Einar swiftly moved to her side, and found himself in agreement. "Back-stroke!" he yelled hoarsly to the rowers. "Havard, can you take us closer? Beach us if you have to: we need to go look at this anyway, I think." His styrsman nodded, his fine, light hair catching the fitful sunlight as it struggled through the clouds. Einar gripped the top-strake, his face set hard, his eyes like flakes of grim, grey steel. Ragna got up from where she had settled against a bale of cloth and came to stand beside him. She did not care for his being around the bondswomen of the house even when she was nearby, and although he had never admitted anything, and she could never prove anything, she remained certain that at least some of the brats aboard this vessel were his.

"I see what she means," she murmured, following his gaze. "That looks like..."

"Like someone dragged two pillars out of the sea, and over the sand to their own house," finished Einar in a grating growl. "Well, if the Thunderer has chosen to let these people take him home, then clearly he wants us to follow." He frowned slightly, tufty brows closing over keen, clouded eyes. "I wasn't expecting to find people here; had it in my head that we'd find new land, untouched. Instead..." his voice tailed off and he lapsed into thought.

"And are you planning to take that home from them, whoever they are?" asked his wife with a touch of worry in her voice.

"We'll see," answered her husband non-comittally. "But I'm not ruling it out – especially if they want the wood for some other purpose than holding a respectable roof up."

"I don't follow, husband."

Einar grunted a laugh. "Do you see any trees hereabouts, Ragna?"

"No, but what of it?"

Einar raised an incredulous eyebrow. "What are they using for firewood then, hmm?"

The look of shock and horror on her face brought a smile to his own craggy visage.

CHAPTER SIX

Einar, Havard and a couple of the other men stood on the sand, staring at the long, deep gashes that led along the shore and then turned up towards the dunes. Around those marks, the sand had been churned up and dug into over and over again, as if feet or hooves had repeatedly pushed into it as a large, heavy object had been dragged away from the beach. Havard looked over at his sister's husband, and then back out to where the boat sat heavy in the waves that pushed onto the shore. From the top-strake, anxious faces could be seen staring back at them.

"Well, I reckon that seals it, then..."

Einar nodded. "Hard to draw any other conclusion, ain't it? The roof-posts *did* come ashore here, and some other bastard's taken them before we could follow."

Havard smiled mercilessly and fingered the long knife that hung along his waistline. "But they left us a path to follow..."

"Aye, that they did. Back to the boat, then: we'll get the rest of the boys together and dig out the weapons. Then we'll follow this trail and see what we find." He looked skyward. "I reckon there's enough of the day left to do it in."

"Want to go further now and see how far it is?"

Einar spat. "I don't think it'll be too long a walk: my guess would be to find some houses just beyond these dunes here. They've got to be living pretty close by; else how would they have ever spotted our pillars, eh? That suggests they're shore-looking folk by habit, and that in turn suggests to me that they don't live very far away at all." He looked up at the tops of the sandy ridges. "No, I think I'll wait until we have our full strength here before I go any closer to 'em. Probability is that we've already been seen, if you think about it: if they spotted the pillars, they can't have missed us, surely? So we go back for the lads and the spears. Then we can climb these slopes and see what lies beyond."

CHAPTER SEVEN

To a visitor's eyes, the homestead of Drosten and Olwen appeared as two distinct settlements. Northwards, a cluster of little square-shaped buildings suggested dwellings and workshops; to the south, all that showed was a pair of grassy, close-set, flattened-out cones poking out of the ground. Only if a visitor went closer could the low stone walls be seen beneath these roofs, and then that newcomer really had to search for the entrances, which were guarded by solid wooden doors. The ground between all these buildings was a good couple of bowshots, Einar reckoned, and the same from where he stood at the edge of the dunes to the foot-worn path that wandered from roundhouses to square sheds. The whole area was trampled level and clean, free of any grass or weeds, but still mostly sand rather than soil. The good growing fields apparently lay further inland, but the homes stood here, between the crops and the sea, on the land that refused to produce anything of worth apart from people.

Einar stopped at the settlement's entrance from the sea. There was no home-field that he could discern, no marker-posts around the houses, although he admitted to himself that such things might be further afield if this was a rich place. He stood, outwardly relaxed and at ease, whilst he waited for his sight to clear, and the sound of hoarse, heavy breathing in his ears to subside. Despite the clouds and the breeze that had followed him and his men from the ship, he was hot in his iron helmet and his mailshirt. The leather tunic he wore beneath the rings only served to keep the heat close to his body, whilst his head felt as if it were boiling. The weight of his round shield across his back was telling on his spine – as was the byrnie – and his sword bumped awkwardly against his thigh at every step. Nevertheless, he had kept taking those steps, his eyes fixed on the trail left by his missing roof-timbers, his mind fixed on the absolute need not to falter or fall on his arse in front of his household, however hard the going might become. This far from familiar territory, rebellion was only a single slip away, and Einar was too set on his wyrd to even consider such an eventuality.

Now, as he stood at the edge of the houses and waited for his shipmates to catch up, he leaned on his spear and allowed himself a slight smile of triumph as he cautiously surveyed the scene. Where was everyone? This many houses ought to hold, what, twenty or so people at the very least; before he had left More for the last time, he had known farmers cram twice that number into their byres and sheds during the busy times, like in the spring when flocks were clipped before being moved to the upper pastures, in the autumn when the crops were gathered in, and whenever the king's reeve came sniffing for scat. He could not believe that his arrival had gone unnoticed: he had caught glimpses of movement in the dunes around him as they had trudged up the strand, and he didn't for a moment believe they had all been due to hares or seabirds. Nor had he seen any reason to be particularly quiet in his approach: let these thieves of his precious pillars hear him coming – and let them tremble in their little houses! Besides which, there was smoke coming out of a couple of these strange, short huts with their shaggy roofs. So there were people here, then. Better, in that case, to stand here a while and let the lads reform, before going any closer. Inside, he was getting frantic with concern to discover what had become of his beloved roof-timbers, those posts which had held his father's – and *his* father's – house up; but he had also learned long ago that a calm exterior outweighed any amount of worry.

   Havard came up beside him, having read his brother-in-law's thoughts more-or-less rightly. "Think there's enough of us to take this place?"

   "Aye, if we need to. I'd rather find out who they are and what's happened to the posts before we start killing people, though."

   Havard grinned. "That's only wise, I'd say. If they know how things work around here, it'd save a lot of effort if we kept 'em alive and helpful."

"All the same, I'm not standing around all day waiting for them to show themselves," Einar decided after a while. "Take a couple of the lads and see if you can find our pillars, eh? Go north, up to that little group of houses, where the smoke's coming from. We'll come along behind and keep some bows at the draw in case of trouble – so don't pick Thorstein among your crew."

Havard nodded and silently pointed fingers at Thorolf and Gisli, beckoning them forward. Einar reached out a hand for a bowstave, which was duly supplied. Beside him as he bent and strung it, lean, thin Thorstein pulled an arrow from his quiver and fitted it to his own bow.

Havard only covered a few paces before a voice called from among the houses. All movement stopped; eyes searched every corner, every hidden place, looking for the speaker. After a brief pause, a man with dark, piercing eyes, greying hair and dressed in a long shirt that reached to his ankles with a cloak thrown over the top, came into view.

"My name is Drosten," he announced, "and I am the master in these lands. I have other men with me, who I will keep concealed for now, until I have your names and your business here." He looked past Havard towards Einar, who stood out somewhat on account of being the only man there wearing any sort of armour beyond the almost mandatory leather cap. "I take it you lead these men?" Drosten called. "Come forward then, so we can discuss whatever it is you're wanting hereabouts without having to shout."

"Think that counts as an invitation?" wondered Einar quietly. Beside him, Thorstein shrugged. "I wouldn't know, lord: I didn't understand a word of what was said."

"I did: but then, I've been around here in years gone by. I wonder how many of the lads caught any of it? Keep that arrow ready," the lord continued, as he handed back the bow, settled his spear on a shoulder and strode forwards. He had the uncomfortable sensation of unseen eyes fixed upon his every move. As he reached Havard, that worthy fell in unasked beside him.

The two men stopped about an arm's length from Drosten, who stood silently, his arms folded, regarding them from rich brown eyes set in a craggy, squared-off sort of face. Both his hair and his beard were longer and thicker than the Norsemen's, but they seemed to suit him. Clearly getting on in years, he still stood straight and tall. Einar could not see any weapons on him, in contrast to his own men who positively bristled with knives, spears and axes. The ship-master regarded Drosten for a moment, and nodded imperceptibly, a slight smile on his lips.

"I am Einar, formerly of the region known as More, along the North Way. This is my wife's brother, Havard. We have reason to believe you hold some property of mine, and we have come to get it back." He tried hard not to show the relief he felt at finding native words coming so easily to his tongue, or the concern at the chance of conversations getting harder as time went on.

Drosten raised an eyebrow. "Hard to imagine what sort of property you're speaking of, friend."

"Oh, you'd know it if you saw it. Them, rather, since there are two. Large timber pillars, all carved and painted; the sort that you might use to hold a roof up."

"I see. Valuable to you, are they?"

Einar snorted a laugh. "If you're looking to get a ransom from us for them, think again. They hold a different value altogether." He swung the spear off his shoulder and thumped its butt into the sandy ground. "I followed tracks from your beach down there, so I'm certain they came this way. But perhaps down to those other buildings. We came this way seeking someone to ask about them."

Drosten managed a smile. "You have keen eyes, sea-rover, and a sharp mind, then."

"I notice you're not denying that you have them. If they are here, and they're safe, I will thank you for bringing them ashore for me; I might even consider giving a gift for such good care."

Drosten shrugged. "If I had realised their owners would come looking for them, I would've left them on the sand, and saved you the trouble of hauling them back to your ship again."

"Ah, well now, there's the thing, you see. These posts weren't just lost off the ship: I sent them overboard deliberately. I sent them into the waves and the currents so that the Gods would send them ashore, and show me where to build my own house in these lands. That's how we decide such things when we have to leave our old homes and make new ones. And here they are, all snug and ready to be put up again." Einar grinned. "So you won't have to help us carry them away after all. Here is where I am told to build my home, and here is where it *will* be built. Whether you want it here or not, it will be built. I've not come this far just to be turned away, old man: you can be friend, and profit from my wealth and my coming here, or you can be against me, and suffer for it." He smiled again suddenly. "But I'd rather not be making threats at all! Surely we could be neighbours, in the fullness of time? Come, then, are you ready to discuss that gift I offered earlier?"

CHAPTER EIGHT

Drosten seemed to have aged years in just an afternoon as he sat by the fireside, staring into the flames. Around him, Olwen, their children and their servants clustered as close as they could, seeking a share of the light, the warmth and any comfort that happened to be going spare. Not that there was very much for anyone of that last commodity.

"Well, at least you got rid of them for tonight," Olwen said reassuringly, reaching out to lay a hand on her husband's arm. "It bought us a little time, Drosten, and Maelchon should be well on his way to the king by now. At least we were able to do that much, even if we couldn't just send them away at spearpoint. Help will come soon; I can't imagine a man like Bridei taking this sort of thing without a fight."

The old man managed a smile. "You're right, of course: we just have to hang on for a few days, until our king gets his warband together and comes to our rescue." He raised his eyebrows in thought. "It's hard to believe we're the first to have had this sort of thing come to pass, isn't it? What with the Northmen coming and going every summer, I suppose it was only a matter of time before some of them started thinking about stopping here permanently. Perhaps the land is better here than in whatever hell it is they come from."

"It is," murmured Olwen, her mind once more turning back the years and remembering her time among these strange, barbaric, dangerous folk. "I recall them saying how much of it is mountain: huge, high walls of rock and stone, and how all their homes cluster at the bottom of these walls, between the stone and the sea, which pushes far into the country in long, deep lochs. I was curious," she retorted to the looks around the fire at her. "I had no husband then, and I thought it worth getting to know these strangers – and it's just as well I did, now, isn't it?"

"That depends on just how well you chose to know them," murmured Drosten.

"This is still my house, Drosten, and my family's children will inherit here, not yours," she replied sharply. "Now if we are to see these monsters off we must be strong, and close to each other, not looking for ways to distance ourselves. I still say that my memories might yet come in useful, and the hows and whys of my coming by them are none of your business. And that goes for all of you," she added, looking around the crowded house. There were silent nods and murmurs of acceptance.

"Well then," said Drosten after an awkward pause, "what else can you tell us of use right now, wife of mine?"

Olwen racked her brains, but now she had everybody's eyes upon her, thoughts would not come. "Nothing at the moment," she admitted eventually. "It was a good few years ago, and a lot has happened since that pushes much of what went on out of my mind. But I'll keep trying to remember."

"What we can do, and ought to do, is get the weapons out and ready," suggested Drosten. "I was able to bluff them today, but that won't work a second time. When they come next, I'll have to have men really hidden, with sharp edges waiting." He looked at his farmhands. "So go and sharpen your spears, all of you. Have your knives ready, and your bowstrings dry and waxed. Tomorrow's going to get nasty, but I'll not just stand aside and let these brutes take this land." He looked over towards Olwen. "Whatever else, I owe you better than to let that happen."

Olwen looked over at him worriedly. "Do you think we have enough men to hold them off? How many might there be, I wonder?"

"I suppose we can pull together around a dozen, maybe fifteen, spears," replied her husband, counting men in his mind's eye. "Some of us have bows as well, of course, and they're even more useful, in many ways. If I hold a core of spears around me out in the open, we can put the archers in doorways and hidden places all around. That would be our best plan, I think. The most danger to these newcomers, and the least exposure for us."

"Except for those of you out in the middle with your spears," answered Olwen. "I can see you and them catching the worst of anything that comes the other way. Did you not say that they had archers as well?"

"It can't be helped," Drosten said with a sad little smile. "There's always a price to pay, somewhere."

"Then I say, keep the price as low as you can. These are my lands and my folk too: I'll come and share any danger there is, and sit beside you. Talk first: see what they want, and then how much less than that they'll actually accept. It might still happen that we and they can come to an arrangement: they must be skilled men, good with dealing and farming; and sailing, come to that. They'd be useful to have beside us, in some ways."

"I'll ask them all of that," Drosten answered, "but I can't see them settling among our other serfs and landsmen somehow. Not after what you've already said about them as a people."

Olwen didn't think it would happen for an instant either, but something in her felt driven to at least try.

CHAPTER NINE

Ragna watched her husband and his companions trudging back through the damp sands of their landing-place, and looked for any clues as to how they had fared. Nobody was limping, or being helped along, so that was good; on the other hand, they were not dancing or singing as they came either, which suggested something other than victory. After nearly twenty years of marriage, Ragna knew her husband, and he was not one to miss a chance of a celebration, however small the cause.

"How d'you think it went?" asked her younger son, Bjorn. Beside him his older brother, Svein, snorted dismissively.

"How are we supposed to tell from up here, fool? The only way to be certain is to wait until the old man bothers to tell us anything."

"That's enough," retorted his mother sharply. "You mind your tongue, or it'll be you fathir's fists that do the talking on you."

Svein threw up his hands in the sort of disgust that only a fourteen-year-old could make meaningful. "Why are we here, mothir? What's all this going about in aid of?" The frown that had seemed to become more and more a permanent feature on his face during the voyage deepened yet further. "Why couldn't we just stay where we were? We were happy there: things were settled and sorted out. Now we're all stuffed into this little boat in the middle of nowhere, looking for a place to start all over again! Why? I just don't understand what he's up to with all of this, I really don't."

"You mean you're still angry that he took away the

chance for you to go off and live with our uncle Grim," muttered Bjorn, but he said it whilst still within reach of his brother and got a slap around the head for his trouble.

"I don't care what your cause for being so difficult is," said Ragna coldly, catching hold of Svein's outstretched arm before he could withdraw it. Her fingers were like steel; they squeezed into the flesh around her eldest's wrist-bones, making him wince. "Heading for manhood you might be, my boy, but this is still your fathir's house, for all that it floats on the ocean, and the usual rules still hold good. If you've got an argument brewing, take it up with him, not with your brother here." She let go and Svein massaged some life back into the joint, wincing with the pain.

Ragna chuckled cruelly. "If you're whining about that, boy, think how much harder it would've been with Grim and his sons, hmm? Or think of the hardships there'd've been had your own fathir taken you over the sea with him in the summers, like you kept asking him to, eh?" She caught his eye, and raised one eyebrow, her lips pursed thoughtfully. "You're fifteen or so summers, son: you're not a child anymore. But if you want to be treated as the man you should be by now, then you have to start showing some signs of being that man, hmm?" Her gaze travelled back to the shore, and the ladder-pole that had been lowered into the surf as her menfolk approached. "Your fathir has a lot to deal with in this business, Svein, and arguments from you over nothings aren't going to help at all." Svein nodded silently, but the frown remained.

It was a difficult age, Ragna knew, as her pale eyes slipped past him to see Einar clambering over the top-strake. And, she considered, having your whole world pulled out from under you, having promises suddenly broken without any real explanation as to why, being taken far away from your friends and playmates, so far that it was unlikely Svein would ever see them again... no wonder he was bad-tempered about it all. She wondered how she would have dealt with such things at that age; probably not so very differently, if she was being honest. But honesty and fair dealing were luxuries out here: the incoming king had shown very little of either quality, and that had made life harder than it ought to have been. They weren't the only ones abandoning the steadings and farms of the homelands, and when Einar had heard the tales of good lands to the west, far enough out in the ocean to be rid of Harald but not so far as to be completely cut off from everything, his head had turned. It was an answer to all his problems – or so he had thought. Ragna waited patiently while he bent and wriggled out of his mailshirt, with the attendant grunting and swearing, and then downed a cup of ale. Svein had gone off to try and be alone somewhere on a forty-foot boat that held twenty people or more, plus all their movable belongings; Bjorn was happy at five or six years old to just lean on his mother's legs and be close to her.

"Well?" she enquired, once her husband had finally stretched and twisted and massaged all the aches and knots out of his well-muscled frame, and then strolled the short distance to where she stood. "What did you find, husband?"

"I found our pillars, right enough, and I found the man who organised to have them taken up to his houses beyond the dunes there," he answered, pointing a hand vaguely shoreward. He scratched his nose with the other hand. "He didn't seem too eager to give up his holdings, though."

"Hardly surprising," Ragna replied. "In his place,

I can't imagine you doing any differently. So then, what next?"

"That's a good question: I would imagine he's sent word out to try and raise some help, and no doubt he and his own lads are sharpening their spears as we speak. I was right about one other thing, though: from the style of his shirt, and his name, and his way of talking, we're right where I thought we were, on the eastern shores of the Orccareyjar." He grinned. "I've been in these parts before. More importantly, this is where people back home said some Jarl or other was setting up in residence. There'll be friends out there somewhere, in amongst all these enemies."

"Don't be too swift to call these local folk our foes," advised his wife. "If this man lives here, chances are that he too has a wife and children. It might well be that his concern for them will speak louder than any wish he has to start fighting and possibly get them all killed." She rested a hand on his arm. "Gentle words might get us further than hard knocks, in that case. And to be truthful, I'd rather you had a bit more thought for *us* before you go picking fights that might see us beaten off just as easily." She paused for a moment and then asked: "Do these people have a name for themselves?"

Einar looked around at the familiar faces. These people had been with him for more years than he could recall; some, like old Ottar, had been bondsmen to his father, whilst others, many of the women among them, had come into his house when he had married Ragna. They had followed him as he built up his house, his wealth and his reputation among the freemen of More. Now here they were, still ready to follow him into a new life, in new lands. But for all their loyalty, they were still only one boat, and not even a full crew of fighting-men, either. Whatever this Orcca-man had in store for them, the likelihood was that it would not be got without hard knocks somewhere along the way. And only Einar among them had the wealth to afford – or to justify – any armour beyond leather jerkins and hats. There was sense in Ragna's words, he had to admit.

"Pictari, Picti, something like that, if I recall right," he said absently, answering Ragna's last question first. "I said I'd go back tomorrow for his decision," he said eventually. "I didn't say I'd go alone, or unarmed. Nor do I plan to do either of those things. In fact, on balance, I think another show of our own force might be a good thing." He stretched the last kinks out of his back, the joints popping audibly. "It would be even better if we knew where some of our fellow-countrymen were, but that's just not to be, I suspect. We just have to hope that there are some between this place and whatever king or lord these natives have, to stop them sending for help." He sighed, and looked around again. "Still, we're here: we made it over the ocean. This is home, or somewhere near to it at any rate; we might as well get comfortable. Get the awning up, boys, and someone start the fire going. We'll eat and drink and settle in for the night, and start believing that we belong hereabouts, eh?"

From his place amid the cargo, Svein glared at his father's good humour. He saw nothing about this place that sang to him of home.

CHAPTER TEN

"How are we going to get enough men here to drive these intruders away?" It must have been the seventh time at least that Drosten had uttered the question, or something like it and leading to the same point. His brows were pulled low over his eyes, his mouth pulled down into a frown, and his cloak wrapped tightly around him as he sat by the fire and considered what few options he appeared to have.

From across the flames, Olwen sat and looked at him mildly. "Are you certain that bringing weapons against them is even the best idea?" she asked tentatively. "Unless you're certain of your ground, and equally certain of the men's quality, I 'd 've said that starting a fight is the last thing we should be thinking of. As I said earlier today, before they first appeared. These aren't just a bunch of our own youths getting rowdy on the beer. Don't forget who they are, and don't fool yourself into thinking that you can succeed against them where so many others have failed – and paid with their lives for the mistake."

He looked up at her. "All that sounds as if you've already surrendered, wife of mine. It gives the impression that your faith in me has died, and that your only concern is to keep your home and your family safe, even if that means giving the home away and having us all living in servitude. Do I guess it right, or have I misjudged you so badly after all?"

She shuffled her stool closer to his. "I don't want to be widowed a second time, if that's what you mean, Drosten. I don't want to see this place destroyed, and us along with it; I don't want to see Rilca or Morgan taken away and sold by these creatures – and they do such things. I 've seen it happen.

"I want us kept here, together, where we can at least look after each other, and if that means we let these newcomers in to settle somewhere in our lands, then so be it. I'll even insist on this point: we at least ask them if they'd take that from us, before we start hurling spears and talking of battles and hardship and war. They're only one boat, and they've been at sea for some days; my thought is that they'll settle for a bit of ground to put a house on rather than set sail again in the hope of getting more somewhere else. And we have those precious posts of theirs, remember, so if they want to go on again from here, they have to go without those, and that seems to be a problem their headman would rather not face." She leaned forward, her hand on his arm. "So play on those weak points, Drosten, and stop worrying about your own. You might yet be surprised at how much you can win without ever lifting a sword."

He patted her hand. "Wise words, Olwen, wise words indeed. I don't see that their being said as much out of necessity as anything else makes them any less valuable, either. Very well, we'll give this Einar the chance to come in peaceably and make a home beside us: there's good space to the south, isn't there? Enough to put a house on? It might even be far enough away to let him think he's won something all by himself."

Olwen nodded. "That's the sort of thing they often think is important. Put it to them; we might be lucky enough that they'd take it. And we lose nothing by trying, after all."

Drosten nodded. "I'd be happier lighting candles in the kirk as well. We need all the help we can get, and we've been good people."

Olwen frowned. "If we've still had no word from Bridei, it might be that the way is shut. It might be that we are expected to deal with this problem without the aid of our Lord in Heaven."

"A harsh price to pay, since we're dealing with heathens."

CHAPTER ELEVEN

Einar looked with distaste at the bag containing his armour as Skapti deposited it at his master's feet. "D'you think I *really* have to clamber into that thing again?" he asked Ragna pleadingly.

She shrugged. "Depends what sort of impression you want to make, I suppose. This headman ashore has seen you in it already, but from what you were saying last night he's the only one that has. On top of which, I've no idea where your better shirt's stowed among this lot." She waved a hand to indicate their cargo. "So all you have to put on a show with is that grimy thing you're wearing now, which I don't think would impress anyone, quite frankly. Better to put the mail over the top of it, and hide the worst of the dirt."

He regarded his wife balefully. "You seem clean and well decked-out, though. How's that happened?"

She smiled sweetly. "I did my own packing: I can find what I need to act the part. And I have no intention of being outshone by any local wife hereabouts, not when our future depends on being the strongest, the brightest and the best."

Einar chuckled. "I doubt there'll be any contest as to brightness!" It was true: Ragna had strung every line of beads and jewels she had between her brooches, and had clipped her whitest, cleanest shawl across her shoulders. The weak sunlight sparkled from glass and amber and silver coins as they all lay across her breasts, nestled in the rich red fabric of her dress and held at each end by the big, boxy shapes of those brooches, themselves gilded, pierced and studded with enamel. She had uncovered her hair as well, wrapping it into a knot at the back of her head and letting the rest of its length fall like a pale golden stream down her back. Einar enjoyed the view for a few moments, tugging absently at his beard. "The only problem is going to be preserving such finery as we get you off the ship," he said teasingly.

Ragna raised an eyebrow. "Well I'm only doing it the once, so I suggest you leave some of the lads behind and have them put the awning up on the beach there. If we're staying here and making a home, I don't see any point in skulking aboard the ship longer than we need to, and it would be good to get the animals back onto solid ground too."

"That's a fair point," answered her husband. "These people must have spears, but how many would be anyone's guess. They're more likely to be guessing at our strength rather better, and if they decide to try and hold out until they can get word away to their friends..."

"Then I suggest once again that you don't dismiss any deal they offer you out of hand." said Ragna firmly. "It's not just our decision here, after all: we invoked the Thunderer to show us the way and he brought us somewhere that was already taken. There's likely to be a reason for that, surely; and until we can see what it is, I'd rather we didn't go around making enemies too readily."

"I'll not sit under some local as his thrall," warned Einar.

"I'm not asking you to. I'm just asking you to consider something other than just being the undisputed Master of this new home you've brought us to. It's hardly as if you were that back in the old country, now was it?"

"No, we paid our dues to Jarl and Hauldr – but they weren't living under our roof. The farm and its lands were mine outright."

"Until you realised that this new king was likely to just confiscate them if he thought it desirable..."

Einar scowled. "Alright, so maybe the place wasn't so much mine after all, not in reality. Felt like it was, though. And my point still stands, for all this bickering over points of law; I should've taken you to the Thing more often, the way you argue. I'll not be so far under anyone here, be they local-man or inganger like us, that I've not got my own roof, held up by my family pillars, and my own fields to live from."

"I thought we lived more from what you brought in from the boat each summer..."

"That's different: that's extras, and luxuries. It's always been the fields that fed us and gave us the basics in clothing; if I'd ever had to miss a summer at sea, we wouldn't have felt it too badly."

Ragna sighed. "All I'm trying to say is that our new life here might not be so different to that we've left behind; even if you're so full of what you want here, I'll settle for a house and enough soil to grow our seed, and we'll have to buy in kine and more sheep anyway, at some point. We don't *have* to be the lords here in order to make a home and a living."

From the look on his face, Einar was clearly having trouble coming to grips with some of these ideas, she thought sadly. But at least this time she was going ashore with him, and there might yet be chances to hold him to less than he dreamed of. Which was sad for her, in its own way, since his wild dreams were one of the things she had always liked most about her husband. When he and his father had come to bargain for her hand all those years ago, he had sat beside her on the benches in her own parent's house and told tales that captured her imagination and her admiration. After he had returned home, she and her father had sat and talked the proposal over. It had been her own enthusiasm for Einar as a husband that had finally swung the deal; and now here she was, wishing he wasn't quite so ardent in his dreams and his ambition. And for what? For the sake of not upsetting the new neighbours? For the hope of a friendly word and a little help now and then, while Einar bent his back and stretched his mind in the building of a whole new life for her and their children? Ragna felt her cheeks reddening in her embarrassment; what sort of a wife had she become in this place? Her eyes caught the rows of sparkling glass and silver ornaments adorning her breast, the proceeds of her husband's trading and looting, placed out for all the world to see. He had made her rich, and now he was looking to make her a Hauldr in this place – and she was trying to persuade him not to. Her mouth pursed in anger. It was a wonder he was even still talking to her.

CHAPTER TWELVE

The local men had put out stools and a single low table in the open ground between their groups of close-clustered buildings. Drosten and a woman Einar presumed was his wife sat in the cool breeze, awaiting their unwelcome visitors; behind them, a dozen or so men stood idly leaning on sharp, newly-cleaned spears, whose long, thin blades caught the glitters of fitful sunlight as the clouds raced past overhead. Two children, a girl of around Svein's own age and a boy who might be a little younger than Bjorn, stood between the masters and the men, as if being protected by both. It was a little far to read any faces with accuracy, but there did seem to be a palpable air of uncertainty, tinged with nervousness. As he entered the yard, Einar slowed his pace a little to survey the scene.

"Well," he muttered to Havard beside him, "there's a rough count of their numbers, eh?"

"And as many again hidden out of sight, I shouldn't wonder. Even if it's only the women and their kids, they're still potentially a problem."

"No doubt about it. So that gives them, what – about twenty?" He shrugged. "Much the same as us, then. Better than I'd hoped..."

"Now take away the handful we left on the shore," warned Havard, "and the need to keep another few back here out of bowshot to watch our own backs, and there's enough more of them than us to give out a good hiding should the mood take 'em."

"Aye, but I don't think it will," replied Einar. "He's got his wife out beside him, look, and I have Ragna with me, all of which argues against starting a fight. Reckon those two are their own children? I don't see any others... maybe we should've brought the boys along after all, not that I think Svein's in the mood for being polite these days. And there are jugs on the table there; no, for all the show of iron, I think we're talking and bargaining today." And with that, he stepped forward. Ragna and Havard exchanged a glance, and fell in behind.

"That's a relief," murmured Drosten to Olwen as they stood in welcome. "He's brought his wife along. He can't be meaning to start anything with her in the way, can he?"

"That's a lot of wealth she's wearing, too," she answered. "Too much to risk getting it – or her – damaged, I'd've thought." She smiled. "We and they are thinking alike, then. This might yet turn into a good day for everyone."

Introductions were made: seats were offered and accepted, and ale poured. Drosten came swiftly to business once the formalities were attended to, however.

"In this place," he began, "lineage is through the woman's line, to the next male children. I'm told it's different in your homelands, and father passes to son. Here, it would be my sister's sons who would inherit my property – but these lands aren't mine to give away. They belong to my wife, Olwen, but our son Morgan here will have them on her death. On his death, however, they pass to his adopted sister's children, so you can appreciate that any deal we make with you over settling here could be overturned in some distant future..."

"This is Rilca," interrupted Olwen, gently taking the girl's arm and pulling her forward. Olwen's eyes never left Einar's face, and the longer they regarded his features, the more trouble clouded her bright, dark orbs.

"Meaning that our staying is entirely dependent on the goodwill of just about everyone around us, since we're unlikely to keep track of who's about to inherit?" asked Einar with a grin. He seemed unaware of Olwen's scrutiny. Drosten nodded in answer to his question, and Einar swiftly translated the bones of the matter for his own wife.

"I don't see that it matters," put in Ragna, forestalling any other answer from her husband. "We are here to settle and make a living, not stop for a summer and then head elsewhere. However we treat our new neighbours will stay with us, and only a fool makes a fight where none need be." She flashed a smile at Olwen and her children. The local woman responded; Rilca and Morgan clung tighter to her than ever, worry in every muscle. Once again, Einar relayed the message in a dialect the local woman would understand.

"There is a long ridge that continues from this place, to the south of us here," Drosten went on. "It has good access to the sea, and fair soil further inland. There are some buildings sitting on it already but they're old ones, ruined and no longer used. We had it in mind to offer you that as a place to settle, if you'd take it."

"That sounds interesting," murmured Ragna in her husband's ear. "Think we could manage on such a foundation?"

"It would be a simple matter to have your posts moved across – when you were ready, of course," added Drosten idly.

"Your terms?" asked Einar warily.

Drosten frowned in thought. "My wife is the legal owner of all this part of the country: it has come to her from various lineages, and is confirmed by our king, Bridei. I can't see that any of her family – or mine, come to that – would sit quietly if we made you a gift of it: you might have to swear fealty to us, become tenants, that sort of thing." He stopped and examined Einar's expression. "Might I ask what your position was in your old home?"

"I remain a freeman. I was never in bond to anyone, not in the way you're implying at any rate: Jarls and kings don't count, since I'm sure you're just as beholden to yours as I was to mine. My house was my own, and it was my fathir's before me. What sort of status in your world do such tenants have, then? Could you promise us our full rights under the law, the right to attend and speak at the Thing, even to demand audience with the king, should we need it?" He tugged his beard thoughtfully. "And while we're about it, what would you be expecting from us in return?"

Drosten's frown deepened. "This wasn't my idea, offering you a home, you know. I'd've sooner sent you off at spearpoint. I've heard tales of your people coming to other parts and demanding everything they could see."

"No doubt the tales were true, as well. We find ourselves in similar boats, friend Drosten, since I'd be happy to trade love-taps with you for mastery hereabouts, and were I to come out on top, I'd drive you and your people into the sea as readily as you would mine, eh? So we understand each other to that extent, if no further. But you don't seem able to get word to anyone else who might help, which seems to suggest that there's nobody around to aid you. We've been here, what? Two, three nights now? And there's no extra spears to be seen from you. But I can't be sure who else sits along these coasts, and whether they'd be friend or foe, and so I can't call on anyone either, for all that your failing to find help might mean that I have unknown friends nearby. And so here we are, facing each other with what we have right now, and needing to come to some sort of arrangement." He smiled grimly, and dropped his hand onto the worn, care-polished three-lobed pommel of his sword. "I've not turned your kind offer down, you'll notice; I'm just finding out more about it, that's all. As such offers go, I'd say it was probably a good one. But I've got a right to know what the price of it is, wouldn't you say?"

Beyond the introduction of her adopted daughter, Olwen had said not a word so far; now she touched her husband's arm to silence him for a moment. "I would be content with the payment of a rent, and a promise of help at harvest and sowing-time, and your oath to side with me in any disputes or other matters that might arise as a result of your settling here," she said. "I might also want a share in any profits coming from the use of that ship you arrived in, since I don't expect for a moment that you'll be giving up *that* source of income. You people put a high value on living well: your lady there shows this well enough. If you are living on my lands, I don't see why I shouldn't have a share in that wealth. But I'll not expect you to work in my fields, or attend me in my house, or any of the other duties my own household fulfils."

"A share of the ship's money *as* the rent," argued Einar, "and other help to be paid for under whatever the usual rules are in these parts. And we are a separate household, not beholden in any way beyond what neighbours or friends might do for each other anyway."

Drosten turned to his wife as if to protest, but she cut him off. "Very well, then. Come back tomorrow and Drosten will walk the bounds with you."

CHAPTER THIRTEEN

"That was too easy," muttered Einar on his way back to the beach. "Why go to such trouble in the beginning if the woman then just gives in to almost everything afterwards?" He trudged through the grass in silence for a few paces before speaking again. "It makes no sense; it also leaves Drosten looking like a fool, and I can't imagine he'll take kindly to that."

"Seems to me that the men here have a hard enough time of it anyway," observed Havard. "If they all inherit from their mothers, what does a husband stand to gain? He's a lot older than she is, from the look of him; think maybe she's a second wife?"

"These folk follow the kirk ways," answered Einar. "They only have one wife at a time. If his first is dead, any kids from that match will have had all the property she owned. His only chance of getting anything is if they let him back in, and if that had happened, why would he have married again, just to lose it all in gambling on having another brat with this woman?" He sighed in expasperation. "It still makes no sense to me. How about to you, my love?"

Ragna shrugged. "I'll let you know when I bother thinking about it. I'm just happy that she did agree to so little." She moved closer to Einar and hugged his arm. "That was well bargained, husband; worth the walk for seeing it done."

He smiled down at her. "I'm glad I could be so entertaining! So: we have the posts, or at least we know where they are, and now we have a patch of land to put 'em back up on. I wonder what this place is like for timber and stone? It might go down badly with our new mistress if we have to break up the boat in order to make a roof."

"He said there were houses on it already. Maybe they still have their timbers." Havard remembered. "If we bring, say, Ketil and Hrafn along with us next time, they'd have a better eye for what we could or couldn't re-use."

"Fine idea," agreed Einar as he topped the ridge and looked down on a beach full of bustle and life. The ship's awnings had been wrestled ashore and its posts set up in the deep, moist sand; the bondsmen had also got most of the furniture ashore, and a fire was set a short way up the slope. As he watched, Skapti and Asbjorn grabbed hold of another sheep and unceremoniously tossed it over the side of the ship, to land bleating and kicking on the sand with its fellows. Einar grinned. "Remind me again in the morning, eh? Tonight, I think we've earned a celebration."

*

Drosten was indeed unhappy. Rather than take his customary place beside the fire, he banged the door shut behind him and stood out in the chill of the early evening. Around him, all the familiar sights, sounds and smells went on as before – but now they felt strange, alien, threatening. Much like the boat this Einar had come in, he felt adrift, powerless in the currents that swirled and eddied around him.

He had no idea how long he stood thus before Olwen came out and gently took his arm. He found no words to say to her, so he waited until she spoke.

"I know I undid all your work today," she began haltingly. "You have to accept that I had my reasons, Drosten. I didn't do it out of spite, or anything else. I did it to stop them thinking of bringing a fight to us, and possibly our losing everything."

"This seems to have become an overriding concern for you," he answered bitterly. "It begins to seem as if nothing else matters: not our honour, not our safety, not even our strong position here in these discussions. We could've held them to almost anything: we could've pulled oaths out of them to be friends and even never to take up weapons against us! We could have been *safe!* And instead, you settled for a share of some future profits that might never come, and a vague promise of help if we need it." He pulled his arm away and turned to face her. "I need to know why, Olwen. I need to know what drove you to undermine me so in front of strangers, and I need to know if, after doing that, you still even want me here."

"Those are hard questions," she replied, "and

there are no easy answers, save to the last one. What I did today was not aimed at you, my husband: you still have my love, my faith and my trust, as you always have. But I don't want anything happening to you, to Rilca or to Morgan, because of these incomers getting less than they might want. I've spent time with such people before, remember, and I've seen what they can be like when roused. There's no stopping them: they would kill us all without even bothering to think about it. They might take us alive, and ship us off to one of their other havens, to be sold on into slavery, and they'd never think anything of that, either. We might never see each other again: would you want your son taken away like that, not knowing if he lived or died, or even where he was? Would you really have risked all this, just for the sake of driving a hard bargain?" She shook her head nervously. "That's too high a price, husband, and one we didn't need to pay. Let them have the place to the south, and let them build it up as they will. I don't care if we never see a scrap of silver from it; if we never see our new neighbours either, that will be splendid." She reached out for his hand again. "By doing what I did, I took away all their reasons for wanting to come against us. We haven't heard from Bridei, have we? Even their headman worked the consequences of that one out. We're on our own, here: either Maelchon didn't get to him at all, or our king heard his message and decided to ignore it. We had the chance to make better friends, more useful friends, out of these newcomers. I chose to do that against holding out the hope of rescue some time in the future."

"Very well; I can see the sense in your actions. But it hurts, all the same."

"I realise that – I knew it at the time, but there was nowhere for me to take you aside and discuss it first. And

I am sorry, truly sorry, for how it must have looked and felt. I could see no other way, though. Einar was already getting restless to my eyes."

Drosten smiled bleakly. "I had that impression, too. He certainly took your offer quickly enough."

"He probably realised that he wouldn't get a better one. He might also, with luck, think it has driven a wedge between us. He would find himself out of his depth if he tried to exploit such a thing – if we keep together, even in spite of what I did."

"For the greater good?"

She nodded in relief. "For the greater good, aye. Will you come back in, and let us be a family again?"

He looked at her askance. "I might not have said as much, but I do share your worries over what might happen to the children if these foreigners turn against us, whatever happens to you or I."

"I'm glad to hear that, but I never really doubted it, truly I didn't. How far do you trust them, then?"

"Me? Not a bit. How about you?"

"Not a lot more, depsite what it may look like."

"Your memories making them seem a bit too familiar, are they?"

She smiled. "How well you know me. It might, after all, be such a little advantage, yet it keeps trying to make itself bigger and more important than ever. I don't know what to do about it."

"They're your memories: what you make of them is up to you. They're like dreams, in that they've only got the value we put on them. If you keep your memories in mind while we deal with Einar and his brood, and I keep taking them at face value, day to day, then between us, we might have the measure of them, wouldn't you say?"

She gently edged him towards the door of their

house. "That seems a wise course, Drosten my husband. We'll be stronger together than apart. Come inside; help me keep these memories away."

CHAPTER FOURTEEN

The land to the south of Olwen's steading was very similar: perhaps a little more exposed, with perhaps a few more stones and rocks poking through the grass and sand of the ridge on which the old buildings stood. There was little of them left beyond broken rings of stone walls and a mass of shattered, sodden, ruined timbers and loose rubble piled in the pits that made their floors. Einar and his companions stood with Drosten and *his* companions, and slowly surveyed the scene.

"Not a lot to work with, lord," commented Ketil drily, as his pale eyes took in the details and his agile mind made plans as to what could be salvaged from it all. Einar shrugged.

"We were promised old buildings: nobody said anything about them being ready to live in. But there's enough stone to do something useful with, surely?"

"Aye lord, easily. D'you want a proper house in the old style, or will you keep to the local ways and rebuild 'em as they are?"

"I'm not at all sure I could get used to living inside a barrel, not at my age. I reckon we could dig all that stone out, knock down what's left, and then sort of connect the floors we have here together, and build the new hall around that."

"So you'll take our offer then?" prompted Drosten. He had stood silently, listening to these newcomers making their plans, and had waited as long as he thought he could before saying anything. By this stage, he reckoned, they should either be far enough into their schemes to make backing out of them unthinkable, or insulted enough to just up and sail away. Sadly, he reflected, it looked like being the former. He would rather they had chosen the second option.

"I reckon so," grinned Einar. "Will you walk the bounds with me and show me how much I get?"

"You can see the smoke rising from my own house, even from here," began the Pict. "I propose that we set the boundary halfway between there and here. There's a stream that's near enough to that point: I'll settle for sharing the water with you, and you get this side while I have the other. Then your land carries on down to the sea on the one side, and goes inland to the top of the slope, until it meets the lines of David's boundary. I wouldn't know where to begin turning that into measurements you might understand," he added, seeing the blank look on the Norseman's face, "but it's marked with stones. You can't miss it," he added pointedly.

"If we walk along it, and you show me where you mean, I'm sure it'll make sense," Einar replied slowly. "And then it must turn back again to the sea at some point, hmm?"

"Aye, where the beach gives way to the rocks of the Tangi. Again, it'll probably make more sense if you see it for yourself."

*

It was evening before Einar and his followers returned to their campsite. Ragna looked up as she heard their approach, and ordered more of their precious stored wood to go on the fire. Peering into the iron kettle suspended on the ship's tripod above the flames confirmed that the night's stew was nowhere near ready, and the art of making bread on a flat stone without a pot to cover it continued to elude her. She sighed, resigning herself to a long period of re-learning all the skills she had acquired at her own mother's side. It seemed so long ago, these days. Since they had taken ship and ended up on this strange, gently sloping coastline, she had lost all sense of time and place. Nothing was familiar here, not even the colours of the sky or the speed at which the clouds raced overhead; not the chill in the rain, the fierceness of the wind, the lay of the land – or the motives of their new neighbours, with their dark hair, their sharp, darting eyes and their lack of stature. Even Bjorn showed every sign of towering over many of them, or those she had seen at any rate. Most of her time had been spent here, making a ship into a home whilst her husband went out and attended to the sharp-ended business of establishing his homestead in these peope's lands. Somebody had evidently given instructions for supplies to be sent down to her, though: her gaze wandered to the baskets of grain and small pots of meat that had arrived earlier in the day, and she wondered about how that had been arranged, and who was really in charge of this settlement they had stumbled into.

     She needed to get out more, she decided as she watched Einar, devoid of his mailshirt today, come sliding and floundering down the sand towards them. The man who had been dealing with them had a wife, servants, a household: they would all have useful information on how things ran hereabouts. All the sorts of little details that Einar would undoubtedly neglect to ask about, that could make all the difference to relations with these new neighbours in the years to come, could be had from the wives and the bondsmen of this place: but he would never ask. So it would be up to her; it would also be useful, she decided, to have her own sources of information and friendship. That way, if Einar and Drosten started having arguments about anything, she had Drosten's wife to fall back on as a method of averting any unneccessary conflicts. She would have to learn the language, she realised; the best way into that was to buy a bondi or two for her own household, and let them teach it. Or to keep encouraging them to come and sell things.

As her husband reached the edges of the campsite, she dipped his cup into the ale-barrel and went out to meet him. "How long until we have proper walls around us, then?" she asked by way of greeting.

"I think we could clear out what's there in a day or two, and then if we wished, we could put the awnings over the top and make our plans," he replied with a smile.

"Think the weather will hold for that long? I'm not wanting to be under this awning through gales and storms," she warned him.

"We came away at the very start of summer," said Einar. "We should be safe for a while, and I don't recall any bad storms when I've been out this way before. There are walls still standing," he continued, recoiling under her baleful glare, "and the floors are dug into the soil. So there's a good base to build on, even if they are all the wrong shape for decent people. Ketil reckons the timber's all gone too far to rescue, so one thing we'll have to do quickly is send the ship back out to find more." He ran a hand through his hair. "That's going to be more of a problem than I'd want, and it gets bigger whenever I think about it. If the rumours are true that other of our folk are settled in these islands, then we might be able to get timbers from them. But finding 'em's going to be the hard part."

"Not really: you send some of the lads out to find friends and timbers, and the rest of you stay here and start building what you can. They could ask about bere and sheep and such while they're going, too, since we'll be needing some of everything, if not this summer then certainly next time around. I know we brought what we could, but it might be best to assume there'll be nothing here to have swiftly; these people will surely need it for themselves. Perhaps my brother would like to go..."

"It's a thought. He's had enough practice at handling the ship after all."

Ragna arched an eyebrow. "And you could always ask our new landlords where they get *their* building-wood from. Somebody sent us food today: there's at least one friendly face here."

"Hmph. We'll see about that. From how Drosten was today, I'd say there's not *that* much goodwill to be had from their direction, and I'd rather not start relying on them too much so early in our time here."

"Einar, husband of mine, that choice might not be yours! If we have sudden storms in a house with no roof to it, it might be enough to finish us all. So *I* say you ought to at least be asking the question of them, unless you're prepared to see your whole family washed away come winter. There must be a reason as to why those houses are deserted, after all..."

"I'd not thought of it in those terms, it's true. Perhaps you're right; there are things I should be asking. I wonder if they'd take silver to build a house for us?" He grinned savagely. "I think Drosten's on the back foot already; if we start turning his own people away from him, there's less to stop us having the best of the place instead of the worst. Yes, there are indeed things I should be asking of them."

Ragna patted his arm. "That's right dear: there are." She said nothing of her intention to ask other things of Olwen as soon as she was able.

CHAPTER FIFTEEN

Drosten had largely resigned himself to an unending stream of these foreigners tramping through his own lands and homestead as they established themselves further to the south. But it was not to be: one of Einar's first acts was to move his ship from its original beaching-place, in favour of one right below the site of his new home. That removed the need for anything more than an occasional visit into his wife's estates, and the faces who did come soon became familiar, their requests predictable. Eggs; milk; meat, occasionally; the odd question, usually in gestures and half-recognised similar words, as to how things were done from time to time. The people who turned up on such errands were clearly servants, farmhands... these newcomers had a name for them, he recalled. Bondsmen? Something like that. Drosten mentally equated them with the men and women who worked for him and Olwen, and saw no reason to learn their names. Clearly, though, it was going to be useful for these incomers to have some knowledge of the local tongue, and Drosten allowed his own people to encourage that learning. As the days went on, some of them became quite proficient, and dialogues progressed beyond odd words into something resembling sentences.

Then, one day as spring turned into summer, as the days got longer and longer and the wind lessened gradually and became warmer, they had a visitor of a different type. This one came with companions, and brought no baskets or bags in which to carry things bought or bartered. As he watched them pick their way over the intervening ridges of windblown, grass-covered sand, Drosten waved a few of his own people closer.

"Hang around the houses for a while," he murmured, "we might need a proper welcome of some sort."

Maccus shielded his eyes from the bright edges of the clouds that hid the sun, trying to make out the figures. "I don't see much in the way of weapons, lord..."

Drosten grinned. "Wrong sort of welcome you had in mind, lad! This one will require standing around and looking smarter than is usual, for a bit." He tore his eyes from the oncoming entourage. "I'd better go tell your mistress. You go and round up those with any sort of decent clothing, and bring 'em back here wearing it."

"There's little enough of that for any of us, lord. We're none of us so wealthy that we can afford spare shirts even."

"I know, I know: just do what you can, Maccus, alright? It's no better for your mistress and me, I promise you."

He ducked into the house, into the main chamber. Olwen looked up from the fire as she heard his approach.

"You look flustered, husband."

"Mm, I daresay. Wife of mine, lady of these lands, there are visitors approaching who I think might be coming to see you more than any other of us."

"Really? Can you see who yet?"

"Not with any certainty, but from the look of 'em I'm betting it's Einar's own wife and her attendants."

Olwen raised her eyebrows. "Now *that's* unexpected, aye!" She looked around. "There's not much

I can do to smarten this place up..."

Drosten raised a hand. "Consider where she lives at the moment, love; I reckon anywhere with walls and a solid roof will feel like the grandest of halls!"

Nevertheless, in answer to a silent, unspoken plea, Drosten sent a couple of the servant-girls in to help clear the place up a bit, and personally checked the level of the ale-cask. Then he and his wife went back outside, and stood at the edges of the yard to welcome their visitors in.

CHAPTER SIXTEEN

Two women regarded each other across a fire. Olwen had found time to pull out her better dress, the one woven from wools dyed in heather and summer berries, the mix that had needed Morgan's own piss to be kept in a bucket and then poured in with the fruits to make the colour stick to the wool. The effect was to suggest lines of darker colour criss-crossing the fabric, but it was fragile in sunlight and so only came out for special occasions. Her shawl was a riot of colours, all interweaved in reds, greens and yellows, a special gift from someone long ago, someone she now found it easier not to think about so often. She had even left Drosten outside to welcome their guests alone, and come back inside to comb her thinning dark hair, making it shine in the peat-glow as it sat on her shoulders.

Ragna had clearly also made an effort to impress, although the style was so different that Olwen might not have realised just how much effort she had made. There was none of the subtle interweaving of colours in her linen that Olwen displayed in her wool; instead, the colours were clear, solid and strong, and the fabric was cut generously enough to give her a fluid, flowing appearance whenever she moved. She wore the gilded brooches Einar had brought back from a trip into the Baltic one time, with the straps of her topdress pinned to them over her shoulders and strings of glass and amber beads hanging between them across her breasts. Her underdress was pink, the sleeveless topdress a pale, bright blue, with complicated bands of some kind of weaving Olwen had never seen before around the top edge. Her cloak hung down over her shoulders, secured by those brooches and hanging down her back, and her sleeves hung down to her knuckles, leaving only dainty fingers showing. None of it suggested ever working for a living – which was the whole idea, of course.

"I thought it was about time you and I met properly," Ragna began haltingly, once they and their respective attendants were settled around the firepit. "If we are to be neighbours, I thought it only wise to come and ask you how matters work around these parts..." she tailed off, unsure of how to continue as her grasp of the local speech ran out. She stopped and looked around the room for a moment; one of her handmaids bent and murmured something in her ear. "Clearly things are very different here to how they are in my old home," she continued, "I don't even know if this is the right way to go visiting." She smiled, a little nervously. "There are so many questions, it's hard to know where to begin..."

Olwen relaxed just a little. "Well, clearly your house is your own, so there's no need to adopt new ways within it – unless you feel you ought, of course. But if your husband is anything like mine, he won't be keen on the idea."

That got a better smile; maybe this wouldn't be

such a trial after all. Olwen realised with a touch of shame that such visitings should have been easy affairs for her; anyone in her position ought to be capable of receiving guests without going into a panic about it. What had happened to her in those years since she had settled here with Drosten? Had they really become so isolated and inward-looking?

"You look troubled," said Ragna gently, peering at her with what might have been concern in her eyes. Olwen smiled and shook her head.

"Oh, no, it's nothing; just stray thoughts pushing in. But what of you, lady Ragna? Did you really bring your whole household over the sea in that one boat? Have you children? How did they take to it all?"

"Aye, we did all that, although it was crowded and the boat didn't sail very well, I'm told. It's my husband Einar's ship, but my brother Havard holds another stake in it, and it's usually his hand on the styrbord. As for the children: well, my two managed well enough, but some of the bondar found it harder going."

"Bondar? Serving-men?"

Ragna nodded. "Something like that. Paid men and women who work for us and are like part of the larger family. Different to thralls – the ones taken or bought, who don't get paid and are owned by their buyers. We let those go before we came away: they've all gone on to neighbours or friends in the old country." She leaned forward. "They can be troublesome sometimes; it's often easier to do without them, and put up with the expense of having proper bondar instead."

Olwen managed to control a shudder. She remembered seeing such people, and didn't wonder that they were a problem to control.

"What of you?" Ragna was saying, "are there

children hereabouts? I thought I saw two when we came ashore to strike a deal that first time."

"Yes: there is Rilca, my sister's daughter, now coming into her womanhood. Rilca? Step forward dear, and be introduced; I'm sure I saw you in here earlier." The girl duly stepped out of the shadows and bowed her head to the visitors. Ragna picked up the cue and gravely bowed back.

"I am happy to meet you, Rilca. I have a son about your age, I would think, although he's not such good company at the moment. I think he's still angry at being pulled away from his old home and his hopes of a fostering with one of his distant relatives – do you folk follow that custom, or is it strictly one of ours? Is Rilca here fostering with you?"

"No, my sister and her husband are both dead some years back, and so Rilca lives here on our family's lands with me. Although I control these estates, they're not exactly mine to own you see; if she has sons before I die, then those boys and not my own son, Morgan, will have this place. I think my husband explained it to yours; I don't remember rightly." She turned back to her adopted daughter. "Rilca, is Morgan around?"

"I think he's out in the fields," answered Rilca. "Shall I fetch him for you?"

"If you would, yes." The speed with which she vanished out of the doorway suggested to Ragna that the girl was happier to be away from all this business. She filed the point away for reference, and the conversation moved on to the sorts of crops that grew best in the sandy soils of these lands, the animals that did well in these parts, and who might be willing to part with either seed or stock.

"You wanted me mama?" came a little voice

suddenly.

"Indeed. Come and say hello to our new neighbour, Morgan. This is the lady Ragna, wife to Einar."

"I'm happy to meet you, Mawgan... you would be Drostensson in my language and custom." She peered closer at him in the dim firelight. "My, what striking bright eyes you have. And such fairness in the hair and skin, too; very noble and fine you look. It's a strange thing, but I reckon my other son, Bjorn, must be close to *your* age, just as Svein is to your cousin's. There must be something in that, somewhere, but probably only the Gods know what."

Olwen looked at her visitor with unfathomable eyes, and wondered what else might lay beneath such a remark.

CHAPTER SEVENTEEN

Wind battered the dunes and the waves that churned beyond them, carrying sand and salt sea into the air and far inland. The skies turned angry shades of grey, almost black in places, blotting out the sun and casting dark, gloomy shadows across the whole of the land. The clouds raced across overhead, like the storm-god's wagon or the fury of a vengeful lord; all the while, that wind raced with them, pushing the wet and the cold deep into the bones of anyone who dared to venture outdoors.

Einar and his followers huddled in the damp stony bases of old, wrecked homes and watched the ship's awnings flap dangerously over their heads. The water was already seeping through the heavy woollen cloth, depsite the layers of fat and oil that were liberally smeared all over it. There was nothing that could be done, though: there was no point in going outside if all it achieved was to bring more cold and wet back in with you. The bondar had found an alcove that appeared to have once been some sort of hearth and had managed to start a small fire. It wasn't doing much to actually warm the place, but it looked good, and it served to promise them all that the storm would eventually ease, and things could be done to make next time a little easier.

Ragna looked across at her husband over the fragile little flames. "We can't do this again..." she murmured. He nodded with grave, serious eyes.

"Agreed. I have a plan, though."

"I just hope Havard and the boat-men are alright..."

Einar shrugged. "We've sailed through worse: it's never comfortable, but the boat's sound and Havard's a good styrsman. They'll be fine, wherever they are."

"You were saying you have a plan? What sort of plan?"

"A plan for making our life better here." He leaned closer. "You know we sit on a bit of a rise here, yes? That's why the wind's hitting us so hard, I reckon: there's no protection from it, and my bet is that this is why the place was abandoned. And you know that our patch of ground's not all that big, when you take a better look at it? Well, I have word that there's an old boundary that Drosten likes to ignore: it runs between his houses and the edge of the land where we first beached. I have it in mind to claim all of that long high ridge as ours, in addition to this land here. I don't know how good these folk are at remembering every little detail, but in his offer, he sort-of included that bit as well."

"I don't see what good that does us, husband. It's

shelter we need, not more fields to try and work. We've got little enough done as it is; I can see us having to buy from our neighbours if we're not to starve come the winter."

"I know all that, but listen. The ground there is higher, and the grass in the dunes gives a measure of protection against these winds. Below the ridge is a good spot for a house; better by far than this."

Ragna looked at him skeptically. "How come you know all of this and I didn't?"

Einar gave her a smug smile. "I don't just talk to these neighbours of ours – when I have to. I go around looking at things, too. There's the stump of one of their fancy stones, the ones Drosten showed me further inland, where even his lands run out and someone else's begin. Looks to me as if it was deliberately broken off, and then someone tried to bury the thing – but the wind keeps bringing it back up." He wiped a drip off his nose absently. "There's a lot of stones up there: I think some of the folk might've been in the habit of burying their dead somewhere by the burn. The lads sometimes come across the grave-markers that kirk-gangers insist on having."

"If Drosten thinks that land is his, by whatever route, I can't see him giving it up just like that, any more now than when we first came here." said Ragna thoughtfully.

"We're a bit more organised now," replied her husband, "and we've still not seen any signs of other folk coming to his aid against us. You leave it to me: I'll not only take that shore, but I'll have them build us a house on it."

Ragna raised her eyebrows. "Now there's a boast..."

But Einar said nothing more. He just settled back

against his patch of the wall, and waited for the storm to subside.

CHAPTER EIGHTEEN

After wind and gales came sunshine and warmer, gentler breezes, that played on the bare skin or set cloaks idly flapping as you walked. The grass looked brighter, greener, as if washed clean by the storms and ready to take on another load of grubby, draining living. Even the air smelled washed and fresher somehow, although smoke still rose from rooftops and the usual odours were still in abundance around the houses and the sheds.

It was a morning that Olwen and her husband might have enjoyed out in the fields together; or, if the workload allowed, they might have passed it by and stayed indoors, in bed, locked in each other's arms and enjoying entirely different pleasures. But not this time: this time, their household came in and demanded their presence outside. This time, there was trouble ahead. They dressed quickly and stumbled out, blinking in the sunlight, squinting to try and work out what was amiss.

Their retainers inexorably guided them shoreward, to where the rest of the settlement stood, noisily talking, crowded around something – or someone. As they came nearer, Drosten heard Einar's heavily accented tones.

"What's going on?" Drosten demanded. He pushed his way through the small knot of his own people to come face-to-face with his neighbour. "Einar, what are you doing? What's happened?"

The Norseman grinned. "I was wondering when you'd show up. You're an ideal witness, Drosten."

The Pict sighed. "Witness to what?"

"You know about the marker stone that sits between here and that path between your houses." It was a statement, not a question. Drosten pursed his lips, but said nothing.

"Well," Einar went on, "I've been asking around, and it seems that this strip of shoreline is another property: it isn't connected to yours at all, as far as I can tell. So I've come to claim it, since it runs into mine on the other side of the burn. And because you don't seem to be using it; and because as a ship-owner, it would be far more useful to me than it will ever be to you."

"None of which explains why you've gathered *my* men around you, and taken them away from their proper work," growled Drosten. "Isn't it enough that you've been buying our grain and meat from us already, and now you have to resort to such nonsense just to stop us growing more? You're own people will need feeding as well, you know; are you so intent on ruining us all?"

"Such claims should be made before proper witnesses," Einar growled back, "which is why I brought all my lads to hear it as well. Care to dispute any of it?"

"Arlen: go and get spears!" barked Drosten. "You others, go with him and stop this nonsense now!"

"That's a shame," said Einar idly. "It means you'll *all* miss out," he added, a little more loudly. Some of the local men wavered; their pace slowed.

"What will they miss, Einar?" asked Olwen, worriedly. "What have you said to them already, that we weren't present to hear?"

"I've had a chance to sort through my belongings; I offered them a share in my silver."

"In return for what?" demanded Drosten.

"Fair payment for building me a house on this

spot. One that will withstand another storm like that last one was. I reckon it's a bit more sheltered here, you see. Is that why your own people left that land you put us on?" he asked suddenly. "Was there a plan to see how long we would last huddled under our sail, until the weather did for us all?"

Drosten pursed his lips in a frown; Olwen's eyes widened slightly. Einar nodded with a satisfied smile.

"Thought so." He nodded towards his own men, laden with spears and axes, dressed and ready for war. "If you want to keep these wolves away from your own doors," he suggested, leaning closer and keeping his tone low, "I'd suggest not standing in my way while I look to my own people's welfare. Now somewhere between you and I, there's still that boundary I mentioned earlier. I know where that stone sits, and I'll even offer to put another one up in it's place. But you'll have your side, and I'll have mine, and I reckon that even as things are now, my spears outnumber yours. I'm even more certain they've had more practice with 'em than your lot: all your lads came out to see us unarmed! Can you imagine that?" He shook his head in disbelief. "That's just careless, that is; asking for trouble, if you ask me. It's a dangerous world." He suddenly switched his attention to the other men still standing around. "So then," he called, "will you come and earn honest payment with me, or will you go back to your fields and your sheep, and hope your fields will give you enough for todays' night-meal?"

The numbers that surged back towards him were answer enough for Drosten. Einar merely gestured that the Orccans go with Havard and his own followers. He stepped closer to Olwen and Drosten.

"I won't let them all come at once, and I'll make sure there's some from my own house to replace them while they work," he assured them quietly. "I have no wish to disrupt things so much that you or we starve from this; but nor will I sit idle while my men die around me from the cold and the wet. You knew those old houses were exposed, and you did nothing to even warn us. Look on this as a bad deed catching up with you. Besides, I don't reckon it'll take all that long to get a smallish house up, if all these lads, yours and mine, can find the way to work together. Then *everyone* can go back into the fields and concentrate on keeping us fed, eh?"

"You have enough people of your own, Einar," said Olwen worriedly. "Why do you feel the need to take ours?"

"Because your lads have put up more houses than mine ever have, and we need to learn how it's done. Because it's a good way of getting them working together and getting to know each other a little better. And, as I said before, because to some extent your own actions made this necessary. This is the weregeld for sitting back and trying to get us all killed in the storms. Should I go on?"

"Why not come to us and arrange it first, Einar?" asked Drosten. "If you're talking about working together and knowing each other better, what persuaded you to come and steal our men for your own work, and not ask for them openly beforehand? Such behaviour does nothing to bring me closer to you."

Einar shrugged. "You and I can afford to be enemies. These lads can't: later in the year, I'm willing to bet they'll be needing each other more and more. You wait: you'll thank me for this one day."

Drosten spat on the ground between them. "Don't lie awake waiting for that day."

SUMMER, 902 A.D.

CHAPTER NINETEEN

Drosten was aware that it had become a habit, almost. Rise from his bed in the morning, have a quick cup and a bite of anything that happened to be close to hand around the fireside. Speak the morning greetings to Olwen and the children; head out, pull open the outer door and step out into the day. Find those whose work was with the ewes and the new lambs, and put them to it. Check on the pigs, in case any of the sows were farrowing yet, and if they were, then arrange to have the fences put between mother and young to stop them being crushed beneath her. Go and look at the barley-field, and make sure his farmhands were picking out the weeds effectively. Then round up a few of the lads, preferably with their dogs in tow, and send them over to see where the neighbours were sending their own sheep across the boundary *this* time.

Drosten scowled in the chill breeze and pulled a comb through the tight hairs of his beard. He had walked the boundary with Einar: the man knew exactly where his own lands ended. Drosten had even put up a stone to remind him when Einar had failed to do so in spite of his offer at the time he had his new house built, but perhaps it worked more as a provocation. Not that any of it was really his, Drosten felt: in some undefinable way, he still looked on the whole place as belonging to his wife, his own family. These newcomers were only temporary; they would get disheartened in a summer or two. After all, had they not come all the way here from good land in their own country? To his mind, that suggested fickle natures and weak wills, easily defeated by time and gentle, insistent pressure. Like making sure they kept to the agreements.

He spotted Rilca from the corner of his eye: she too was heading in the Norsemen's direction, and a little quicker than his own emmissaries. He frowned; there was no reason for her to be so keen on keeping their new neighbours out of trouble – was there? They had a son about her age, he recalled; perhaps it might be wise to ask Olwen to have word with the girl, if only about the facts behind where babies came from. Drosten would rather she took it further and suggested that she perhaps go back to spending her time with her own people, as she always had before, but he also recognised that such pleading would probably be futile. Einar and his crewmen were new, unusual in so many ways, and he could see the attraction they held for everyone in his household, even if he chose to dismiss it himself. He was still stinging, he realised, from the way so many of them had rushed to help build Einar's new house for him, in return for silver they couldn't spend. Now where was the sense in that?

Even his own wife seemed to have taken an interest in them, he recalled gloomily. But then he might have expected that, given how readily she had agreed to let them settle in the first place. And there was another bone of irritation for Drosten: there had been agreements of payment for using the land, and nothing had so far been seen in that regard. All he ever did seem to see was a flock of scabby sheep roaming wherever they pleased, sometimes accompanied by a shepherd who didn't seem to care about boundaries or marker-stones. And always, it seemed, a different member of Einar's retinue, whenever

Drosten went to protest.

He thought about telling his own men to be sure and take the dogs with them, and set them loose as they got closer. That would be another escalation, with the possibility that somebody might get seriously hurt; and Olwen had told him enough tales of the pride these northern people took in their weapons, and their readiness to use them. Was he ready for proper fighting? Probably not; and almost certainly, Olwen wouldn't be. Not after what had happened to Rilca's father and Uoret, her own former husband. No, then, he would have to settle for more harsh words, which would undoubtedly be ignored as they always were. One reason he had taken to sending others over to push the sheep off their land was that he was becoming sick of spouting the same old phrases and demands, and watching the silent, sarcastic, faintly dismissive smiles he got in return. Perhaps it was time to make a proper visit over to Einar's new house, so recently finished and sitting proudly in the shelter of the dunes. Drosten hoped the ghosts of the other, older house would rise up and choke the newcomers, and thereby save him the bother.

He could have kept a list of all the little annoyances and implied insults that seemed to make up a large portion of his life these days: but he didn't want to. He knew in his own heart that his temper was getting shorter, his anger more ready to burst out at whoever happened to be closest. It was not a fair thing to burden his own family, his own household, with: they remained steadfast and loyal and supportive of him, however much they might seem to side with the newcomers. His orders were still obeyed, his place by the fireside unchanged. But it was getting harder to control himself. Yes, he thought, it might definitely be time to go and confront the new master of the southern lands in his own new home. Remind him who his real master was; remind him that, if he chose to ignore the boundaries agreed only a season ago or less, then Drosten might choose to do the same. The idea of this hulking, brutish Northman fuming impotently as his neighbour's cattle went trampling through his barley-field finally brought a smile to his craggy features. He finished with the comb, and went off to gather up a handful of his farmhands for company.

CHAPTER TWENTY

Rilca ran as fast as her legs would carry her over the uneven, sandy soil. Long grasses, their heads heavy with seeds and reaching almost to her chest, whipped at her body as she dodged lithely past them, but there were always more to come, trying to snare her and bring her down – if the rough, pitted ground didn't manage it first. Her dark chestnut hair, a little lighter now in the long days of summer when the sun almost never set, streamed out behind her; green eyes scanned the path ahead, the lie of the grasses to either side, the humps and dips in the ground around her. But they always came back to the small dark sheep that stood huddled among those same long grasses, and the grim grey boulder that sat beyond them.

Whilst her eyes stayed firmly fixed on where she was going at such a breakneck speed, her ears strained behind her, waiting for the inevitable sound of others from her household coming along in her tempestuous wake. It was happening more and more, she knew: whoever Einar had dumped the job of tending his new flocks on wasn't up to the task, and the bloody animals had wandered past the marker-stone her step-father had put up only at the end of this past spring. Once the Norsemen had come ashore and taken the land her aunt had offered them, Drosten's first act had been to get the stone carved and set up on the exact point where their land turned into the neighbour's. It was a simple enough concept, Rilca thought: somebody puts a stone up to mark the edge of their land, so you keep your livestock on your side of it – unless you were intending to start a fight over it. She at least was beginning to think that this was exactly what craggy old Einar had in mind, and she had heard a good few of their household muttering the same thing. After all, hadn't he then stolen the ground between their house and the sea, almost as soon as he was ashore?

None of which actually had any direct bearing on why she ran so fast to intercept these small, scraggy, bleating creatures before anybody else from her side of the border could. Oh no: she had no interest in the sheep at all, and cared not a whit where they chose to crop the grass. Sooner or later somebody would come and round them up, and they would be pushed back to their proper pastures by Einar's men or Drosten's. The end result was always the same; only the level of cursing and yelling seemed to vary. Rilca didn't care. She had other reasons for running.

Suddenly, she grinned, her eyes lighting up with more pleasure than just fast running could account for. A figure had risen up out of the tall grass: perhaps he had heard the pounding of her feet as she approached, or perhaps he had finally decided that the fallout from letting his sheep wander was not worth the effort today. Rilca hoped the first was at least part of the reason for his appearance, but was sensible enough not to totally disregard the latter. He waved as she burst through a denser clump of grass, and bent to retrieve a spear.

At least he's not scowling all the time these days, she thought happily. Even the worst, most stormy of tempers had to blow itself out eventually, but in Svein's case it had taken a good few moons to do it. She thought it had been worth the wait, though: his smile beamed across his wide cheekbones, and reached deep into his pale blue eyes under that long, impossibly light fringe that seemed to have a mind of its own in the winds of this place. He was tall and lean, like his father, she thought idly, but hopefully without the nasty streak she always suspected lay just below the surface in Einar.

"Lost your sheep again?" she asked teasingly as she reached his side and leant gasping against him. His chest was solid, firm, his ribs clearly felt and the sounds of his own breath loud in her ear.

"What would make you bother about that today, when you never have before, hmm?" His answer came in the same light-hearted tone as her initial question, but as always, Rilca thought she sensed deeper, more anxious undercurrents. This time, she chose to ignore them – at least to begin with.

"I'm not bothered; I'm just asking the question to find out why you're out and about so early in the day."

"It's not early!" he laughed. "It must be heading for day-meal time at least: all the rest of the lads are long out in the fields. Have you come looking for an invitation?" he asked suddenly, hopefully. He reached out to steady her as she pulled herself upright and nearly fell into a puffin-hole. "I'm sure there'd be enough to feed another one: there usually is. I reckon they're starving you over there." He nodded back the way she had come. "So who's on your tail today, to come and shout at us about these bastard sheep?"

Rilca laughed. "I'm pretty sure it's only that sort of reaction that's stopped Drosten sending men out to spear 'em already! To be honest, though, ours wander just as much, although never in this direction."

"That's 'cos this land's not so good," answered Svein with a touch both of smugness at knowing the reason and annoyance at the fact behind his answer. "Sheep with any sense always seem to know where the best grass is to be had, and these ones, though bloody-minded and small and a pain in the arse with all their wandering about, ain't stupid. There's better grass up on these ridges, and better still beyond the paths to your houses. I don't think anyone's ever actually brought them this way: we've never needed to, not since the day they came off the boat, and it's not *that* long ago. All fathir has to do is keep sending someone out to bring the sodding things back again, before your step-fathir gets all irate and difficult – again."

Rilca looked over at him, head cocked and hands on hips. "That part, Svein, I don't need to be told! For what it's worth, he seems to take it out as much on the rest of us as he does on you lot. I just wish he'd stop trying to achieve the impossible and settle down to something like the life we had before..."

"Before?"

"Don't *you* start trying to get all irate with *me*! For all that you and I have come to a sort of friendship, we're the only ones, I think, who have, out of all the folk who live hereabouts. It can't be argued against: things were different before your father came and brought you all along with him. It's just one of those things." She shrugged, trying to indicate how little importance she gave the matter. "Drosten never used to be as harsh as he is now. Something's getting to him more and more, but nobody, not even my aunt, can put a finger on what it might be. It's having all sorts of ill effects around the household."

Svein raised an eyebrow. "Sure it's not just that we're here now?"

Rilca shook her head. "It shouldn't bother him: these lands were never going to be his anyway, not the way things run for us. When aunt Olwen dies, her inheritance goes to Morgan, as her son – unless I've had a son by then, in which case he gets it all." She brushed wayward hair out of her eyes and pretended not to notice the sudden, burning stares of her companion. "No, it's something else, or maybe lots of little things, all building up inside him. I just hope he's got the sense to speak it all out before it bursts him."

"Fathir says that he's the stubborn, hard-headed type."

Rilca snorted. "He can talk!"

That brought another smile, and even the beginnings of a laugh out of Svein. Then his eyes slid past her, towards a knot of men coming more slowly in their direction. "Aye aye, here comes trouble," he murmured. "Want to make it look like you came to do their job for 'em?"

"What's the point? They're coming over anyway..."

"Yes, but it might put you in a better light with Drosten."

"I'm starting to get beyond caring, Svein, I really am," she replied despondently. "Nothing seems to be right, or done well enough these days, by any of us."

"So what are you going to do?"

"I'm going to stand here talking with you, until

they come. I notice you're not doing anything to round up the sheep that are causing all the trouble."

"Well, no..."

"So then, we're both going to catch it from somewhere or other, aren't we?"

"I know just what you mean about being beyond caring," the lad muttered. He looked back towards the oncoming figures. "I'm really not in the mood for this today, but nor am I in the mood for letting you carry blame for things you've not done wrong." He straightened up and shouldered his spear. "So I'm going to drive these fuck-arsed sheep home again, before those other prats catch up with us. You care to come, or will you head homeward?"

Rilca beamed a smile. "That's two invitations in a morning, Svein; you're getting eager."

He grinned back. "Give me one good reason why I shouldn't be?"

"Ah no, that just spoils the fun!" She turned to go, then looked back at him over her shoulder, green eyes flashing and hair tumbling down her back. "I'll see you again soon enough, Svein."

"That you will," he murmured under his breath as he tore his eyes away from her and back to the sheep. As if they could read his intent, they were huddling closer together and watching him with unblinking, impassive eyes. He brought the spear down in a sweeping motion behind the nearest group, sending them turning and running back the way they had come. "That you will," Svein repeated, before turning to collect the rest of the flock and starting for home before the Orcca-men could even shout a greeting.

CHAPTER TWENTY-ONE

Svein saw no reason to hurry homeward, even though there was no point in dawdling either. He knew what he would find in the new house, so recently built and which had allowed them to abandon the ruins of the houses some previous tenants had also left behind to rot and moulder in the wind and rain that seemed to continue all the way into summer without respite. His father would be sprawled comfortably in his High-Seat, between his two precious bloody pillars, those rotten lumps of wood that had landed them in this miserable place to begin with. No, he decided, he took that last statement back: this place had Rilca to brighten it up, and he found himself thinking more and more that she did indeed brighten what might otherwise be a miserable and comfortless existence. So: his father would be in his customary place, handing out the jobs around the farmstead, overseeing all the work from a safe distance whilst being careful not to get too close to any of it himself. He would probably be on his second or third horn by now, too, but Einar didn't seem to get drunk from it early in the day. And he usually stopped between the day and night- meals. Mothir would be doing much the same in the smaller *stofa* at the end of the house, but in her case there was more actual doing and joining-in with the spinning and the weaving, and keeping a closer track of what the farmhands and bondar had to say. Sometimes, Svein got the idea that his mother knew more of what was going on than his father did; he couldn't remember whether it had ever been so in their old home, but he found more and more that the details of that old life, details he swore he would hold close in his mind for ever, were fading away, swamped by the here-and-now, and the harsh business of everyday living. What he was more certain of was that he had a larger share of the chores and household tasks than he had ever had before: hence his being out with the sheep this morning. At least in this place, he thought, there was no need to shepherd the animals up to higher pastures through the summer, as they had always done in the old country.

Once he had gathered them onto the wide, meandering path through the dunes the sheep were happy enough to make their own way home, with only an occasional whack from the spear being needed. He cajoled them through the improvised gate in the rough fence they had made from any scraps of driftwood, odd branches and bushes that had been close to hand, and back into the ruins of those old houses, which seemed far better suited to sheep than to men. Then he headed back northwards, over the burn, along the top of the ridged dunes and into the slight dip behind them that marked the site of his new home.

It looked a lot like the house they had left behind in More, he had to admit: the lads had done a good job on it. It was maybe a little shorter than his people were used to, but then it had been put up largely by Drosten's own men, and resembled their own squared-off homes still further to the north. It boasted a low-hanging roof covered in fine, green turf, and good stone walls around the big posts that held that same roof up. A single porch pushed out from the grassy mound at the southern end, with the strong wooden door framed in its barge-boards. It even boasted stone paving leading up to that door, and a storm-sill to try and keep some of the wet and mud out. There was a second doorway in the north-eastern corner, but nobody used it very much. It was more for throwing the ashes of the fire out than anything else, and had nothing in the way of porches or fancy paths. The bondar had rapidly fixed a curtain up over it to keep the draught to a minimum, and Svein suspected that it wouldn't be long before it got blocked up completely. So he went in by the proper entrance.

Svein was already almost as tall as the door was. He pushed it open and ducked both himself and his spear through it, entering a narrow passage that spanned the width of the house. At the near end, yet still almost lost in the gloom, stood an ale barrel and a milk-vat, side by side on stone slabs to keep them cool. One side of the passage was formed by the end wall of the house, whilst the other was a wooden partition with a doorway into the main hall. At the far end, another door led into a little room where his mother kept her weaving. The light from the hearth was the only illumination out here, making the hall a natural place to head for as quickly as possible.

Einar looked up as his eldest son entered. "You're back early," he grunted. Svein regarded him for a moment before replying.

"I brought the sheep back from their roving when I saw men from Drosten's place heading our way. I wasn't in the mood for getting sworn at today."

"Surprised you chose not to stop and chat with his daughter again."

Svein's face hardened into a frown as he took a place at the opposite bench. "What's that supposed to mean?"

"You're barely fourteen summers, Svein. Since we started finding others of our countrymen in these islands, I'd've thought you'd be looking to their houses if you're thinking about making friendships – or more."

"Since when did that become a problem? What

does it matter if I talk with Rilca from time to time?"

"Aren't you listening, boy?" growled Einar across the peaty haze of the hearth. "We might have had to strike a deal with these dark people when we first got here – but now that's changing. Now we find friends and cousins every time your uncle Havard takes the ship out. Drosten's folk are retreating further and further as Haralds' mean ways send more and more of our own people westwards. He's becoming isolated, alone... doomed, and his family with him." He tugged at his beard as his hard grey eyes regarded his son. "It's something that's been on my mind a lot, even since the day we first got here. Drosten's got no support he can call on; that's the only reason he bargained with us at all in the first place!" He tapped his empty cup on the edge of the wide bench that made up their seats. "You start getting fond of his daughter – or any of them, come to that – and one day, you'll find your heart full of pain and misery. Because one day, not too far away, they're going to wind up dead, or in thrall to whoever takes the rest of their lands from them. And no son of mine is destined for that sort of wyrd. So you forget them – her. If it's friends you're looking for, there's plenty of good men here have sons and foster-kids; if you're thinking about marriage already, I'd say you were still a little young for it – but if you really want to, we'll start looking for suitable girls. It might need a trip eastwards before we find the right match, but I'm willing to consider it if you're serious..."

"Stop it!" blazed Svein suddenly. "You know damn well that's not what you meant!"

"Then stop getting so friendly with those who will soon be beneath you," came the reply.

"Has all this got aught to do with sending the sheep out over towards Drosten's lands every day?"

"Just getting him used to the idea, is all."

Svein shook his head. "I don't see that there's any need for it. All this other talk of friends around us wherever we turn is just bollocks: Havard's had the ship out once, just once, so far, and it took him over a fortnight to find anyone willing to sell us the timber for this roof! I was in the room when he told you all about it, remember: I'm not like Bjorn, who's too young to question the shit you feed him day after day. And I go out, and I talk to people, both ours and Drosten's. I'll find my own friends."

"Bold words for one so young."

Svein shrugged. "I was saying to Rilca only this morning that I'm pretty much past caring, right now."

Einar's gaze never faltered. "We'll see how that goes, as time goes by."

Svein got up again and prowled along his side of the hearth. "I still don't see what you have against Rilca and her people. It's not like they're *Saami* or anything."

"They're not our people either, though, are they? You only have to look at 'em to see that. They're shorter, darker, narrower in the face. They think differently; they have strange ways, to our minds at least." Einar leaned forward. "I'm not saying any of this just out of spite, or just because they're different, although many might think that to be enough of a reason to keep a distance from 'em. But the world is how it is: there are the strong ones, and the weak ones. Right now, more and more, Drosten and his kind are becoming the weaker out of them and us. It began long before our little ship arrived on these shores; it must have done, or their king would've sent men to help drive us away by now. But it didn't happen, did it?"

"Someone said that they'd sent messengers, and never had a reply. I think mothir told me it."

Einar smiled. "Your ma's a canny one, and she puts more effort into listening to the gossip from over there than I ever have."

Svein smiled back, crookedly. "Well doesn't that just prove my point, then? What's the use of shutting ourselves off when there's good information to be had all around us? I don't ken why you do this, fathir, I really don't. We couldn't even have got this place built if it weren't for them. I don't understand what it is you're trying to prove with all this, but all it says to me is that you've lost your bloody mind." He peered over the top of the iron pot, now taken off the ship, that hung by its chain from the roof-beam. "Is this ready yet?"

"How should I know? Go ask Hildegard, or Yrsa, or one of those."

Svein glared at him. "Bloody good idea," he muttered, and stomped back towards the room at the end of the passage.

CHAPTER TWENTY-TWO

Ragna looked up from her embroidering as Svein pushed the inner door open. "It's awful hot in here," he declared. "D'you want this left open awhile?"

"I'm fine with it closed," she answered, "it means I don't have to listen to your fathir rambling on."

Svein grimaced. "I've just come away from that, so I'll shut it again gladly." He leant his weight against the planks, which pushed back into their frame. "I brought the sheep back: Rilca came across to warn me there were others on their way, and I got off before they reached me." He moved into the middle of the room and sat on a vacant stool. "Any ideas why fathir's so against

Drosten and his people these days?"

Ragna idly brushed hair away from her face before answering. "It's a strength-and-power thing between your fathir and Drosten. They're like two *holmgangar* facing each other across the duelling field, waiting for one of them to make a wrong move." She sighed. "It's got a lot worse as summer's gone on; I suppose he's none too happy about you being friendly with Rilca either, although if he had any wits, he'd be encouraging you both."

"Why so?"

His mother straightened on her own seat and looked at him seriously. "Drosten's people, for a start, aren't his: they're Olwen's people, if we're being strictly correct about it. She's the one who owns it all: the land, the houses, the people, everything. That's how these Orcca-folk arrange matters. You'll inherit all of this," she indicated their own house with a wave of her hand, "when your fathir dies. But Olwen's son, Mawgan isn't it? - he'll only inherit his mothir's property if young Rilca hasn't had a son by then." She smiled sympathetically. "It's a complicated way of doing things, if you ask me, but that's how I had it explained. And," she held up a warning finger, "Rilca's sons will only inherit because Olwen's sister is dead already, and died before she had any sons. Had that been different, then Rilca's brothers would've got everything."

"And how does that bear on my being a friend towards Rilca? Who mentioned most of this only today, as it happens..."

"Really? That's interesting... but did you not hear what I just said about Rilca having sons before Olwen dies, and what that does to her own child?"

Understanding dawned on the boy. "Fathir was

saying that if I was looking for a wife already, he'd start sounding out some mysterious friends he claims uncle Havard has found while out sailing."

"Well then, that just confirms that your fathir's not thinking at all, doesn't it?"

"What do *you* think about it?"

Ragna put down her cloth. "I think you're too young in many ways to be considering marriage just yet, although I've no idea what sort of age is proper for our neighbours."

"What about being friendly towards them in general?"

"I do it all the time, or hadn't you noticed? That should give you the answer to the question, surely." She regarded him with serious, pale blue eyes, and reached out a delicate hand to brush the linen of his shirt. "Your fathir has his own ideas of how things should be, Svein, and there's little can be done to dislodge them at the moment. All we can do, sometimes, is keep our own counsel and watch how the wind is blowing on any given day. But if you want an easier time of it, I'd keep your friendliness towards Rilca out of his sight when you can."

"Pretty easy to do when he doesn't come outside very much."

Ragna raised her eyebrows. "I don't know where you get that idea from: he's outdoors more than he's in, most days. Now that the summer-days are here he spends most of his time in the few fields we've managed to put under the *ard,* and checking on the health of your sheep." She chuckled. "How else do you think he knows about you and Rilca meeting up so often, hmm?"

"Maybe it's me who's not been paying attention."

"Ah, you're young still, and full of joy at the world – well, some days, anyway. Just ignore your fathir when you can, and try and be careful around him the rest of the time. But don't disregard his words completely, though."

"Why not, when you've just as good as said they don't matter?"

"Because there's always the chance he's right. He talks to people too, you know, even if they aren't the same ones that you and I do. Nothing is certain, Svein: nothing at all. What's more certain is that when winter comes, we'll be needing more food than we'll have from our own lands. Like it or no, we're probably going to be buying off Olwen and Drosten, and if they're short as well it's likely to get difficult."

"Even more so when the old man's talking crap half the time. I only came in to see if it was day-meal time, and even that's got complicated."

Ragna shrugged a smile. "Maybe you'd be better off out in the fields again, eh? But you're right: the day-meal can't be far away. I sent Signy into the dairy earlier: she ought to know, or be taking care of it at any rate. Why don't you go find out, eh?"

Svein stood up. "I'll do that." He looked around the dim room, lit only by its own smaller hearth and a range of rush-lights set in bowls around the walls. "Where's Bjorn?"

"Ah," said his mother, her smile broadening. "More than likely he's off down to the shore with Mawgan."

"Right," muttered Svein. "I can almost see why fathir's getting so annoyed at it all. Is there anyone here but him that isn't spending all their time with the neighbours, instead of working our own place?"

"I've no idea," answered his mother with a laugh. "You can make a hobby of asking them, if you like."

CHAPTER TWENTY-THREE

The day-meal came and went; after the hubub of the bondsmen's chatter and the gossiping of the housemaids, the hearth felt quiet and still. Einar enjoyed this time, when the world around him slowed and he could, to some extent, be alone with his thoughts. Those who sometimes shared his company around these moments, Havard and Thorfinn, Skapti and Halvgrim, knew not to talk too loudly, or interrupt if their lord felt like discussing things. Today was a day for sitting quietly and waiting; the clues were all there in Einar's face, in the way he sat and the speed with which he emptied his cup.

Finally, however, he stirred. "Tell me more about these people you met, Havard," he growled gently, "those who came from our own country and sold us these timbers. Give me their names, their strength and the place they call home in these islands." He leaned forward on the bench. "Tell me how they conduct business with any of these local folk; tell me what they told you about their own strengths and the strength of their neighbours." He stared into his empty cup, unseeing, his mind far away amid troubles that might not even exist. "I need to know where we stand in relation to these folk, these Orcca-men: which of us is the stronger, and the more likely to drive the other out."

Havard sniffed. "Drosten been yelling and shouting again?"

"That's not got anything to do with it..."

"Brother-in-law, it might have if you're thinking of taking some sort of action against him. The only reason I can think of for asking such things is your wanting to know if you can rely on help from outside..."

"So then, tell me what I need to know!"

"We've only just got here," retorted Havard, a touch of impatience in his voice, "we've not even had a summer under our own roof yet. We've bought their help in putting this house up, we've had food and help of all sorts from them; we've even taken a huge extra chunk of land off them without offering anything in return for it, and you're *still* looking to start a fight already?"

"I am if my men keep getting harassed over where the animals roam, over where we put our *bere*, over what we're doing in our own household... there seems to be no end to it, some days. Everywhere I turn, I find Orcca-folk talking to my family, making friendly as they can, worming their way in and trying to keep us under their thumb... I said when we first arrived – before we even set out, I said what I was coming here to find – and it wasn't to sit on leftover fields and be subject to some craggy-arsed little man who doesn't even own the lands he's trying to rule!" He thumped the table that stood between them across the width of the house. "It's not right, Havard, and I'll dare you to say that you'd stand for it in my place. It's getting more obvious, too, the more the days go on: the responses more swift, the language more belligerent, as if they're looking for a fight just as much. I'm just concerned to strike first, before they can get help from somewhere – which is why I want you to tell me of the people you found when you took the bloody boat out!" he finished in an exasperated shout.

"Alright, there's no need for yelling and such; I just wasn't sure how much more there was to tell. I didn't hold back on the gossip when I came home, now did I? So you tell me what you want to know about, and I'll try and provide it."

Einar glowered at his bench-mates before

speaking again. "I want the *hauldr's* name, for a start..."

"He's Ottar, a son of one Hrafn from Oslofjord, right under Harald's nose."

"Not a name I know at all, and I've been down those ways occasionally. And how long he's been here?"

"That's harder: around four or five winters, he said, although he admitted that he was losing count. The place looks well-established, so it must be at least that long, I'd've thought."

"And were there any of the local men already sitting there when he decided to settle?"

"I didn't think to ask. Sorry. I was more concerned with trading for timber, like I'd been asked to."

Einar waved the apology away with a smile. "It doesn't matter really, though I was curious. Alright then, what else? Ah, yes: who else does he know here? Are there enough of us to set up a Thing? And is there a Jarl come westwards from the old lands, or is it all just rumour and lies again?"

"He mentioned a couple of names, but without getting into details of where these other people were. He didn't mention anything about Jarls, or Things; I got the impression that, much like us, he's on his own and making it work without any sort of support."

Einar raised an eyebrow. "Think he'd like some support? Where is he, this Ottar, in relation to us?"

"He's a day's sail down the coast heading southwards in a big, wide bay, and I think he'd welcome a friendly face well enough – he certainly made us feel at home, and couldn't do enough for us. Thinking of paying a visit, then?"

"It might be worth the trip, aye. Did he bring his family over with him?"

"Not that he mentioned..."

"That's a pity: Svein's getting restless, and a little too friendly with the neighbours. Especially that girl of theirs. If I could find him more suitable playmates, I'd put some effort into bringing them together." He growled a sigh. "So what we have, then, is two households, Ottar's and this one, sitting a day or so apart with very little in the way of Orcca-men around them." He stroked his beard absently. "Why are the natives not sitting on this land already, and why don't they do anything to try and get it back?" he wondered quietly.

"Maybe they've got troubles of their own elsewhere, that we haven't heard about," suggested Halvgrim. "Or maybe there's not enough of them, for whatever reason, to band together and do it."

Havard stared at his brother-in-law across the fire. "It was only earlier today you were complaining that Drosten's lot were being too active in trying to get this place back! So which is it, Einar?"

Einar rubbed his eyes. "I don't know: I can't keep it straight in my head." He peered into his cup again, but it was definitely empty, and liable to stay that way. "Ah, enough of it. Come on: let's go out and get on with the day. Maybe some fresher air will clear my head a bit."

CHAPTER TWENTY-FOUR

Once the eating was over and the jug had gone round, Ragna read her husband well enough to take her own companions and retreat back into the weaving-room. There, among the skeins of newly-dyed wool that hung from the rafters, the baskets full of raw fleece newly plucked from the backs of the sheep as they began to moult and the little stack of cloth that sat beside the big loom on which it was woven, she and her friends could talk more freely. The little hearth was already stacked with peat, leaving the air smoky, hot and dry. Thora had collected another jug on the way through, and they settled onto the various stools that cluttered the floor around the raised platform at the end wall.

"He's gnawing at these problems he thinks we have with Olwen and her family more and more," said Ragna when they were all comfortable and taking up the tools of their work.

"Aye, lady, but what to do about it?" replied Gytha cautiously.

"Now there's a question," admitted their mistress. "It's hard to know what's for the best when he's in this sort of mood. Sometimes it'll just blow over, but other days it nags and nags at him." She teased out a stubborn knot in the fleece before setting her spindle spinning again, watching the thread twist and lengthen as it headed for the floor. "I'm mostly concerned that he doesn't set anything off that will come back to haunt us later on; I can't believe that Drosten hasn't got the means to collect more men should it come to blows between them and us."

"The lady of the house there seems friendly enough towards us," agreed Signy, brushing golden hair back from her young face. "It's hard to see what the master would want to go upsetting things for – if I've followed it right," she added hastily. Ragna smiled.

"Oh, I think you've got it well enough. I don't understand it either, beyond my husband's stubborn refusal to accept that he could be master here without being the Jarl as well."

"Ah," said Gytha sagely. "This other man's not in his dream of our new life here, then."

Ragna looked hard at her. "I don't think I could've

said it better, Gytha. That's exactly it! Einar brought us here expecting to find empty fields and open land just there for the taking. Instead, his pillars washed ashore in a place already lived in, and I don't think he's come to terms with that yet. Perhaps he never will; perhaps the Thunderer intended him to do for Drosten and his family, and make this place ours rather than simply moving in where nobody was before. Perhaps Einar has to work for what he wanted..."

"Lady, if that's so, then what about the rest of us, who've taken the trouble to be friendly towards the lady Olwen and her household?" asked Thora. "Doesn't that put us against both our own lord, and the will of the Gods?"

"If we've worked it out right, then I suppose it does," admitted Ragna reluctantly. "But we could've got it wrong, even then."

"All of us together, lady?" queried Gytha. "I find that unlikely, to be truthful."

"Aye," said Ragna softly, "so do I. I'd put more trust in our thinking than in my husband's, sometimes – though not a word of such outside of this door! I think he's having enough troubles already, without having to worry about our loyalty as well."

"There's no doubt of our allegiance," protested Thora. "We're just helping him to think, aren't we?"

"*I* think," said Ragna slowly, "that it might be a good time to go and visit the lady next door again, and try to find out what's going on on her side of the marker-stone. All we're doing here is guessing, and trying to do anything on that sort of basis just isn't going to work. We need to find out *facts*, and then we have something definite to go on."

"Your pardon, lady... but are you sure that's

wise?"

"Arranging such a thing won't be easy with the lord so keen *not* to talk to them," observed Signy.

Ragna smiled. "You're wrong there: it couldn't be easier." She beckoned to the younger woman. "Go find Svein for me, would you Signy? Tell him I need something doing."

CHAPTER TWENTY-FIVE

Drosten had gone to look over the pigs, to see if one might be big enough for an early slaughter. Rilca was away with Danna and a couple of the other women, helping where she could, learning everything she was taught. Her neice was growing up fast, Olwen knew: her hair seemed longer and more windswept every day, her eyes more alive and bright with excitement and the joy of discovery. She was on the verge of womanhood, which was both a good and a bad thing, the way the world was now. A year ago, Olwen was sure she would have found more happiness and pleasure in watching her adopted daughter growing up, and in explaining how the household was run, who did what and why... all the knowledge Rilca would need when the day came to start the search for a husband. But now, she found little to be happy or joyous about at the best of times. Her heart was troubled, her soul uneasy. And it was hard to see any way out of her dark, grim place that would not involve walking through places even darker and harsher than this.

She wondered, as she idly fed the fire and tried to work up some enthusiasm for her daily tasks, if this mood might not have descended upon her anyway, as the years passed and some things got harder to keep inside. Would something else have occurred that brought all her old memories to the surface after having been so carefuy buried for so many years? Would she still be feeling this way even if Einar and his boatload of pirates had not come washing up upon her shore? Why did it have to be here? What sort of fates or forces governed such things? It would have to be a cruel world indeed that let such things happen purely by accident. Why her shore? Why *him?*

Her dark eyes roved around the round little world of her house. They took in the benches clustered around the firepit, the sheepskins scattered across the floor and piled in the little alcoves where they all slept, alone in their dreams every night. She saw the woven rugs that hung from the walls and from the rafters, these last making a sort of partition wherever they hung, dividing the room into little curtained-off parts, a segment for every set of tasks. From outside, little gusts of wind ran playfully under the curtain, puffing little motes of dust and soil up from the bare earth of the floor. She had lived here for a good many years: it was all intimately familiar, and yet in these moods it also appeared alien and strange. Unable to shake the gloom into which she was sliding, she leaned over and began to collect the eating-bowls from by the fireside.

"I'll help, mama." A little hand grabbed the edge of one of the clay bowls and lifted it towards her. She smiled back into grey eyes and fine, sandy hair, set in and around a pale, round little face that beamed a smile in return.

"Where did dada go?" Morgan asked.

"I think he went to look at the pigs," she replied, forcing herself to concentrate on the question, on the actual words, rather than on the stream of searing memories that tore through her head once more. "He was thinking about having one butchered, since we're low on meat. Would you fancy fresh pig?"

"Yes, but sheep would be nicer still."

"We can't kill any of the sheep just now, little one: the ewes are still suckling, their lambs are too small, and we've already eaten all of last year's spares. You know how it is: we eat the new rams every year, save maybe one or two, but we keep the ewes so that they can make more lambs." She shook her head decisively. "No, Morgan, it's the wrong time of year for killing sheep. Maybe in another moon or two, though. You'll have to ask your father."

The lad thought about it for a moment or two, then seemed to lose interest. "Where's Rilca?"

"Rilca's working with Danna, Bethan and Gwen today, so she can't go with you to play. You know it always gets busier in the long days, what with the barley growing and all the newborn animals."

"Would you come, then?"

"Where were you thinking of going?"

"I don't know. The shore? The fields? Or I might go and see what Be-yorn's doing. That's a funny name, isn't it?" He tried the sound of it again, "Beee-yorrnn. Be-yornn. Be..."

His mother gently put a hand over his mouth. "Shh: enough now. You go out; I'll come and find you in a little while, and maybe you could help me with the bread-making, hmm?"

Morgan nodded and slipped out of her grasp, skipping round the firepit to the big outer door. She watched him go with mixed thoughts once more.

Was it wise to distract him from the Norsemen next door, she wondered; the way things were shaping between Einar and her own husband, closeness and familiarity might be the only weapons that could save them when the fighting eventually broke out – as she was more and more certain that it would. She felt powerless to stop it: perhaps part of her even wanted it, wanted the bloodshed and the maiming, wanted, perhaps most of all, to see either Einar or Drosten dead at her feet. The worst part, the scariest part, was that she realised that it didn't matter which. She would make her peace with one or the other of them, either one, on any terms they chose. But having a truce with both was going to become impossible. There were too many points on which there could never be agreement. And the biggest point was the one that had just gone happily running out to play.

Why, why, *why* had Einar washed up here? Was this the Lord's way of punishing her for sins long forgotten? Was it the devils he prayed to having a sick and twisted joke, feeling their strength in this new land? Bad enough that any of these wicked people turned up at her house... but *this* one...

CHAPTER TWENTY-SIX

Her husband Uoret had died, died in his own bed in the prime of his life, without a mark on him, without leaving her any reason to go seeking redress from anyone. It happened, Olwen knew; there had been others she had heard of over the years before and since, but that knowing had not prepared her for the huge and sudden void that had opened up within her as she gazed down upon his pale, cold corpse that morning long ago. The servants, his relatives, her own family, had joined at the graveside, howling and wailing, screaming their grief and anger to the heavens and the hells. As was customary, his sister's son had inherited their clan's lands – and his sister had never been very keen on Olwen. It had not taken long for her place in the household to lessen, for her seat to be moved further out from the fireside, for the welcome to grow colder. She had gone back to her own sister's estates here in this place, where the dunes looked out to the open sea and the winds came howling back with ice and rain in their teeth. Arwen and Drem had no male children, only Rilca; Olwen's own sons were already dead, having barely lived beyond a year. She had wondered if perhaps early deaths ran in Uoret's family. Nothing seemed to make her hurt and pain any better; everywhere she turned, even in this new place, she found reminders of her old life, her man, their own life together, now cut short so unfairly.

They had been tumultuous, troublesome times: not for either the first or the last time, eyes had scanned the ocean waves to the very horizon, looking anxiously for signs of long, lean ships with broad, square sails, that brought danger and despair in among their other cargoes. The word to war had come often from David, Bridei's uncle and the king of the time; Uoret had answered it whenever the call had come, as had Olwen's own brother-in-law. One time, one time of storms and danger and confusion, only her husband had returned, with dark circles of tiredness under his eyes, the dark marks of bruises across his body... and darker shadows of grief and terror set deep within his eyes. Those wounds never really healed, she thought, and she had wondered if they had also had a hand in his death soon after. Arwen, her own sister, wife to Drem, and Rilca's mother, had followed him into the grave within a season, and Olwen had found herself totally, utterly alone. She and the young girl had clung to each other desperately in those dark days, finding no comfort, but at least they gave each other no extra pain either.

Grief had filled her: blind anger and rage at the cruelty of a world that could do such things and carry on uncaring, had filled the spaces left raw and bleeding by those she had known and loved. What purpose could there ever be in a place and a people that had let this happen? Why should she heed the quiet words and hidden motives of those distant branches of her own family and clan that were all she had left by way of company? No; she looked elsewhere for reason, for understanding... for recompense and perhaps even a new beginning. When word had filtered through that the Norse men had set up a trading camp, and were announcing their intent to stay until the summer faded towards winter, she had found her thoughts unable to stray far from them. Eventually, her feet were compelled to follow, regardless of the warning words that trailed behind her from her own people.

Olwen had only ever known small, cosy houses, built in circular patterns into the soil of their native land, full of warmth and comforting features. Suddenly, she had found herself adrift among alien worlds and ideas. There were no houses for these sea-rovers; instead, they came ashore with sharp-cornered tents, rectangular in shape with their woollen fabric stretched over garishly painted triangular frames, clustered together in a chaotic jumble of noise, smell and cargo. Piles of timber, whole trunks of long, straight trees, lay in the grass alongside bundles of fabric, mountains of animal skins, sacks of soft, downy feathers, and barrels of slimy, oily fish that stank whenever anyone went downwind. As she took her first hesitant steps among them, all she could hear was the hubub of foreign speech, nasal and differently accented than the tongue she was used to. All she could see was colour: red, blue, green, yellow, in solid hues instead of her own familiar mix of threads, dyed purple and mauve with the local heathers. All she could smell was fish, overlain with thick woodsmoke and the indefinable odours of ships and salt-laden men. All so very strange and bewildering to a woman in the pits of grief and despair, who had never got closer to the ocean than the sands above its shore, had never dealt with men outside her own close family. Her world had suddenly felt even smaller and more inadequate than before.

Somewhere in the outskirts of this sprawling, vibrant, colourful, worrying, threatening place, Olwen had wavered – and then gone forward. Those who had accompanied her, a cluster of servants and farmhands, a few relatives, even fewer friends, had turned curious and concerned eyes in her direction, wondering what had got into her head this time, in a time of so many strange thoughts and deeds that many of her household wondered if she even had any mind left. Those whose own convictions prevented them from going any closer to these new, outlandish visitors were left behind; Olwen, having started, walked resolutely onwards, into their midst. As her short, dark figure entered their strange, chaotic world, as she walked closer and closer to their people, their tents and the ships drawn up on the gently sloping shore, fair heads and bright, light-coloured eyes turned to look, to watch her progress, and to wonder what she had come there for. She had stood silently for a long while, her arms folded and her shawl wrapped closely around her, as the wind blew hair out of her face and put stinging tears into her eyes. Eventually, one of these odd-looking men had ambled over to where she was, and thrust a cup towards her.

Einar. Although it had taken some time to work out that he was telling her his name. But it had been a start. Almost alone among his people, he had been willing to take the time needed to find out what Olwen had come to them for. Clearly she wasn't buying, and she seemed to have nothing to sell either. So who was she, and what did she want?

"My husband is dead," she began haltingly.

"You saying we killed him?" He had some knowledge of her speech, then, which suggested he had been this way before. Perhaps, she thought, he was some sort of leader or chief among them.

"No – or not directly. But some among you killed my sister's husband, who fought by his side. They sent my own husband home to me damaged, wounded, weak. He died soon afterwards."

"So you are here to seek a *weregeld* for your sister's husband? Why? What is that to you?"

"Here, we recognise descent through the women, not the men. My sister only has one child, a daughter. It is in her name that I come."

The Norseman had regarded her through cold, grey eyes. "I think there is more to it than this."

"What makes you say that? How could you know what goes on beyond this place where you spend your summers?"

He had brushed the question aside. "So you have come to ask payment, in your niece's name, for her dead father. Why does the girl not come? Is she still just a child? Why doesn't her mother come?"

"Her mother is dead also, and she's barely nine years old. That's why." She had glared at him defiantly. "So who do I talk to in order to get what I came for?"

Einar spread his hands wide. "We have no leader here: we are all equal, independent, come together as much by chance as anything else. I couldn't even say for sure if whoever gave your brother-in-law his death-blow is here at all – and that's allowing that he actually met his death at the hands of a countryman of mine. Which can't be proved..."

Dark eyes had met and held the grey. "There will be someone here, the man with a bigger ship, or more cargo, or more of those silver rings you all seem to wear on your sleeves; someone whose voice carries louder, whose thoughts carry more weight than those of some others." She sighed. "I'm not such a fool as to think that one of you is going to stand up and admit to the deed: there'd be no way you would've known the names of those you might have killed, whatever the circumstances of it. We're nothing to you: I've heard the tales of the things your people have done in other places, to other folk..."

"But you came here anyway."

"Yes I did."

"Without anyone else to speak on your behalf or support your claim against... someone."

"I have companions, those who work under me. I was not so foolish as to come completely alone."

Einar's eyebrows raised. "You are *hauldr* in these lands, then?"

"What does that mean?"

He grinned, a crack in the ice of his demeanour so far. "It's a name for the person who owns the land and has command over others."

She nodded. "That would be me, then, yes."

"Well now, that perhaps changes things. You're a landowner, with wealth of your own. We acknowledge that in women or men, unlike in some other places."

"Does it mean your people are more likely to give me a hearing because of it?"

"You still have nobody to accuse," Einar pointed out. "You cannot give a name, or even a place or a time when your relative was killed; you can't even be sure he died at our hands, as you've said yourself." He shook his head. "I wouldn't give much for your hopes, lady, I really wouldn't. But I admire your bravery in coming among us like this."

"Bravery will win me nothing by itself, though," she had replied bitterly. "There is nothing to show for my coming here, from what you say."

"Perhaps: but even bravery should be recognised." He had held out a cup, and indicated the stool next to his own. After a moment's slow hesitation, she had reached out for both. It had stretched into a long season after that; slowly, imperceptibly, her companions drifted away, until one day even Einar was packing up his belongings and stowing things aboard a ship he claimed to be his. It was not long after he had pushed that boat out into the grey waters, after she had stood and watched as the oars had snaked outwards and splashed into the water, that Olwen had realised that she needed, more than anything else, to find another husband. She had enjoyed the company and sharing of the days more than she had expected, but now she knew that she wanted it to last longer. It was time to go back to her own people, and seek out another who would properly take the place of her dead, sweet Uoret. Before her belly swelled too much to avoid even more mistrust and loneliness.

CHAPTER TWENTY-SEVEN

The more she sat and thought, the more convinced she became. The more convinced she became, the deeper the darkness around her felt. A secret kept for six years is hard to bear, she reflected wistfully: but she had borne it well. She might have gone on doing so for who knows how long – until Einar came striding into her yard. She had recognised him instantly: the eyes, the build, the particular walk he had. He had evidently not realised who she was – had the years altered her so much, she wondered, or was it that so much might have happened to him in between that he had simply forgotten? She could not for the life of her decide whether his failure to remember was a good thing or a bad. His lack of memory had at least allowed her the time to try and decide when and how to tell Drosten that his beloved son might not be his at all.

That was a tale she was not looking forward to telling. Quite apart from whatever such truths might do to her own reputation, what about Drosten? How was he likely to take such news? Gentle and kind though he generally was, Olwen could not imagine him just accepting it quietly and then getting on with things as before. She could only see hard words and long, stony silences between them from now onwards, and if his attitude towards Einar wasn't hard enough now, it wasn't going to get any softer. Yet she had not rushed out and married him simply to hide her deeds of that long-ago summer: there had been other reasons, matters to do with inheritances and ownership of property – and plain, simple loneliness, a desire not to be alone any more. That had been an unexpected parting gift from Einar, which had also sent her back among her own people with a purpose that seemed more like her old self, the one everybody had known before Uoret had died, the woman with a drive to get done what needed to be done.

Drosten had been an ideal if unlikely choice, and Olwen had found him genuinely likeable and receptive to her overtures. With their marriage, intricate power structures slid back into their accustomed places: she was anchored once more, and Rilca with her, safe within the familiar patterns of her own people. Morgan had arrived some moons afterwards, and nobody had thought to question that he was Drosten's progeny. Olwen had seen no reason to encourage such thoughts, had even convinced herself over the years that he was the legitimate child of her husband. Memories of her crazed season among the Norse had faded, sunk to the bottom of her mind and lain there untroubled, with no reason to disturb them. But now they were up on the surface again, vivid and clear in every detail, and Morgan was not Drosten's child. You only had to look at him to see that, she realised, and wondered how she had managed to not see it for so long. She had lied not only to her husband and her family, but to herself as well. None of them would be thanking her for it now.

And then there was the kirk... it didn't seem very likely that the priest would be especially welcoming either, regardless of her position hereabouts. When she had been married before – on both occasions, thinking back – Resad had been very clear about fidelity and faithfulness both to husband and God. It was part of the divine way of things, and somehow, she suspected that the technicality of being unmarried at the time of Morgan's conception was not going to be enough to blot out the likely sin of the subsequent deception. She knew

in her bones that everyone would sympathise with
Drosten and the awkwardness of his situation: Olwen
recalled that heads had shaken and tongues had wagged
when she had first sent her messengers to his family,
sounding out the possibility of marriage. It had made a
sort of sense: she needed a father-figure for the coming
child in order to conceal her own foolishness of the
summer, and she had genuinely felt that need for
company which had driven her into Einar's bed in the
first place. That hadn't changed. But Rilca would benefit
also, and the farmhands would rally to a headman in a
way that, for all that inheritances came through their
mothers or their aunts, they would never quite come
together under a woman. Olwen's property lay on an
exposed coast, a long, thin strip that stretched more along
the shore than it headed inland: it was a harsh place to
wrest a living from, and her ancestors had already
abandoned one settlement in favour of higher, more
fertile ground slightly more to the north. It needed strong
leadership, shot through with a gentle touch and a
forgiving, flexible nature. Drosten had taken to it all, and
had slowly pulled them through hard times and
unexpected setbacks, to the point where the household
was secure and comfortable. He had been a good father, a
caring husband, a strong leader of the men, a careful
planner. Olwen, too, had worked hard at her end of the
bargain, and had thought the bad times might perhaps
finally be behind them.

 She smiled bitterly. So much for hope, then.
Whatever comfort they had been enjoying up until this
spring was about to be torn away from them all, with no
idea of where they might end up after the storm had
abated – if it ever did. This was the sort of trouble that
might live on until she and Drosten and Einar were all in

their graves, and their offspring might or might not bother to repair the damage they had left behind.

Olwen felt tears stinging behind her eyelids. It would be so easy to just sit and weep by her fireside – but she couldn't. There were bowls to wash, chickens to feed, Morgan to play with, bread to make, meat to cut and start stewing. Regret was an emotion she had no time to indulge. But she would have to make time to work out how she would say what needed saying. Something in her guessed that she would have to say it soon.

LATE SUMMER, 902 A.D.

CHAPTER TWENTY-EIGHT

There was a definite change in the looks and the attitudes of those around him: Drosten could feel it even at times when nobody thought he was looking. Where he had been used to respectful, open faces, now he saw clouded eyes and carefully concealed expressions; where once he had carried authority, now he seemed to hold only pity. There was no doubt that all these people he had got used to thinking of as his own folk were concerned for him, and were sympathetic in their responses, but Drosten found he would much rather have everything as it had been before.

But before what? Before he had been told that the boy he had doted on as his own son, had been told over and over was without doubt his own flesh and blood, was not any of these things? Before the ship carrying his actual father, a heathen raider who had never returned to show any interest in the lives he had so carelessly destroyed, had once more appeared over the sea, to land and make trouble at his own doorstep? How in the world had *that* come to pass? There was so much coastline to these lands... and he made his way here. The likelihood of that was minimal, surely, but Drosten did not care to speculate on the deeper inferences of such an admission. He had already decided that his world was shattered enough already, without doing anything more to enrage the Almighty, or whatever other powers might be involved. Olwen had already suggested that perhaps Einar's own devils were testing their strength; as if admitting her foolishness of so long ago were not enough, now she chose to compound the sin by even suggesting such beings might exist. If she truly felt that way, why not go and move in with her former bedmate?

In spite of an instinctive assurance that he would get a friendly hearing from any of his farmhands if he chose to talk, Drosten was reluctant. They were the servants: he was still, regardless of all that had been said and revealed, their master. It was not seemly to discuss their mistress's shortcomings and transgressions with them; it bordered on a breakdown of the natural order of decent society to even consider such a thing. He sniffed to himself. It was the sort of thing his neighbours might do. Perhaps if he said such things often enough, they might even become true.

Yet part of him recognised that he needed to talk everything over with *someone*: if he did not, he could only see a long life of silence and bitterness stretching out before him. Or perhaps it would not be so long: something inside him seemed to have already given up the struggle to go on living. After all, what point was there in long life it it held no joy or pleasure? And, he discovered, he had no joy in his wife any more. He frowned in thought. With such matters going through his head, it was clearly time to find somewhere quiet to sort through them all. He needed, even if he didn't want, someone to talk to. But who?

"A bitter blow," said a voice by his shoulder suddenly, making him jump. He turned to see the speaker.

"You crept up quietly enough, Conyn," he muttered. "Care to do the same to our neighbours and take a burning torch with you?"

Conyn the blacksmith chuckled. "Come into the

forge, master: it's warmer than standing out here staring into space, and there's enough noise can be made to cover anything you don't want heard."

He slid backwards, out of sight unless Drosten followed him. The forge was set in its own little building a short way apart from the rest, surrounded by darker soils tinged with ash, a smell of hot iron, heat and a rumour of noise. In some ways, it existed within its own little world: for all that Drosten's people had long since stopped venerating blacksmiths as being close to godhood, something of the old aura still clung.

Once inside, the air was dark and warm, even though there was only the faintest glow coming from the hearth. Drosten looked around him, peering into the gloomier, furthest reaches of the hut. "You not particularly busy just now, then?"

Conyn loomed out of the dark air, swirling with dust and ash, placing a large, battered wooden ale-cup into his master's hand. "I'll be getting the fire up later on, but it's early yet. There's time to sit and talk a while, safe in the surety that anything said will never escape these walls."

"Hmm. We don't seem to see much of you Conyn, it's true, and yet you're always here or around somewhere."

"Keeping occupied," smiled the smith cryptically.

"Had much from our new neighbours in the way of work?"

"Odd bits here and there: not enough to consider moving, if that's what you're asking. Nothing worthy of telling you about, either: no weapons, nothing like that at all. Mended a pot, lengthened a chain..." he leaned closer. "I was more concerned about you, though, master. You have the look of someone who *needs* a safe ear to whisper things into."

"Really?" answered Drosten caustically. "I can't imagine why that would be!"

Conyn turned surprisingly sad eyes towards him. "I make the offer in good faith, master: I can listen, I might even be able to suggest a few things... I've had my share of bad happenings over the years. I've stood more-or-less where you stand now, which isn't something many men can say. As a result, anything I do offer by way of advice isn't just an opinion. It's tempered by my own experience. That might make it worth a little more; then again, of course, it might not. But I still say that you ought to talk matters over with someone. I simply offered a place that won't let your words out, and an ear that's connected to a closed mouth."

Drosten exhaled heavily. "I appreciate that you mean well, and I shouldn't take my grief out on you either. But the words don't come too easily just now."

"Perhaps it's just that there are so many of them, clamouring to get out."

"Or maybe they're trying to bury themselves deeper, where they can't do any harm."

"Harm?" Conyn snorted derisively. "It seems to me that you needn't be overly worried about causing anyone any extra pain or grief, master. You've taken your share already."

"Nearly seven years I've been her husband," Drosten suddenly announced, as if some inner cask had been broached and his thoughts set free. "Everyone around me thought it sudden and unexpected at the time, but it made its own sort of sense, especially with Rilca to consider as well. Olwen was the only living member of her family branch left who could take ownership of this place; she was widowed, she was alone in the world after not one death near to her, but a whole series of 'em. I'd buried my own wife some years before; my sister's sons had our estates and while I was still just as welcome there, it wasn't home without her any more. And Olwen sought me out, not the other way around." He grimaced. "Now I know why..."

"She's never seemed the type to just do something like that without some degree of real feeling in it as well," said Conyn quietly. "My guess would be that, if she'd not found you to her liking for your own sake, she'd not have taken matters any further."

"Perhaps: we'll never know for sure now, or at least I won't. It feels as if I can't trust a single thing she says, ever again."

"These things ease with time, master..."

"So I've heard: but do I want to give her that time? The thing is," he continued without waiting for an answer, "I've called Morgan my son since the day he was born. I've looked after him, watched him grow, taught him his manners and his behaviour: taken pride in him, 'cos he's a fine lad. Do I just turn my back on him now, simply because he's not my blood after all? How do I get rid of all that pride and feeling that's built up and up all through his life; can I turn him out to fend for himself without making myself an even worse criminal than his mother is in my eyes right now?" He rubbed those same eyes wearily. "I don't think I can, Conyn, however much I perhaps ought to."

"That's a father speaking," replied the smith, "and there's nowt wrong with that. Even when he abandoned his own family to go off and follow some upstart warlord against the Gaels, I never stopped loving my own lad. Even though it left us short-handed at home, even though he emptied the house of everything he could sell in order to buy his weapons, we still took a pride in him and what he did. He's dead now: killed somewhere or other, I don't remember where."

"I don't remember ever hearing about that..."

Conyn smiled. "I don't recall ever telling you, that's probably why."

"I thought about just going away," Drosten continued after a pause. "Go back to the old lands perhaps, or try and get through to Bridei with news of what's happening around here. It's been half a year and we've not even seen a taxman from him: something's up. What sort of king forgets to collect his dues, eh? I didn't feel I could stay around Olwen any more; funny how such things can change so quickly."

"There was a deal of provocation, though," said the smith. As he spoke, his eyes never left those of his lord and master, but his hands were busy: prodding the hearth into life, gathering odd scraps of iron and bronze together, arranging the tools of his trade close by.

Drosten nodded. "That there was. But then I decided not to. There's more at stake than just my pride, more than just the fate of this place and all the folk in it. Oh yes," he grinned at Conyn's raised eyebrows, "I reckon there's a great deal more implications than a lot of you have realised." He leaned forward, his face earnest. "If I go, it doesn't really affect who owns these lands later on, after Olwen dies. That's the way of things. But it might mean that our newcomer neighbours to the south get a hold of it, and that *will* change things, because their sons inherit from their fathers. If I go away, who protects Morgan from Einar's ambitions? There's the blood-father, and the son he could use to get whatever he's after here. Morgan's too young to run this place: he wouldn't have a clue how. But as his father, Einar could come in and do it for him – and put the two households together as one. But it would be a Norse household, and I wouldn't give much for any of your chances if that were to happen, would you?" He shook his head. "There'd be a lot of blood spilt, and lives lost, and all because I chose to take my hurt and anger elsewhere. Olwen wouldn't stop him: I don't think she'd know how. Or if she did see the danger, could she stand against him, the mother of his son? He never came back to find her, you know: she means nothing to him. He didn't even seem to recognise her when they first met again, out in the yard here." He managed a lopsided grin for a brief moment. "I wonder what he's making of all this?"

"Hard to say," ventured Conyn.

"Mmm. And I've no particular wish to find out, either." He sighed again: the brief humour seemed to collapse back inside him, giving way to the gloomier aspects that his workmates had come to know so well just lately. "It's him I blame for this as much as her, you know," he went on, but whether he was still talking to Conyn or not was harder to say. "It's bad enough that she bore his brat, and worse still that she chose to hide the fact under marriages and pretence; I don't think right now that I'll ever forgive her that. But he's in there too, sharing the blame: what sort of man does that to a woman, knowing – hoping, expecting – that he'll never see her again? What sort of man lets a child loose in the world without even caring about it's future, and whether it gets someone to call father, hmm? It's callous and cruel, and just what I'd expect from northern men who come raiding and killing and taking what they will, without regard for the rest of us. Some father he'd've made if he *had* stayed around..."

"And yet he has sons of his own," observed

Conyn, "and they don't seem to have turned out too badly."

"Is that what you think? Maybe it looks different to you in here; all I see is the older one sniffing around Rilca like some fucking dog after a bone. It all smells of just trying to get themselves in here, of not being satisfied with what they were given, when we needn't've given anything at all! You only have to think back to how he got that other house built to see how his mind works: he's cunning and ruthless, cold and hard, is Einar. It brings us back to the question of who gets this place in the end: if Einar's lad knocks Rilca up, then if that kid's a boy, he gets the inheritance over Morgan. See what I mean? Not content with taking the basis of my marriage away from me, not content with fucking up my whole bloody life these days, now he and his children are trying to take everything we all have! Einar gets greedier by the day, and he's encouraging his children to do the same. To not care about any of us, or about what happens to us. And she encouraged him, that first day: she set all the rules and the expectations." Drosten shook his head sadly, his shoulders hunched and his eyes bleak. "I can see nothing of a future for us here; and I can see no way of avoiding what's coming, short of bloodshed."

"And with no word from the king..." began Conyn.

"...We're on our own," concluded his master.

"Then we all need you to stay: there's no leadership to be had from any other quarter."

"Not even from your mistress?"

"You said what you said, sir. How can we trust her judgement, when she's already let these newcomers in so readily?"

"You think she did that just on account of

recognising Einar as Morgan's father? Once I might have argued the point, but now I'm not so sure. Perhaps it's true: I can't imagine any other reason for doing what she did. I'm not so likely to leave, Conyn: as we said, where would I go? And I can't abandon Morgan: or Rilca, come to that. I've known him as my son for his whole life, and that doesn't change overnight. In my own mind, he's still my son – and I'll keep him as such, if only to piss Einar off about it. He'll not take this place without some sort of fight – although Rilca might be a better bet from his point of view. She's as likely to follow in her aunt's footststeps, I shouldn't wonder; she certainly seems to be enjoying the attention his boy's giving her." He rubbed his face and stood up. "I wish there was something I could do about that side of things, but without neighbours to call on for fresh young men who might catch her eye, I don't see what can be done. Well, one thing at a time, I suppose; one thing at a time."

He put his cup down on the edge of the forge's piled turf hearth. Conyn looked up at him.

"If you ever need to speak your mind, master, remember where I am. My lips remain sealed."

"I'll remember. Thankyou. I wish I had more to give you in return."

"Just keep fighting for us, sir. That'll be payment enough."

CHAPTER TWENTY-NINE

The High-Seat pillars still smelled faintly of the sea, and their once-bright paint remained faded and pale in the flickering light of the hearth. They had been placed far enough apart for two people to sit between them, side-by-side in the most important seat in the house, but now only one person sat there. The other for whom the arrangement had been made refused to come between the posts, refused to join her husband in the place of honour. Across the fire from him, her face shone white but her eyes blazed with anger and outrage.

"How is it," she ground out from between stiff lips and clenched teeth, "that I never heard of this before now?"

Einar glowered back at her from his cushions, his cup firmly in his hand. "What was to tell, Ragna? It was long ago; I went away for a summer, as I always have up until now, and I came back home to you at the end of the season. Enough happened even after I left the place to drive it from my mind, and I wasn't intending to go looking for the woman – or any child. And I didn't know she was pregnant when I left, either, don't forget..."

"That makes no bloody difference to me!" she screamed suddenly at him. "Isn't it enough that you thought so little of me and your children that you took her to your fucking bed in the first place? What got into you, Einar? How many other bastard brats of yours are there around the whale's road, hmm? Planning on taking more trips to go and look for them, too?"

"I didn't bring us here to find a child I never knew of, or a woman whose name I could barely pronounce, and who was just available for a moon or so one summer long ago!" he shouted back. At the ends of the hall, those bondar unlucky enough to have been inside when Ragna had come storming in were now finding reasons to go and work elsewhere. Neither their lord or lady noticed.

"I thought we had a marriage stronger than this," she said eventually, her eyes still flaming and her breathing harsh and heavy.

"We do: we always have had..."

"How can you sit there and say that, with this news still fresh in our ears?" she responded incredulously. "You arsehole, you have a *son* in this place! Are you really going to try and convince me that you knew nothing of this? That it wasn't planned?"

"How in all the worlds could I have plotted this, woman? Eh? Tell me that before you let fly with any more of this bloody nonsense, or I'll not listen." He slammed his cup down beside him, and hunched forward to look her more closely in the eye. "I went over sea for a short season. I came ashore somewhere in the Orccareyjar, along with a lot of other ship-men, and we set up a market. Sometime within that market, this woman, whose name I didn't know, and whose business I had to find out through what little of their tongue I had, came along and demanded weregeld for some deaths in her family that she claimed our people – not me, you'll notice – had caused. I offered her my help, since yes, she had some attraction, and I was intrigued. And yes, I bedded her: I can hardly deny it, now can I?" His eyes became harder, and his tone more insistent. *"But I came home again afterwards.* I never abandoned you, or our families. All the wealth I made, all the wealth I have ever made, has come home with me at the end of every summer. And apart from this one time, I have been faithful, and I've not taken other wives, or even knocked up any of the slave-girls I've traded. You've made your thoughts on that clear enough over our years together, and I've never wanted it any other way. Really; honestly. What would you like me to swear that truth on?"

"It's bad enough that you ever even *thought* of doing it just once," grated Ragna. "What did she have that I didn't, hmm? Were you so unhappy in your home that you felt the need to do such a thing to me?"

"I didn't do it to you!" Einar yelled in reply. "It – just – happened! Can't you see that? There is no plan, no plot, no dissatisfaction with you, or with my children, or with my household. What does it take to drive that home?"

"More than you can ever give," she answered, "short of turning back those years and making it so that Mawgan never existed."

Einar sighed and settled back in his seat. "As you say, then, more than I can give."

"Do you regret it?" Ragna asked after a moment's silence between them.

"Regret what? That I took Olwen to my bed long ago, or that the child came to be because of it, or both? I suppose I might regret the first: but I've only just found out about all the rest of it, after all, so perhaps it's a little soon to say. I've lived the years in between not knowing about him – or about Olwen, really – and not even thinking about them, so none of this has had any effect on my decisions or actions. And have I not been a good man to you otherwise?"

Ragna grimaced. "If I'm being honest, then yes, you have. I've had nothing to complain of in our years together – until this came along."

"How did you find out? I can't believe Drosten or his wife just out and told you..."

She scowled across the fire at him. "If you weren't so bloody-minded about our neighbours, you might've known about it sooner as well: but you won't even talk to them, let alone go visit. Have you not even laid eyes on the lad? Well, where all the others over there have dark eyes and dark or reddish hair, and narrow, thin kind of faces, Mawgan has grey eyes – your grey. And fair hair, again like so many of us. And he has the roundness of your face. He sticks out an ell or more among them: there was little enough left to guess."

"Still sounds a bit dubious if that were the only grounds you accused me on. So you must have had something more: I know you well enough to realise that. Any number of our folk have grey eyes, too..."

"His mother was the giveaway. *She* knew, the moment she set eyes on you again; after all these years, she knew. Why else would she let us on these lands so eagerly, even above the protests of her own husband? And useful that they only married just before Mawgan came into the world, too. And she's nervous around any of our people: twitchy, frightened, never saying much." Ragna shrugged carelessly, but the look of distaste never left her features. "I began to wonder, and then one of their bondar mentioned that her mistress knew our tongue and our ways, through having spent time among our folk long ago – before they married. *Then* I asked her outright. I knew before Drosten did, although not by very long."

Einar shook his head. "I never even recognised her."

"Oh, I noticed that, too. So did she, but in some ways that was useful to her, since it meant that she might yet keep it all a secret, even from Drosten. But not now. Now it has all come out, I think."

"You sound regretful about it."

Ragna looked over at him with steel in her eyes. "Perhaps in some ways I am. In others, though, I'm not. I have no wish to live in ignorance of what you do, husband. I do not wish to appear such a fool as Drosten now looks to be." She took a step closer, but still made no move to come and sit beside him. "This proves to me how right I've been to keep a close eye on you whenever you were at home, husband: will you tell me truthfully how many of our bondswomen's brats are yours?"

"You're making too much of this, Ragna..."

"What! How *dare* you even think such a thing! I don't see that I could *ever* make too much of such behaviour! Now will you answer, or shall I go around our own house and ask the questions I put to Olwen, hmm? It's the wrong time of year for you to be out on the ship now, Einar: you'll have to stay here and endure my questions and my anger as best you can – but trying to avoid it won't help, and trying to put the blame back on me somehow won't get you anywhere either. Now, will you answer honestly? If you even know the answer?"

Einar glared. "The answer is easy, since, as I said before, I've not been unfaithful beyond this one time. So none of these kids are mine. And once again, I ask what you'd like me to swear that on!"

"You can make your oaths on those bloody pillars, that caused all this trouble to come about."

Einar shifted round slightly to look at the High-Seat posts. "Funny that they should come ashore here," he mused quietly. "Why here? What's all this *really* about?"

"I seem to remember telling you that you'd done it wrong when we couldn't find them," answered Ragna, "and don't try shifting the attention onto them, either. The Thunderer may have sent them here, but it was your insistence that we followed."

"And wasn't it you who said we shouldn't try and second-guess what was going on?" he retorted sharply. "I'm not trying to avoid the wyrd of what I've done, Ragna," he went on, "I'm just trying to understand it, and not make matters any worse."

"Then I suggest you get up off your arse and start actually talking with our neighbours, and start trying to live alongside them," she replied. "We've not been given the means to be rid of them, for all that I find myself thinking that perhaps I'd rather Olwen weren't here after all. I've got better things to do with my days than worry about where you're stuffing that prick of yours the whole time."

"You needn't be concerned over that," Einar assured her. "I have no intention of chasing anyone other than you. Svein, though, might be a different matter."

"I have no worries in that regard," said Ragna. "If Svein wants to get in with Rilca, I'd encourage him."

"How can you say that after the roasting you've just given me?"

She stared hard at him. "Because he's not my husband, you dolt! You have no idea of how things work in these lands, have you? For all that you've been here before you've really not got a clue, and that refusal to learn anything is likely to do us more damage than anything else." She sat down opposite him with a heavy sigh, and looked bleakly around the hall before continuing.

"These local folk inherit through the women's line. It means that whatever you and Drosten do to each other doesn't matter: it all goes on as before. If Olwen dies – or when, rather – if Rilca hasn't married and had a son, then Mawgan inherits: not as Drosten's lad, but as Olwen's. But if she hangs on until her neice is having children, then any boy child from *that* line gets it all." She looked at her husband sourly. "I thought you'd said that Drosten had explained all this."

"He did, but he also said that I'd never be able to keep track of who was in line to inherit. So I didn't bother about it."

"Like you didn't bother telling me about Olwen all those years ago? Because it wasn't going to matter any more?"

Einar shifted uncomfortably. "Something like that."

The fire and harshness was creeping back into Ragna's tone. "Well it all fucking well matters now, don't it? Time to start paying attention, husband, before you get us all killed from your idleness. The Gods have put us here, and they've given us your old by-blow for a neighbour and a landowner. You'll never be Jarl here unless you put your mind to killing them all – or until you start working out how their system works, and start using what's happened to your – our – advantage. So which is it going to be?"

Einar grinned crookedly. "Much as I'd love to destroy 'em all and just take what's there, we've never had the power to do it, and I can see that nothing's changed in that regard. So I must agree with your wisdom, wife, and start to rethink my position."

"A wise decision. You can start by laying off Svein about his friendship with Rilca."

Einar looked at her in distaste, before his expression slowly changed to one of calculated interest. "Looking to the long term? Thinking it'll end with them producing the son that inherits Olwen's properties?"

"It wouldn't surprise me. But if that's our aim, then we have to allow him to marry her properly, and make it all legal in her family's eyes."

Einar rubbed his beard. "I wonder how they'd take to that?"

"All her close relatives are dead, remember. There's only distant cousins and such. They might not count, for all I know."

Einar thought for a moment. "And how does all this stand with your anger at Mawgan's very existence, and my part in that?"

"I'll let you know when I'm ready to. But any child of Rilca's would cut him out – leave him with nothing."

"That's harsh..."

She shrugged. "So is our way of giving Svein everything when you die. There'll be nothing left for Bjorn, just as there was nothing left for Havard when my own fathir died. Grim got it all."

His eyes narrowed. "If we are to weather this as a household – and we have to, for the sake of the rest of our people here if not for us – then we must be united in our aims as the rest of this mess unfolds, for I can't see it being finished just yet. The Gods only know what Drosten's had to say about it; if I was in his shoes, I'd be sharpening a spear with my name on it."

Ragna looked up sharply. "And on what basis do you say that, you who never even talks to these people?"

"Drosten's made his position clear enough before now: he'd rather we weren't here, and now he has the best of all reasons to drive us away. We should make ready."

Ragna snorted. "If he comes after you because of Mawgan, I'm likely to lend him my whetstone!"

Einar nodded. "That's only fair, I suppose, although I still maintain that I had no way of knowing there was a child involved, and I'll remind you that I never went seeking the woman out since that summer, either. She could've approached any one of the ship-men there that year: she came to me. I've no idea why, wife of mine, I really haven't, although the way our pillars came ashore on her lands might suggest there are greater powers than ours at work here." He suddenly looked worried. "What if Redbeard doesn't want these Orccamen killed? What if we're supposed to work alongside them, and Mawgan is the key to it all?"

"Then I have to either bring you round to that idea or let Drosten be rid of you, wouldn't you say?" She threw her hands up in expasperation. "It's only what the rest of us have been saying since we came here, Einar, and suddenly you've found a reason to listen? How obtuse can you get?"

"Yes, alright, I hear you. We'll – I'll – let 'em alone, and we'll see what comes of it. But if they come making trouble, I'll defend this holding. Olwen might have given it to us in the first place, or some of it at least, but we made it. I'll not have it taken away, not even as weregeld for a brat I never even knew I'd fathered."

Ragna sighed to herself. She supposed it was a step in the best direction.

CHAPTER THIRTY

"What happens now, lady?"

Olwen looked up to see Danna and Gwen standing just out of the shadows. They looked worried, upset, uncertain; emotions that their mistress could echo and amplify manyfold. She shook her head, red-rimmed eyes staring starkly from a pale, drawn face.

"In what way, Danna?" She found herself unable to formulate answers, even sentences. All she could manage was simple questions, requests to her housewomen to make their own questions easier to understand.

"Your husband spends no time with you, lady; the other men are distant and mistrustful. Your children go unnoticed; for your own part, if you'll hear it, you sit here and nothing happens around you." Danna knelt before her mistress, her face full of concern. "We need you whole and still a part of our livelihoods here, lady, or else the newcomers will surely swamp us."

"You know all of what has come out," murmured Olwen quietly. Danna nodded mutely.

"Then how can you ask what you do, knowing what sort of a woman I've become over all these years?"

Gwen shuffled forwards. "Mistress, we only see a change in you since this news came out. Up until then, you were our mistress and we followed you gladly. We still would, if you would just come back to us."

"We have only heard the bare facts of the matter," added Danna. "We know nothing of the reasons behind what happened, but we are certain you'd've had good ones. For all of it."

"I wonder," replied Olwen in the same hollow tone. "I wonder if they really were such good reasons, now all this has come to pass."

"Lady, please," implored Danna, tears welling in her eyes. "We have been together for a good many years: that's true for most of us who live and work here. Why can't the past just lie and be done with? We all have to go on living, working the fields, tending the flocks... raising our bairns... and your lad needs his mama. He doesn't know what's going on: he only sees his mother upset and refusing to move from the fireside while he has to beg for his food from the rest of us and his neice spends all her time with the son of the man whose fault this all is." She stopped suddenly. "Your pardon, lady: I wasn't meaning to speak so to you, and especially not in a time when what you need most are kinder words."

"I might need them, Danna, but do I deserve them? I have no answer to that." She rubbed her eyes tiredly. "I feel like the storm-wrack, the mess left behind when the gales blow themselves out. Oh, Lord, how did all this come to pass? Live on I might have to, but how much is there to live for? Morgan stands between two different peoples; now he's only half mine. What if Einar claims him and takes him away? I've lost one husband through his dying, and now another through his anger and shame – and I have to take the whole of that burden. None of this is of his doing, and yet he stands to lose the most. I ought to do something to take that burden too – but I cannot think what. I can barely think at all. I'm so tired: sleep escapes me, and the world looks dark and unwelcoming. No, I fear there is no haven for me, no matter where I turn. So why turn any way at all? Why not just sit here and let it all end around me?"

"Because *we* still need you, lady," replied the bondswoman gently. "And it won't be long before your husband has need of you, too. Summer is turning: it'll be harvest-time any day now, and soon after that we have to look at putting the rams back in with the ewes, and giving the bull his work, too. Doing nothing doesn't make the problems go away. If anything, Lady, I'd say it's likely to make them worse. It's another of those times when we really do need every last pair of hands, every sharp mind and memory of what gets done and how we do it. Besides all that, isn't Einar more likely than ever to move against us if he sees you sitting here with no will to move, and your husband preoccupied with this trouble? I for one have no wish to live under his rule, Lady: I'm pretty sure it will be harsher than any we've had before, wherever we've been." She reached out and took her mistress' hands in her own. "We need you with us," she implored. "We need you to put all this to one side and help us hold this place against the storm that's surely coming. I'm willing to bet that there's less disruption over this in Einar's house than there is in ours. He'll act on it, and soon."

"It is a low opinion of him that you all have, isn't it?" observed Olwen dourly. "Was it this low before you found out that he was Morgan's true father?"

"Pretty much, Lady. He's not done much to help us think any better of him."

"Every time we see him, it's because he wants something from us," added Gwen. "There's no sign of friendship for it's own sake, no sign of wanting to settle down among us and work his land in a peaceable manner." She shuddered. "He's a thief and a troublemaker through and through."

"Vik-inger, they call them," murmured Olwen. "Water-dwellers, or something, it means. Men who live on their boats and make a living by taking from others. I got the impression that even their own people weren't very happy about them. There's been no word from his house, then?"

Gwen shrugged. "Not that I know of, Lady. Were you expecting any?"

Olwen sighed. "Not really, I suppose. Given that he just sailed away that summer all those years ago and that I've not seen him since until now, no, I'd not be expecting any word." A sad, crooked smile creased her face briefly. "I'm not expecting the lady Ragna to come calling any more, either. I would imagine that her reaction to this news of mine has been greater than his, and not in a good way." She turned her weary eyes up towards the faces of her companions. "You're right: I should stir from this hearth, and get doing again. Sitting here changes nothing, and the story had to be told. I should find Drosten and try to make some sort of peace with him, if only against Einar and his brood. The men will need their spears and bows, I shouldn't wonder. And these lands are still my family's property, in my charge until either Morgan comes of age or Rilca starts having babies – which appears to be some way off yet, thankfully."

"I wouldn't say that too loudly, Lady," warned Danna. "She's spending a lot of her time with Einar's lad these days."

Olwen's eyes clouded over once more. "That's not good," she murmured. "That's not good at all. Has she not seen the trouble that can come from such behaviour? Has she not seen my fate and learned something from it, these last few days?" She reached out a hand to grab Danna's arm, and painfully hauled herself up from her stool. "Then it's definitely time to be up and about."

CHAPTER THIRTY-ONE

The wind always blew in this place. These days, Svein thought sourly as he stepped outside and into the lee of the dunes, it seemed to be blowing just as harshly indoors as it did out. Relations between his mother and father appeared to be at an all-time low, with hard words, lots of shouting punctuated by long, stony silences, and things being thrown, sometimes seemingly for no real reason. Perhaps, he ruminated, it just made them feel better. He was spending a lot of time outside these days: it was quieter, and he had room to think under the wide, tempestuous skies of these strange new lands he now had to call his home, where clouds ran in ragged dark patches rent by stormy winds and the morning mist covered even the gentlest of slopes, coating everything and everyone in a chill, sodden drizzle.

The sharpness of the wind hit his face, stinging it into little reddened patches as he picked his way across the sandy yard, towards the rougher ground that separated their house from the lands of the Orcca-men. Some of those hollows were deeper than they appeared, but they were also constantly shifting under the influence of winds and rains. At least, he thought as he wrapped his cloak tighter around him, there wasn't any rain just now – although even his limited experience was suggesting that such conditions could change in an instant and without very much by way of warning. You always took a cloak when you put a nose out of doors in Orcca-land.

Clearly, with the news that had recently come to light, lots of things were likely to change in their little world. There was suddenly a lot more to think about, and long-term considerations were becoming more and more important as people put their minds to sifting through the problems raised by the news of Mawgan's real parentage. Svein had not yet spoken about it to his own little brother; he wondered what Bjorn would make of it all, but in the usual brotherly fashion, he doubted that there would be much in the way of insight or wisdom coming from *that* direction. Or was he being too harsh?

He needed someone more his own age to talk things over with; someone whose own future might also take a turn for the worse because of this business. He quickened his pace, and turned slightly to head a little further south, towards the burn. There was a spot on its banks, a little hollow where it looked like otters might once have had a nest. It was carved into the bank a short way, out of most of the wind, and seemingly not many people ever went there. But Rilca knew where it was, and Svein found himself hoping she could be there today.

They had no signs, no way of making such arrangements between them: they had to rely on luck and the goodwill of the Gods for a meeting to happen. Today, though, the Gods were with them.

He caught sight of a flash of bright colour amid the wildly waving grass that crested the slight rise above the burn, and smiled to himself. His own word-hoard seemed to be bursting inside him, straining to get out, and he would have put silver on Rilca feeling the same way. He found himself wondering how she saw the world more and more these days, and wondered what it might mean – or what it might one day lead to. He was pretty certain that harsh words from his father would be in there somewhere, but such matters were for another day. Rilca was here, and she was here now, and so there was only the here-and-now that mattered to him. He slithered over the top of the little gully that held the burn at its bottom, and plonked down hard beside her. She smiled.

"I was hoping you'd be here," she began.

Svein nodded. "I hoped the same. There's a lot going on, and it feels like we only have each other to talk to – to me, at any rate. How about you?"

She nodded. "Everyone seems far too caught up in their own side of things to worry much about anyone else." She shook her head. "I don't like it this way."

"Life's always easier when there's nothing to disrupt it. My people say that the challenge is only in those times when it gets tougher, though."

She smiled. "And how are they coping with that challenge right now?"

He laughed. "Fucking badly, if you ask me! Mothir and Fathir spend all their time together shouting and chucking stuff. She won't even take her seat beside him at the moment."

"Is that bad?"

"About as bad as it can get, short of walking away and leaving him completely."

"Think she will?"

Svein snorted. "And go where? I know my uncle has a share in the boat, but he doesn't own it; neither does Fathir, not outright. If she wanted to go away from him, she'd have to walk, and I can't see that happening. The only place she knows of in these parts is your own mothir's, and what sort of welcome would there be, eh?" He shook his head. "No, I think they'll just have to keep on at it until they can make some sort of peace between them. That's why I'm out and about so much these days."

"Mmm, me too."

"It's not going to make managing the harvest any easier either, is it?" he said after a pause. "Times like this, we should be pulling together to get it done – if this weather ever breaks clear for a bit – or we'll all starve. Your folk have any way of dealing with such problems? Any tricks or secrets we ought to know about?"

"No, just wait for clear days and hope they come soon, before everyone's so shredded that they *can't* work together any more. Although it might already be too late for my aunt and uncle."

They fell silent, with just the sounds of the world around them: the rush of the wind, the running of the burn, the rustle of grass above their heads. Further away, sheep bleated and cattle grumbled, but those were noises of another world, one where it was the adults who caused all the trouble and were unable to find a way out of it. Eventually, though, Svein stirred into speech again.

"So how does affect you, all of this? Come to that, what about Mawgan?"

Rilca sighed heavily. "I feel for him: he knows

something very bad has happened, and he sees his mother crying by herself almost all the time, and I'm pretty sure he's worked out that some of it at least is his fault in some way – but nobody's sat him down and tried to explain it all. How *do* you tell a six-year old something like this, anyway?"

"How can it be his doing? He didn't ask to be my fathir's lost son, after all. That's not fair, trying to put any of it on his shoulders; your aunt and uncle should know better than that."

"They're too wrapped up in it all to realise, Svein. Try not to be too harsh on them: at least, not yet."

He raised an eyebrow. "Any particular reason?"

"Yes, they're falling apart!" The girl's own worry and confusion suddenly began to spill out of her mouth. "My aunt's kept this a secret from everyone – *everyone* – for nearly seven years, and it might've gone on being secret for ever. They were happy, Svein: they were content with their lives, we all were, and there was nothing to upset matters or give us any cause for concern. I would've found a husband in a few years, Morgan would've inherited when aunt Olwen dies, Drosten would've probably gone on living here until the end of his own days, and we could have been happy with that. But now...

"Now," she went on after a resolutely deep breath, "now everyone is bothered that your father will want Morgan as his own son, and through him, take the land away from us. There's a lot of our folk have been saying that was his purpose since he first came here, and now more are starting to listen. It probably doesn't help that Drosten's always been one of 'em. He's starting to see himself as the defender of our lands and livelihoods, more than anything else. I couldn't even say if he still thinks of my aunt as his wife after this: although I don't think it's because she got knocked up before they married. That's been known before. I think it's because of how it came to be, and with who..."

Svein shrugged. "He's welcome to his opinion. I'm not sure how I'd feel if I were in his place, so I'm willing to give him some room on it."

Rilca reached out a hand to take his. "It doesn't sound very nice for you I know, but I can't think of any other way to put it. He blames your fathir for his problems, and who's to say he's not got some cause, eh? But it goes too far to blame him for settling here, and to try and make out he did it deliberately, when he didn't even recognise my aunt on meeting her." She sighed, and bowed her head, watching the ripples in the water as it ran past her feet. "He's using Einar as a convenient devil to hang all his troubles on," she said at last, "and he's working up a real anger about him even being here. It wouldn't surprise me to find blood at the end of his path."

Svein snorted. "If it comes to that, my own reckoning is that my fathir's earned whatever he gets. But if Drosten wants to play at love-taps he's likely to end up the worse for it. Fathir's a seasoned traveller, a good man with sword and spear, and long experience of how these things tend to fall out. I may not like him much on a day-to-day basis, but I'd be a fool not to see his strengths. You might want to pass that along if you get the chance, 'cos if Drosten does decide to take him on, there'll be no stopping the old man once he gets ideas of vengeance in his head. And he's said before now that he sees your people as the weaker power in the land, and I would imagine he can make up a case for helping you all on your way into the next world if he's provoked.

" Mind you, Mothir's furious with him, as you

might well imagine, and on that basis I can't see her even allowing Mawgan into the house to visit Bjorn, let alone be fostered with us. So I don't think you need worry about his being taken away from you." He rubbed his chin. "That would go for your aunt, too: I don't know how things work in your people but with mine, the woman is free to leave a husband if he doesn't measure up. She just has to say the words before witnesses at the bedside and the door, and she's free of the marriage. But if Olwen were thinking of taking herself away from Drosten and into our house with Einar, Mothir would never stand for it. She keeps him away from the bondswomen for fear of his making bastards with them; your aunt would never even make it through the door." His gaze left the girl by his side for a moment, and wandered back towards the low green mound of his own home. "She worked it out, you know: she knew before any of this got out from your aunt. So she's had longer to get used to the idea, and try and work out what it all means: but she's still too deep in her anger to think straight." He dug a stone out of the loose soil at his side and idly dropped it into the burn. "I've no idea what fathir's thinking: he's said very little about anything lately."

"And is that a problem?"

"Aye: it means he's using all his energy for thinking, and say what you will about him, thinking is one of those things he does far too well. If he's hatching a plan, it will be bad news for whoever it's aimed against."

"That has to be Drosten and my aunt, surely?"

"That would be my guess. As I say, he's not giving much away just now. Hard facts are hard to come by. But if I do hear anything, I'll get word to you as soon as I can. And remember what I've already said. For my part, I'm happy to try and put him off the idea of slaughtering you all if I possibly can"

"That's a generous offer, Svein." She smiled at him.

"I've no wish to have our friendship destroyed by old people who can't see what happens after their own deaths," he replied awkwardly. "I want to have you as a friend on our own terms. One day, perhaps I'd like it to be more than just friendship that we share – but that's for another day. I'll not put myself forward whilst all this is going on around us."

Rilca gave him a long, appraising stare. "You grow into your manhood more every day, Svein Einarsson," she said eventually. "And if I'm being honest, that man is one I'm admiring more and more. But you're right: nobody would appreciate hearing such things right now, beyond you and me."

"So," he continued, taking her hand once more, "we stay true to each other. We have no secrets, no lies, no loyalties above that to each other. Even if our families end up killing each other around us, although that would be a hard one to keep out of."

"We ought to try, though."

"Yes: we ought to try." There was another long silence after that, but their hands remained closed around each other.

"This must have consequences for you as well, surely?" The girl asked after a while.

"I'm not sure... in the old country, the older son gets it all, everything there is, although some people have been known to arrange a division of their property after they're dead, to try and give something to each of their sons. Perhaps Fathir had something like that in mind for Bjorn and me; if he did, then it would mean if he wanted to take Mawgan in as well, he'd need a third share for him. So, a little less for Bjorn and I than might otherwise be, but I think that would be about all the difference it would make." He rubbed the stubble of his chin as he thought further. "I reckon if he wanted to do that, it would be to try and get hold of your aunt's titles and property – but if I understand it right, that might not even happen..?"

She arched an eyebrow. "You learn fast, then, and no doubt you've made a plan to get around it too!"

He leaned back on the damp sand. "Hardly for me to say, though, is it?"

"I admired my aunt for a little while," Rilca confessed, deftly turning the subject away from her part in the labyrinth of inheritance possibilities. "I thought she'd been so brave, going amongst your people all on her own and demanding things of them, for all that she didn't come away with much. But to have something like this to hide for so long, maybe even for a lifetime... I think that rather took the shine off it for me, when I found out the aftermath of it. It doesn't seem fair somehow: none of it does. It's hard to see that anyone gets to win much out of this, and that can't be the right way of things either, can it?"

"I've no idea," Svein admitted. "I'm just keeping a close eye on Fathir, and trying to second-guess what he's about to do. Would he go and murder your aunt and her husband? If he thought it would get him closer to winning her lands, he might. He'd get Mawgan into the bargain, too – and you, I suppose. 'Cos if Olwen is dead and Mawgan's still a child, don't you get it all?"

She shook her head. "No. Only any sons I have get even a look in." She turned a little to face him. "But I'm betting you knew that already."

"Aye," he replied warily, "but as I just said, I wasn't planning on acting on it. Or not without your being willing to," he added hopefully.

"That's a hard one, Svein: if your father's already killed off the rest of my family, how am I going to have any real say in what happens to me? For all your good intentions – which I believe, by the way – could you stop him? Honestly?"

"Probably not: he's the one with all the skill and the time for planning such a thing. But I might be able to get you a warning: I'd certainly try everything I could to do it."

"I know you would, Svein. Truly I do; and I trust you to do it as well. Hopefully he'll think of some other way."

"Hopefully, yes," agreed the lad, "but maybe not very likely."

CHAPTER THIRTY-TWO

Einar stood in the partial shelter of his porch and stared out through mists and rain at the blurred shapes of sand dunes. He could see nothing more; beyond the low humps of the nearest mounds, all was just grey and indistinct. Drizzle had turned the stones of the doorway shiny and slick with wet, feeling cold through his plain leather shoes. Even his thick hose and his heaviest woollen kirtle couldn't keep out the autumn chill, and he could feel water soaking into the linen shirt underneath.

"We need this storm to blow over," he murmured quietly, wrapping his arms around his chest and exhaling clouds of steam into the chill air beyond. "How in all the worlds are we supposed to get the harvest in with this hanging over us?"

"At least we don't have to move the sheep around like we used to," observed Skapti, clustered with some of the other bondsmen behind their master. "They can stay where they are all year round, according to the Orccamen."

Einar turned to look closely at his followers. "Nice comb," he grunted. Thorfinn grinned.

"Got it from across the way: young Moren, Bran's son, has a knack for 'em."

Einar raised an eyebrow, then shrugged to himself. Everyone else was settling in far better than he felt he was, and the irony was not lost on him. What to do about it remained the problem.

"What do they say about this weather, then?" he asked eventually, after another bout of staring out moodily at the grey wall of mist. "There's no point standing here and just looking at it," he decided, "we might as well go back inside and make our plans in comfort. Come on lads: back to the fireside, and you can tell me what our neighbours have to tell you whenever you go over there. Like it or not, we're here now, and it's still better than if we'd stayed under Harald's nose. You've all got used to the idea: it's about time I did as well."

Behind his back, eyebrows were raised and looks of wonder exchanged. Then they all followed Einar back to the hall, where the fire was bright and warm and drove away the outside world for a little while. Their neighbours remained, as did the climate on this coast; but it was easier to discuss such things, and others besides, when there was no need to look out on them.

"I speak with Rhodri from time to time," ventured Eyjolf once they were back on the benches and the cups had been filled. "He helps the smith over the way sometimes, but otherwise he's one of Drosten's labourers out in the fields. He digs peat, too, which is a useful skill to have in these parts..."

"And what does he say about the clouds and the rain?" replied Einar. "How do they usually judge when there's likely to be a patch of clearer sky, eh?"

Eyjolf shrugged. "As far as I can tell, lord, they don't. They just wait for it as we do, it's so unpredictable. But as soon as it does come, they work swiftly, or at least they always have before. I think our coming has upset things a bit."

His master snorted incredulously. "A bit?? You think? The only reason I've not had some of you boys out on the boat fishing is because I've been expecting old Drosten to come at me with spears and fire the moment my strength was less than usual! Yes, Eyjolf, I'd say we've put matters all to cock over there, and more than just a bit. It's all been an unexpected turn of wyrd and no mistake; and no clear advantage to be had from it either."

Havard looked across at his brother-in-law. "Wouldn't you say having Olwen trample all over her own husband to give us the land here was an advantage, Einar?"

"Mm, I suppose. But then again, given the strength we went ashore with that first time, who's to say anyone else wouldn't've done the same? We were pretty impressive," he recollected with a smile.

"We need to make plans for now, not then," Havard reminded him. "Harvest is coming, for them and for us, and the way things are right now, neither of us is going to get everything done that needs to be. This weather just makes it worse. We need to strike some sort of bargain with Drosten, offer our help in his fields if he'll do the same for us." He leaned forward in earnest. "But we have to do it as separate households: one whisper of treating us all as a single place, under a single master, is liable to send him against us the way things stand – even if we offer to put him in command."

Einar stirred in his seat at those words, but Havard held up a hand. "I'm not saying we do it that way: I'm saying that he's unlikely to accept it even if we offered! Gods, Einar, will you listen?"

"Small chance of that!" said Ragna with a laugh, coming in from the other room and collecting a jug.

"Some of us are going to have to go over and see him," Havard continued once his sister was out of the room. "I'll go if you want me to, but I'm not willing to go alone, and I don't see that any one of us should really have to. So we'll draw lots, and a little group of us can go. Einar can't: not this time. Brother-in-law, your place is here, in your own house and your own fields, doing what you can do by yourself and keeping out of Drosten's sight for a bit."

Their lord grinned. "You speak nothing but sense, Havard. Much as part of me would still like to go over and get this settled once and for all, now ain't the time. We need those extra men, as you say, and the Orcca-folk need the same. This ought to be an easy bargain to strike: the only hard part might be Drosten's attitude, as you say." He looked around for his little chest. "If I can find the silver, I'll put some out for you to take as a gift, help sweeten the way a bit."

"It would be money well spent," declared Thorfinn. Others nodded their agreement.

"Right then, it's settled," Einar went on. "Make some lots and decide who goes: Havard, as Ragna's brother and my styrsman, I think you ought to go: but I'll not insist if you don't want the job. There's likely to be little thanks in it." He pulled a bronze ring, a little circle of knotted, plaited wire from his finger and set it on the table. "Except from me, that is. I've backed myself into a corner, been doing it ever since we got here in some ways, and now I need help to get out again. You'll have my thanks for doing this."

Havard reached out a hand and took the offering. "I'll do it gladly," he replied. "This corner wasn't all of your making, after all. There are other wyrds tangled up in this place as well; it's time for us all to tread carefully."

By the time the lots had been drawn, and the obligatory weapons collected to make a polite showing, the day had begun to brighten. Clouds still filled the wide expanse of open sky, but they were white and grey smudges rather than looming black monsters, and a weak sun shone through them like a blurred golden smear, giving a strange, shining cast to the land beneath. Havard, Ketil and Skapti wrapped their cloaks tightly around them, shifted spears onto shoulders, and set out into the remnants of the wind.

"Reckon this is going to clear any more?" wondered Havard.

"It might do," ventured Ketil. "It seems to me that we often get the best of the day just after dawn, but it will sometimes clear up again past the day-meal." He sniffed through his bright ginger beard. "Problem is, it often clouds over again every night, so we don't really gain anything. What we need is a few days of good, dry sun before we can start cutting. At least, that's how we always used to do it. Perhaps it's different here."

"I can't see it being that much different," said Havard. "It's not as if we've come halfway around the world, now is it? We didn't go very much to the north or the south when we came over, either; no, I reckon the climate's going to be much the same as it was back in the old place. If there's any difference, I'd say it was because there's no mountains in these parts. I've no idea what that would do to the weather, but I'm willing to bet it does something."

"I'll be happy enough if it just stops us having to move the sheep around so much!" laughed Skapti.

The walk into Olwen's lands – not Drosten's, Havard reminded himself – was only a short one. He thought he spotted a flash of bright colour on the line of the burn, but was not inclined to go and investigate; his business was with the lords of this place, and they spent most of their time in the circular houses just to the north of the stream. Nervousness increased as they got nearer: none of them had had any contact with Drosten since the news of Mawgan had come out, and they had no idea of how to approach the man. Havard had planned to rely on straightforward boldness and brash, but now that was starting to seem like rather less of a strategy. He was glad, suddenly, of his spear on his shoulder.

"How long until someone sees us coming and heads out to meet us, would you think?" wondered Ketil idly.

"I see 'em already," came Skapti's reply. "From the bondar's places to the north there."

Havard came to a sudden decision. "Go to them, then," he ordered. "Maybe we can arrange it between those of us actually doing the work, and leave our masters out of it."

"That sounds like an easier way," agreed Skapti.

"I'll settle for less arguments to have with those I'm trying to talk to," murmured Havard.

"Aye, they ought to be willing to listen, at least.

We're trying to make life easier for 'em, after all. Recognise anyone yet?"

"I don't see Drosten, if that's what you're asking," muttered Ketil, shielding his eyes against the bright clouds overhead and leaning into the wind. "I think that's Bran to the left of 'em, and maybe their own Havard... I can't say beyond that. There's too much sting in this wind."

"It's good enough," Havard reassured him. "They're people we know and can deal with."

The two little knots of men met in the ground between the two settlements. "Not the best of days for paying visits, Hevedd," Owain greeted them with his local form of the name. "What brings you away from your fireside, that we have to come away from ours?" There was a smile with the words, for which the Northman was grateful.

"We've come with a proposal to make your sad little lives a bit easier come harvesting!" he laughed. "We were on our way to find your master Drosten and put it to him, but when we saw you coming out it seemed far better to talk with you directly, and keep our lords and betters out of it. They'd only find things to argue over, after all..."

"That's a touchy subject with many of us," said Bran in a low voice. "But I can see the sense in the plan. You'll forgive us if we don't invite you any further, but what with things being as they are, it would go hard with us if we were seen to give you any sort of welcome just now."

Havard nodded. "I understand, although it's sad that it's come to this. There are times when I could cheerfully smash my brother-in-law's head in, and this is one of them. But my words, although they come from him as well, are meant for you men, rather than for your master directly; we were only going to put our proposal to him because he *is* your lord, and it's only right that he hear it. But I'm thinking he might hear it more readily from you than from us: especially if you dress it up as your own idea."

"This sounds like a lot of trouble and difficulty," said Hevedd with a touch of uncertainty. "What is it that you're wanting, exactly?"

"We'll offer to help you in harvesting whatever you have need to," answered Havard promptly. "I should've said that first, but I have a habit of going on a bit. This season doesn't feel right to any of us over the way there: it's different back in the homeland, the summer lasts longer and goes straight into winter. We've never had this bit in between. Is it always like this? Our thinking was that if there's only a few dry days in which to get the barley in, you're going to need every pair of hands you can find. Now I know what Einar's done in the long-ago, and I can begin to understand how Drosten might not want anything to do with us. But if the harvest isn't got in, everyone starves. Am I right?"

"Close enough," agreed Bran. "What's the price for your help? What has Einar seen that he wants now?"

"I'll overlook that," said Havard with a tighter smile than before. "All we ask is that you do the same for us. Our fields run alongside eash other, after all; it's effectively just one big harvest, shared between us. We're all facing the same problem: we came here on Einar's behalf, and with his agreement, since he couldn't see that coming himself would do anybody any favours."

"He's not wrong there," agreed Owain. "Alright then: we'll put it to the master and the lady. We'll send somebody over to you with a reply, hopefully before nightfall. It's a good plan to my ears: I'd rather we lived and worked together than kept on being apart, whatever happened to cause it. And I'll add that it's going to be easier dealing with you, Hevedd, than with your own lord across the way. We get plain talking from you, and no devious schemes or hidden motives. A favourable answer is more likely because we don't have to mention Einar's name to our own master."

"For what it's worth, Einar had no idea that your lady was who she was when we washed up here," answered Havard with another, easier smile. "In fact, I don't think I can remember him ever speaking her name before we came. However this has come to pass, it wasn't at his doing, you have my word on that."

"Nonetheless, it's happened," said Owain. "It's up to us all to try and get over it, now."

CHAPTER THIRTY-THREE

Drosten seemed to have aged still more in the time since the longest days of the summer. The brightness was gone from his eyes and his movements were slower, more deliberate than before. When he did stir himself, it was with sighs and quiet groans, as if every bone and muscle ached. His hair and beard were paler and thinner than before, and his skin seemed full of wrinkles. But the grim set of his mouth was unchanged, and the look of distaste whenever Einar's name came up was as plain as it had ever been. When the Northman's proposal had been put to him - without the need to mention Einar's name at all, Owain discovered - he waved the messengers to stools around the fire and then sat, motionless and quiet for a long while.

Olwen sat a little way away, watching the rain slowly steam from her visitor's cloaks and seeing the damp from their shoes form little puddles in the floor around them. In the flickering glow of the fire their faces seemed to alter and change moment by moment, making it almost impossible to read the expressions. She could not see her husband's face from where she was, but she did not need to. She knew all too well how his face would be set.

Drosten seemed to have withdrawn into himself: the silence stretched longer and longer, with only the hissing of the peat as it burned and the little sounds of the house around them to offer any respite. Eventually, she could take it no longer. "Surely," she began tentatively, her voice sounding loud and harsh in her ears, "surely this can only be a useful thing that they offer? The more hands we have for harvesting, the easier it will be."

Heads and eyes turned to look at her, as if she had only just been noticed. It was not a comfortable feeling, but then she was unable to remember the last time there had been much comfort in her world.

"We thought so, lady," Bran finally ventured. "But Hevedd was insistent that we bring it to you as well. I assume he didn't want to risk further upset by just arranging it among those of us likely to be out in the fields, without your agreement."

"That was unusually thoughtful of them," grated Drosten eventually. "I wonder what the real reason for it is?"

"Need there be one, beyond realising that if we don't get the harvests in, we'll all be the worse for it?" replied Olwen.

"I've yet to see anything in Einar that is simple or straightforward," Drosten said. "I don't see as how this need be any different. You mark my words, there'll be something more to it."

"Hevedd has always been honest and open in his dealings with us, lord," Owain ventured. "It's just as likely that this is all his idea, and he's just put it to Einar as we are putting it to you."

But Drosten had lapsed back into silence again, as if he could divine some hidden motive by just staring into the flames. Olwen looked at his hunched back with pursed lips.

"Are you willing to take his help, husband?" she said at last.

"What does it matter? Do what you like; I can't argue that the help won't be useful. They can send as many of their lads as they want to come and cut the barley with us, and aye, we'll give them the same in return – so long as there's no upsets in between. Go: take the answer to them. Let me sit and think."

*

"If we waited while he sat and thought on every matter that's brought to him," muttered Owain once they were safely back outside and out of earshot, "there'd be nothing done around here at all!" He huddled deeper into the folds of his cloak, its fringed ends dangling wetly in the mud. "I find myself cursing their Hevedd for making us go to our own master instead of just agreeing something and then getting on with it."

"That's the way it goes right now," answered Bran. "But at least he said aye to it – after a fashion."

"The way he said it suggests there might still be trouble ahead, though," murmured Hevedd. "If we're lucky, the sun will shine for a few days, we can all get the work done, and our lord back there might not even stray from his fireside."

"Sad ways for our thoughts to run after so many years," Bran reflected as they trudged onwards, back towards their own clustered dwellings. To the seaward side of them the newcomer's house, the one they had lent a hand in building, loomed black and solid through the drizzle. There were no signs of life: Havard and his mates must have gone back already. Owain rubbed his beard and slowed his pace. "We ought to go over there now and let them know..."

"I'm up for it," said Hevedd. "Let's see how Einar's welcome compares to that our own lord gave us, eh? Oh come on!" he said, exasperated at the sudden shocked looks of his companions. "It's only what nearly all of us are wondering these days, isn't it? I'm even willing to bet that Hevedd welcomes us in and speaks on our behalf if need be, too! And the sooner we can deliver the message, then the sooner we can get together when the weather clears. We were told to take the message back here after all, so Drosten can't even accuse us of going behind his back or undermining his own authority..."

"What little of it he has left," muttered Bran, but in the wind and the rain, his companions failed to hear him.

"Aye, I suppose it's not like we're looking to stay for days on end," smiled Owain suddenly. "Our own people won't miss us for another short while, and in this wet there's nothing so urgent waiting that we can avoid this. Come on then: it's another while beside a fire, getting dry, and maybe even a cup or two in it somewhere. Let's go find out how our neighbours are today."

CHAPTER THIRTY-FOUR

The clouds began to thin a day or so later, whilst the winds got a little stronger but shifted more to the west, coming across the gentle slopes that stood behind the settlement instead of straight in from the sea. They were drier from this direction, with little of the usual salty moisture that turned every iron object rusty within a day if it were left unattended. Men from Olwen's estates came to Einar's house more and more often, bringing news of what the weather was likely to do, and saying that this was probably as good as it would get. It was time to harvest.

"Very well," nodded Einar, rising from his High-Seat when he heard the news. "We'll meet you on the line between our fields, and we'll throw lots or something to decide where we start, eh?"

"Start rounding up the lads," he advised Havard as soon as the visitors had gone from the room. "Take Svein with you as well: he's big enough to do his share after all, and a day or two's strong exercise might do him good." He looked towards the end-room where Ragna and her ladies seemed to be spending more and more of their time these days. "I'll go and organise blood and ale for the other bits."

Skapti followed his gaze. "There much to be had by way of friendliness from that direction, lord?"

Einar grunted. "In many respects, no, things don't seen to have changed since Olwen said her piece about me and Mawgan. But when it comes to ensuring a good harvest and fertile soils for next time, I think there might be a little more flexibility than if I were asking something for myself."

"You have my sympathy for your own position, but I'm still glad about the rest of it, then."

"As we all ought to be. I've no idea how well our seed has done in this place: we had no real time to prepare the ground, but we weren't so late with the planting as I'd feared we might've been. The season seems shorter here: things grow faster, I suppose, what with it being a bit warmer than we've been used to." He put his cup down and stretched his arms wide. "Come on: up on your feet! Get your working-shirts on, but I doubt it'll be warm enough for taking breeks off. The sooner we're out there, the better. I'll not be accused of lagging behind and putting the crop at risk."

There was a general noise and bustle as his companions sorted themselves out. Living in the one house as they did, the wall-benches were stuffed full of bags and bundles at the back where spare clothes and belongings were still stowed away, having never been unpacked since their time aboard the ship. Now was the moment for opening satchels and leather-wrapped parcels, and digging out old, worn-through garments that were not suitable for wearing in the hall, but were still perfectly good for hard work in the fields. Out in the narrow passage and on the platforms that sat amid the roof-timbers at either end of the room, men, women and children alike went hunting for the iron sickles and long knives that made cutting wheat and barley so much easier. They had none of the large baskets in which to carry the harvested grain, and nowhere to thresh that grain from the chaff. Einar's brow furrowed as he stood and thought of solutions to these and other problems.

Ragna opened the door to her own little chamber and looked out at the noisy scene. "Harvest?" she mouthed at her husband.

He nodded. "Are you willing to provide ale and blood to help it along, my wife?"

"Gladly: this feeds us all, although I do wonder what Olwen and her people might have to say about it being done."

"I don't care what they think: if they want to have their kirk-man come and chant over their crop, they're more than welcome. I'll not interfere. But I'll stick with what I know on my side of the stone, thanks."

She gave him a long, hard stare. "That's your concern, husband, but only right and proper after everything else that's been going on. But in that regard, it's going to look very odd if you're not out in the field with everyone else, yet I can't see your being there not attracting some kind of difficulty."

"No, I'd been thinking that, too. Stuff 'em," he declared defiantly, "we need the grain cutting, and any flax that's in along with it this time. There was little enough wool on the sheep's backs when we clipped 'em in the summer: some linen would be most useful. So I'm going. I'll not hide from old Drosten forever over this – or over anything else, come to that."

"Somehow, I thought you wouldn't," said Ragna with a twist of a half-smile, "but don't go back to letting your concern for your reputation get in the way of good sense and plain manners."

"Or of politics?" he asked craftily. "Would you rather I sat indoors like a scared old fool, or went out to meet whatever comes our way head-on, and before it makes its way to you?"

"Your foolishness has already come home to me," she snapped back with a scowl. "Don't go compounding your errors, Einar. And don't be so cocky as to think you've been let off from your past misdeeds, either. Now go and get the harvest before you waste the day with this. I'll bring the jug and the bowl, never fear."

CHAPTER THIRTY-FIVE

Einar strode out in his usual shirt. He only had the two, and the better one was certainly not destined for such work as cutting bere and heaving the grain-heavy stalks into tight bushels. It was dusty, dirty work, full of scraps of plants, mud from underfoot, and sweat that soaked inexorably, irresistably, through the layers from the flesh beneath. Hands got grazed and sliced by sharp, cut edges to the bere-stems, bruised by the knocking against the stalks as they were gathered, and banged on stones as they were collected from the ground. Fingers ached from the constant grasp of sickles and knives, and the bending of stiff stems into circles with which to bind the stacks. No, it was definitely not good-shirt work, and so his everyday green garment, stained by years of wear and the grease from his mail (for it also doubled as his war-shirt), was called into service yet again. But he took the precaution of having his linen one beneath it as some protection from the work, and wound long strips of thick, heavily woven braid around his hose, all the way up to where his breeks ended above his knees. Hot he might get, but it was better than being bloodied and bruised.

His household trailed behind in a long, ragged line: everyone who could be spared was dug out and pressed into service for what was arguably the most important task of the year. Blood-moon, by Einar's reckoning, was not for some time still – they hadn't even had the Winter Finding yet, when the days were as long as the nights – and the slaughtering that took place then was usually managed by just a handful of the men. But harvesting always needed every hand that could be brought to it. Gathering the grain pitted man against the weather, and also against time: leave it too long and the grain rotted in the husks, useless and fit only for ploughing back into the soil. They could not afford to have that happen: nobody ever refused the call to harvest. Einar might forgive his people many other things, but that would never be one of them.

It was a fair day for it, he had to admit: the wind was not too strong, and drier than was often the case. The clouds were high and thin white in colour, which meant that every once in a while the sun could shine down on him from a small window of open blue, and put a little warmth onto his back. His axe felt good in his hand, whilst at his midriff his knife banged and bumped at every stride. All in all, it felt like a good day to lead his people in their yearly battle with the spirits of the soil. Up ahead, coming from the Orccan settlement, he could see a similar string of people to his own. He smiled, which he knew they wouldn't see, and waved: which they would.

His smile faded, to be replaced by a puzzled frown. None had waved back, although faces were clearly turned in his direction. He glanced back at his own folk, but saw nothing amiss to his eyes. So what was this about, then? He looked over again. Was Drosten there?

He was. He stood by the marker-stone, stiff and remote as his people filed past him into their own fields. Einar's brows knitted in thought; he felt more than heard when Havard and Thorfinn came up beside him.

"Think that's trouble up ahead?" he asked quietly.

"Hard to tell: he's had a while to brood on his woes, but the word is that he brings it all down on us."

"On me, you mean?"

Havard nodded. "Pretty much. As for the rest of 'em, it's hard to say. But if he's here, they're more likely to side with him than with us."

Einar sighed. "It had to come someday; we couldn't go on avoiding each other for ever. I don't really care what it takes, but we came here to help with a harvest, and that's what I plan on doing. So we'll go and present ourselves, and then just set to work, alright? We'll do it his way if that's what he wants; what's important is the grain we get from this. Pass the word, Thorfinn; Havard, you're with the lads in my stead while I go deal with this old fool."

Drosten waited like a statue as they approached. Despite himself, as they got closer, Einar paled. This was not the confident, strong headman who had confronted them so long ago, only last spring. This was a man weighed down by troubles and cares, whose woes now almost bent him over, and whose eyes showed none of the sparkle and life that had so impressed his unwelcome visitor. More than anything else, it was the shock of Drosten's aspect that brought home to the Northman the full impact of his past actions. Then he steeled himself and shrugged it off. He hadn't meant for any of this to happen. It was Drosten who had got in his way, and then refused to move.

"So then," said Einar jovially as they came within earshot, "are we ready for this? Where had you in mind to start, neighbour?"

"If I had the strength left in me, I'd drop you where you stand, so smug and bright." The words came out in a long, low growl, through lips that barely moved in the thinning straggle of beard around Drosten's face. "Is it not enough that I have had to endure everything else you sent me, without coming here and finding your face pushed into my own? Are you after my people's grain now as well?"

"Nothing of the sort," snapped Einar, stopping where he was and hoisting his axe onto his shoulder. "We all came out here in good faith, as good neighbours, to lend a hand with the harvest so that we *all* might be sure of eating over the winter. One of your men brought me a message that we'd be welcome, for that if nothing else. Was he wrong? Or is it that you've changed your mind about it all?"

"Your men's hands are due some work on our side of the stones, if you remember the agreement my wife struck with you. Perhaps you remember her as well: all alone in a place full of strangers, looking for help and getting only deception and lies, and then a child into the bargain, hmm? You could not begin to imagine the depths of the humiliation that has caused me, and the anger that's grown out of it."

Einar scratched his nose. "Probably not, no. It's not something I say very often, but if I could undo what happened all those years ago, or if I could change where my posts came ashore, I'd happily do it. But it isn't to be. These things came to pass, and with no regard for what had gone before, or what might happen after. I can offer you a weregeld, but I can't see what good it would do you, and I doubt you'd take it anyway. In the meantime, we have a field to cut and if we don't get on with it we'll all starve later. Havard can tell the lads to lend their hands among your folk: we can do that side first. From your words, I think you and I might be talking here for some while."

"Don't look to over-rule me even in my own fields!"

"I'm not: I only instruct my own lads, and they'll take their lead from you. Hard though it might be to believe, I've not come here looking for trouble."

"Yet you carry an axe..."

Einar stared at him in disbelief. "My folk always carry weapons outside: you know that. This is nothing special; there's no extra reason behind it." He cracked a sudden smile. "If I'd wanted to cause you harm, Drosten, I could've done it already."

"What are those women doing?"

"Women?" Einar turned around to follow the other man's gaze. "Ah, that's Ragna and her mates, come to bless our side of the field. Blood freshly gathered, and ale long kept, a gift for the powers that grow the crops as thanks for allowing our harvest. No doubt you'll have something similar, hmm?"

Drosten watched as the distant figures stopped at the edge of the barley and solemnly poured things from a jug and a bowl. "Not these days," he murmured. "There seems to be a great deal we don't have, or don't do, any more."

"Still no contact with that Jarl of yours? I don't seem to be having much luck in that respect either."

"We don't have trust," Drosten went on, seeming not to hear Einar's words. "We've lost our luck, and our place in the world. Where once our people stood strong, now we are scattered and lost; we can't even get to the kirkmen any more. No messages, no visitors, through this whole summer..." He turned watery, weary eyes on his neighbour; Einar could see no spirit in them, no life or energy at all.

Suddenly, without warning, Drosten simply

collapsed at his feet. Einar took a leap backwards with a shout: around him, men looked up, and then looked for a weapon.

"What happened?" shouted Havard, pushing through the barley with Owain and his son Cadwy close behind.

"He was talking, he looked at me... then he fell." Einar was already on his knees beside the man, running his hands across the points where he ought to feel life. But there was none. "I can't find his heart," he said eventually, "and there's no breath. Drosten is dead, and you have my oath that it was not at my hand."

Owain made his own inspection: around them, more and more of their men were gathering. "There's no wounds on him," Owain confirmed, "so there's no cause for anger at anyone here. Our master has died, seemingly just because it was his appointed time."

"So what do we do?" asked someone. Further away, Einar saw Ragna out of the corner of his eye. She too was coming closer, but there seemed to be far too many of Drosten's men between them all of a sudden. He found himself wishing she were away back to the house already: this place could still get dangerous. He had stood up and left his axe on the ground, laying blackly beside Drosten's pale, lifeless face. He wondered how long it would be before Owain's words failed to hold any weight with his fellows – and how far away his own men were. Einar thought quickly, but it was Havard who spoke.

"Some of you should perhaps take him home," he suggested, "and do whatever needs doing before we come together and make a grave for him. We can't leave this field untouched, though: the rest of us will have to stay and work on. My lads and I are willing to do that while you all decide where you ought to be, but don't forget that we still need this bere to be cut before the weather turns again." He looked to Einar to confirm what he had said with a raised eyebrow.

Experience told Einar that he needed to keep these men moving, working, away from dwelling on this event. Let them mourn in their own time, later, after the work was done. Long, long ago, when he had been barely a lad, his uncle had taken him abroad for a season. It had been a hard trip: they had pulled away from somewhere – and he couldn't now remember just where – with four of their number dead in the bottom of the boat, and a good half-dozen more wounded, their blood oozing stickily into their clothing. There had been no time to sit and cry, or shout at the Gods, or even sew the wounds shut: those of them left had been pushed to the oars by the master, and driven to row, and row, and row, until they were far our to sea, where nobody could follow. Then, and only then, had there been time for tending to the injured, and mourning for the dead. It had seemed harsh to Einar at the time, but it had kept him alive. He had learned the lesson well. Now he had to apply it once more: but was it what these folk did? Was he, without realising, making matters worse between them again?

"Aye," he said in answer to Havard's silent enquiry. "Havard here knows what to do, and we'll keep our word in this. My men will follow his lead, and Havard, you know most of these from Drosten's household, yes? Then there should be no problem in sorting it out. I will either stay or come with you, as you wish." He said this last to Owain, who still stood motionless over his lord.

Ragna had reached the scene by then. "What's this?" she asked. "Drosten dead?" She made her own examination of the prone figure. "Dead indeed, husband," she murmured quietly. "I wonder what happens now?"

From slightly further away, Svein watched silently, his eyes clouded. He had seen the whole affair, and knew that his father had not even struck the other man. But how to convince all these others, all the Orccamen who had been expecting just such a thing for so long, that it was so? And what of Rilca?

He stepped forward. "I saw it all, and if it will be of any help, I'm willing to go and be witness for Olwen..."

"That would be 'Lady Olwen' to you, lad," growled his father. "And what makes you think they'd believe you when you tell them I had no part in it? More likely they'd tear you apart in order to be avenged on me. No, Svein, that won't do. This is a matter for them, and them alone. We can have no place in it."

"This one time, I'm agreeing with your fathir," Ragna added. "Our faces would be no comfort in that house just now: not that I think they ever have been, on reflection. Your back is better used here, though: of that I *am* convinced. So, go get your sickle."

AUTUMN, 902 A.D.

CHAPTER THIRTY-SIX

Keen, pale eyes watched from beneath long fringes of fair or pale reddish hair as a ragged line of smaller, darker figures shuffled out across the windswept, rain-threatened landscape. Grass whipped around their legs and long kirtles as they stumbled onward, their burden carried low between four of their number. They got over the line of the burn only with some difficulty, passing the tightly-wrapped bundle over their shoulders as the land dipped into the water, which gurgled onwards as if unconcerned by their passage or the reasons for it. Above, held motionless by the winds, seabirds watched silently - as silently as the folk who walked slowly onwards, and as still as those who watched from the shelter of their southern doorway.

"It's an odd way for things to fall out," mused Einar quietly at length. "If he'd been felled by an axe, it'd be different. There's something not right about just dropping down dead in your own fields."

"I know what you mean," agreed Havard. "It's not how I'd want to end up." He cast a sideways look at his brother-in-law. "Mind you, there's been a lot of things not quite right around here for a long while..."

"I'd be hard-pressed to argue that one," admitted Einar. "There've been things I'd do differently the next time around, or even if I could go back and have another try at them the first time. You did well when it happened, though. Olwen's lads rallied to you in a way I thought I'd never see. I owe you a lot for that – we all do. If you hadn't stepped in as you did, the barley would still be in the fields, ruined and finished. Winter wouldn't be looking anywhere near as bright as it is now."

Havard brushed the comment quietly aside as he watched Drosten's final journey into the old kirkyard, where every spade put into the soil seemed to pull up gravestones, or the remains of those who ought to have stayed beneath them. "If they're putting him to rest over there, we'll need to find somewhere else for planting next spring."

"There'll be room enough, don't you worry. After all, what's to stop us moving out into the Orcca-folk's lands now? Think Olwen's lads would fight for her to that extent?" Einar rubbed his beard. "Not that I'm thinking of taking any of it by force: I think we know them too well, and owe them too much, to let that happen. But they might take silver for another patch of ground, or they might look more kindly on our putting our crops together as one, now that Drosten's gone."

"From what's been said to me, I reckon that last approach might take you a lot further than trying to prise it from them with a spear. Granted, they're not especially happy with her as their Lady these days, not since the story about Mawgan got out, but they have a tie to the land, and to the place. It's an *odal* thing..."

"Ah: the place where you belong, where you have inheritances and blood ties. That says it all. Do they have something like *odal* in their laws, then?"

"I've no idea: I just say it on the grounds of what I've seen and heard from them."

"Fair enough." Einar fell silent for a while, as he watched the procession cluster around a freshly-dug grave. The wind carried snatches of sound back to him: chanting, possibly crying – or was that the gulls? He couldn't tell. He squinted into the sting of the breeze, trying to make out individual figures. Was Olwen there? Or her children? Burials were always awkward times: the living demanded certain behaviours from each other, or something was deemed wrong with the occasion. Even ship-men had their customs and taboos, but they generally managed the disposal of dead comrades with a minimum of fuss. Often through expediency: enemies were notoriously averse to allowing you burial rights on their lands.

"I can't see anything in this wind," he finally admitted with a growl. Havard gave him a look of mild surprise.

"And what were you expecting to see, brother-in-law?"

"I've no idea... Olwen perhaps, and if Rilca has gone with the body, then it's likely that Svein's there somewhere as well." He scratched his beard again, and wondered where his comb had got to. "I wonder what Mawgan's been told about it all, and by whom."

"That's not going to be easy, whoever gets the task."

"No indeed. It might've been useful to let him be welcome here, but I don't see that happening anytime soon..."

"Ragna still being difficult about it all?"

Einar nodded glumly. "I had hoped she might have cooled a little by now, and been amenable to talking round, at least some of the way. But not so far."

Havard clapped a hand on his shoulder. "I can't promise anything, but I'll have a word."

He went back inside, carefully propping the makeshift door back into place behind him. Einar stood alone, his cloak wrapped tightly around him, and watched the little smudges of the funeral party through the rain as they finally laid their old master to rest. One day it would be his turn, he knew: such was the way of things. He had seen enough of life that death held no terrors, but he found himself hoping his end would be a little more heroic than Drosten's had been.

CHAPTER THIRTY-SEVEN

Once the body was in the ground there was nothing else to do. Drosten was gone; whatever tears were needful to shed for him had all fallen onto the damp earth piled beside his grave. He would live on in the hearts and minds of his people – for a little while. At least until the necessities of everyday living reasserted their supremacy in thought and action. Then, like so many others before him, he would gently, gradually, fade.

Even Olwen found herself resigned to his passing in a way that she had not experienced before. When Uoret had died, in such a similarly sudden manner she thought now, her grief had been as huge as the skies and as deep as the oceans. She remembered thinking how it might never end, how her aching for him might never cease, or even diminish with the passing of the years. It had been that depth of emotion that had sent her wandering into the Norsemen's summer market, still looking for answers she could never have possibly got. She had been younger then, too. This day, with so many other wounds still raw and bleeding in her soul, her husband's death was just another rip in the fabric of her being. Her shock at its sudden coming would pass; life would have to go on, in one form or another. She sighed as they all tramped back to the houses, her head bent low, her gaze unseeing at the grass and heathers that bent under her foot. The darkening clouds over her head seemed a perfect echo to her mood. Beside and behind her, her companions somehow sensed her feeling and kept a respectful, silent distance.

Olwen's head only raised as they reached her own house and the little cortege began to break up. Conyn the smith headed back to his own dark, strange little world, his face grim and covered in worried, angular lines. Owain, Bran and the other men quietly headed back to the fields in which the animals grazed unconcerned, oblivious to the troubles felt by men. She looked around. In the strips of land that separated her holding from Einar's, the barley stood neatly stacked and only awaiting its moving into the drying-house. She rather suspected that some sort of deal had been struck with her neighbour to which she had not been party, whereby all the grain would be stored on her land. Einar might have used his silver to get himself a house built, but he evidently hadn't thought about what other buildings he was going to need. Come to that, had he even mentioned a boat-shed? Surely he wouldn't be intending to keep it out in the open through the whole winter? There'd be nothing but firewood left of it by spring if he did.

She felt rather than saw when gentle hands guided her through the doorway and sat her by the fireside. Danna was already placing more peat over the tired little flames by the time Olwen realised where she was and began to focus on her surroundings again. Tired: that was how she felt. Like the flames, struggling to carry on, seemingly weighed down by so many burdens...

A face swam into view: Rilca was kneeling before her, worry in every feature. "Are you alright, aunt?" she was saying. "Do you need anything?"

She smiled wanly. "Only sleep, and rest, and an end to all these troubles," she murmured. "Probably a bit too much to ask, just now."

The girl shrugged noncommittally. "Two of the three are easy enough, but I suspect it's that third one that'd do the most good."

"Well, we'll see," Olwen replied. "Who knows what may come next, hmm? I'll be happy if Einar over the way there doesn't try and take advantage of all this. Which reminds me, niece of mine, that we must talk someday soon."

Rilca scowled. "About Svein?" Her body was already tensing for an argument, but Olwen hadn't the energy for one. She patted the girl's hands.

"Aye, about Svein, but not just about him. It's a talk we'd've been having around this age of yours, whatever the circumstances. But it's not so urgent yet, I think, that it can't wait for a day or two longer. When I'm a bit more awake, which I suppose I'm going to have to be now that Drosten is gone from us." Her voice caught at that last sentence, and she suddenly found herself on the edge of tears once again. From the fireside, Gwen pushed a cup of ale into her mistress' hands.

"Here, Lady, this will help. There'll be stew soon, and good bread."

Olwen looked over at her. "And tomorrow is a fresh beginning?"

"If you wish it so, Lady, aye."

Olwen sipped the ale, strong and laced with heather-flowers. "That would seem like a fine idea. We need to break out of this season of misery we've had so far. We need prayer, we need effort, we need new ideas all around us. I've lost two husbands now; last time, I went looking to incomers for comfort, but all they've brought me is sorrow and trouble. Now they are sitting here beside us, but I'll not look to them for answers this time." She looked up, her eyes brighter than anyone had seen them in weeks. "I've sat in their shadow long enough. It's time to walk in the sun again."

CHAPTER THIRTY-EIGHT

Gwen, Danna and the other women of Olwen's household made their way homewards in the last light of the day, that time when shadows lengthen, colours dim, and the roughness of the ground underfoot becomes lost in the grey of evening. Their beds lay northwards, amid the smaller, newer little huts, beside husbands or less formal partners, or with children left over from marriages been and gone; or with aged, lonely parents now equally adrift in the world. People clustered together, for warmth, for company, for some lessening of the loneliness that might otherwise overwhelm them. And wherever they congregated, they talked.

"What d'you think's brought about this change of heart suddenly?" wondered Gwen as they entered one of the larger buildings in the little huddle of roofs. "And more importantly, d'you think it'll last?"

"What's that?" asked Owain, looking up from a half-mended shoe. "More goings-on with our lady?"

"Drosten's barely cold in the ground," commented Bran as he got up and poured ale. "It's a bit soon for making bold decisions, surely?"

"But if not now, then when?" replied Danna. "What's wrong with finding the strength for another try at life whenever it happens?"

"I don't know, but it just feels a bit wrong,

somehow."

Danna sat beside him. "You men felt more attached to Drosten than we did, I'd guess. You were out in the fields with him more than us, and you spent less time with the lady. So you'll be closer to him than to her, and I'd even go so far as to say that you'll mourn him deeper and longer than she will. But as we were coming away tonight, she seemed more alive, more ready to take on the problems that surround us, than she has since Einar and his crew arrived here. We're going to need all our strength in dealing with whatever comes along next – and something will, you mark my words. I can't see Einar leaving us alone now that Drosten's not here to help protect us."

"Scant thanks we gave him when he lived," murmured Hevedd. "I can't help wondering if maybe we all had a part to play in his dying so suddenly..."

Heads turned to look at him. Eyes turned harsh and accusing.

"Well, how many of us still have the silver Einar paid us for building his house, eh?" went on Hevedd defiantly. "Remember how Drosten wanted us to turn aside, take up our spears and send Einar away? But we didn't, did we? So don't any of you start glaring at me that way. We all had a hand in it."

"There's no arguing that point," admitted Allun after a moment's silence. "But we tried to be loyal in other ways. None of us went over to Einar as... what's the word he uses?"

"Bond-something," supplied Conyn from the corner.

"Aye, that's it. We all stayed here: and apart from the house-building, we rallied round him whenever he needed us. And before the Northmen came at all, we were as steadfast as any lord might have wished for."

"Nowhere else to go, though, was there?" muttered Danna. Allun looked across at her.

"And did you ever want to go elsewhere, Danna? Where would you have gone, that would've suited you as well as this place, eh?"

"Enough," said Conyn again, putting down his cup. "The point is that we should be ready to follow our lady's lead, if lead it turns out to be, and look to our futures. Drosten knew as well as any of us that Einar and his gang aren't just going to sit on their patch of ground and be content with it: that's not their way. My worry is that without strong leadership, we don't have the means to stand against them – or the skill, either, come to that." He leaned forward into the firelight. "We are duty-bound to follow our lady's will in these matters: we can keep the place going, attend to all our usual tasks, aye, but when it comes to relations with our neighbours, we don't have the right to decide how it's done. That's her place. We can only follow. For myself, I don't know whether this new mood you're speaking of is going to last – what if she's not strong enough any more to maintain it? Do we slide back into the bad ways of this last summer, when everyones's been moping around as if the sky were falling?"

"It pretty much did for her," Danna reminded the smith sharply. Conyn merely shrugged.

"That changes nothing. If we have to rely on her for leadership, then it might be up to you women to keep her propped up enough *to* lead! Think you're strong enough to keep doing that, day after day, with Einar's wolves sniffing at the door?"

Gwen frowned. "We can't do it forever..."

"I know. Now you know it too. If the Lord is with

us you won't have to, and the lady will pull herself out of her pit. But we can't rely on that happening right now, no matter what she says to you. Realistically, we're pretty much on our own – without a leader who can lead us."

Owain stirred uncomfortably. "Are you suggesting we put one of ourselves forward to do the job? That's pretty dangerous talk, Conyn."

"I don't know what to suggest," admitted the smith wearily. "I'm just looking for ideas at the moment. Short of just going across to Einar and surrendering everything we have in exchange for an end to his ambition, I can't think what to do. And I'll not put my head into that yoke just yet."

"If it were their Hevedd in charge instead of Einar, that idea might have a bit more merit," mused Owain. "He's an easier, more honest man in his dealings, and more inclined to be friendly towards us. But it isn't, and so it's not worth talking about, I suppose."

"We could spend endless nights discussing what to do," pointed out Bran, "but nothing changes the fact that it's not our decision anyway. What happens to us is up to the lady. We might as well go to our beds for all the good we can do; then at least we'll be rested for whatever the day brings."

"I'll settle for another day of just doing the usual work with nothing to disrupt it," decided Owain. There was a general chorus of agreement, and people started sorting out their blankets, wrapping themselves against the inevitable draughts and creeping as close to the fire as they dared.

Only Conyn stayed where he was. He stared deep into the dull glow of the banked firelight, long after his companions were all snoring gently around him. But he found no answers to any of the questions that would not let him sleep.

CHAPTER THIRTY-NINE

The days grew ever-shorter once the harvest was finally in. Once more, Olwen watched her own farmhands work alongside those from Einar's steading as the sheafs were gathered into every empty hut or shed that could be found, and the long process of winnowing began.

They had worked well as a single entity, she had to admit; furthermore, she could admit it without any of the grudging, unwilling emnity that had characterised Drosten's attitude to such things. Einar had come from a place very similar to this, if not so spread-out: alongside his adventures aboard ship, he had been a farmer when at home. He was familiar with the seasons for planting and harvest, for lambing and putting the ram in. To have adapted so quickly to new lands and new ways all around him was, she decided, little short of miraculous. Could Drosten have done so well, she wondered quietly. But that was a question without meaning now. Drosten, her husband, was gone.

She squinted at the figures out in the barley-field, strained her ears for the sounds of talk that drifted back to her on the breeze. Ah, she had been right: there were Rilca and Svein, working side-by-side again. It seemed to be happening a lot more, she reflected, and whilst she was certain that they also spent a lot of time together away from the rest of the men, it couldn't be denied that they did their share of the work together as well. As if they were already wed... which they couldn't be of course, at least not in Olwen's eyes or the eyes of her folk. That required ceremonies, and formal betrothals, and the agreement of the kirk – none of which they had even asked for as yet. She knew nothing of how Svein's people did things: were they perhaps already man and wife in Einar's eyes?

Olwen had desperately hoped that something good, like an end to the troubles between her own house and that of Einar, might come out of her husband's death. Suddenly, it seemed a forlorn hope.

"What catches your eye, mistress?" asked Danna beside her suddenly, passing a cup of ale.

"Ask who, rather than what," Olwen replied quietly. "Tell me Danna, how much do you and Gwen see of Rilca in the house these days?"

The younger woman pursed her lips in thought. "About the same as usual, Lady, although she knows most of what we could teach her already. She's as good at the fireside as any of us, she knows about milking the cows and birthing the lambs, she watches the skies and the seasons and the length of the days, and she knows what they all mean. Is there something wrong?"

"Only that I worry when I see her beside Einar's boy so much of the time."

"They do seem to have got very close, Lady, but I couldn't say that she's neglected her work because of it – at least, not as far as I've seen."

"Nevertheless, when she gets back, send her to me. There are things I think I ought to tell her; things I should've said long ago."

Danna looked over at her mistress, at the lines of worry and memory etched into her face. "Aye Lady," was all she could think of to say.

CHAPTER FORTY

It seemed to Rilca that it had been such a very long time since there had been music in the house. People used to sing and play, she remembered; there had been bright firesides, laughter, pleasure in the life they had in this place. But such things seemed to have faded over the moons. Now the nights were largely silent, with only the occasional hiss or crackle from the peat on the fire to punctuate the stillness. Words were murmured rather than spoken; she didn't even know where the bone whistles were these days, although she hoped Arlen still had his drum somewhere safe.

Morgan seemed to have noticed the changes as well: his little face was solemn, the mouth pulled down in a perpetual frown that Rilca found she hated to see. He looked paler, too, somehow, and he didn't run around like he used to. His time seemed to be spent mostly keeping out of people's way – even his mothers'. Rilca suspected he spent much of his days alone, just sitting in the dark somewhere. Something deep within her knew that wasn't right.

So, even when Danna had come looking for her as everybody had made their way homewards in the last of the light and told her that her aunt had asked to speak with her, Rilca went looking for her little cousin instead. It was no easy task: nobody seemed to have seen him, which only really served to confirm her fears. But then, she thought wryly, wasn't she as much to blame? Had she not been so busy with other matters – and other people – that Morgan had been able to slip out of her view as well? It was not so long ago that they had been almost inseperable: she recalled a walk along the beach in search of shellfish. They hadn't been down that way in God only knew how long: not since they had found Einar's posts, in fact. And since the man himself had arrived, they hadn't gone to the shore at all. Rilca didn't even know if Morgan and Bjorn were still playing together: how likely was it, since everyone had learned of his true parentage? Probably not very, if she was being honest.

  She struck out in that direction, however, since she couldn't immediately think of any other place to begin a search. It was always possible that the lad would see them all traipsing homewards, and take himself back to the fireside: but she wanted to be sure, or at least to try and have some idea of where he was spending his days. Part of her wanted to promise to do better for him, but another part accepted that such promises were far too likely to be broken by simple circumstance. A third part whispered in her head that, if she went shorewards at this sort of time, there was a chance of having Svein to walk beside her.

  And so it proved. "What brings you this way when all the work's done?" he asked when he caught up with her. "I can't say for certain what sort of welcome you'll have if you're looking to come home with me, but I'll stand up for you whatever they say about it."

  She smiled at him in the deepening gloom, her hair caught once again in the wind. "That's a kind thought, Svein, but this time I'm looking for Morgan. Do you know if he still comes over to see Bjorn these days?"

  Svein frowned in thought. "No, I wouldn't know, and I don't recall seeing him hanging around either. Is he missing, then? Should we both search for the lad? If he's out in this for too long he'll never find his way home before he freezes to death."

  "That's right Svein, look on the bright side," she

muttered crossly. "He's not been seen much at all, anywhere, for some while, even though he's in every night. I just wondered what he's been doing with himself: he's turned very quiet and withdrawn lately. I'm worried about him: it's not a natural childhood he's having right now, and God knows it'll be over soon enough."

Svein shrugged. "Fathir would say that he's heading for working age: he says it of Bjorn, too. If you want to ask my brother, I'm sure I can get you in and out before anyone takes offence at you – although maybe these days they wouldn't. I have to admit I've rather stopped listening; perhaps it's time to start taking notice again."

"Good idea: they might go back to including you in what they're planning if you do that."

Svein smiled wryly. "Alright, I hear you! What do you want me to do to help you in this?"

"Well, if you've not seen Morgan, there's not a lot you *can* do, I think. But asking Bjorn's a good idea. If I wait outside perhaps, could you go in and ask him?"

They were nearly at the dark bulk of Einar's house: the grass was shorter here, where the sheep clustered in the lee of the building to shelter from the wind as it whipped across the dunes, full of salt and sea-wet. Bjorn led her along the side to the far end, where a stone path offered more even, but also more slippery, footing up to the porch. There was room within it for two: Rilca reached up and kissed him quickly before he pushed open the door and vanished inside. A blast of heat escaped around his body; left in the cold on her own, Rilca shivered.

She waited; it seemed like the night was stretching on around her and heading for dawn before Svein reappeared. "Come on inside," he said urgently, and beckoned her closer.

"What's happening?" she asked warily. Unseen, one hand went down to her belt, and the small knife she carried there.

"Bjorn is happy to tell what little he knows, but the old man suggested you come in and ask him honestly for yourself. Mothir agreed: you're welcome here!" The relief in his voice couldn't be concealed.

"Come on," he urged, leading her down the dark passageway. She had an impression of a door in another part of the wall, as if leading to another little room, but things were moving too fast around her, and in her own head, for any real understanding. The heat was almost unbearable; from a gap in the wall, a blaze of light shone outwards and the sound of voices became gradually louder as they approached. Svein squeezed her hand in reassurance: she kept the other firmly on the comforting bone handle of her knife.

Svein led her into a long, hot room, with wide benches along either side. There was a crowd of people, but her eyes were drawn to the two painted and carved posts that stood in the middle of one wall. She knew what *those* were, and she also instantly recognised Einar as he sat between them. So where was his wife, the lady who had visited her aunt – before the tale of Morgan's conception came out. Rilca realised that, welcome or not in this place, she still had need to tread carefully.

"Be welcome, Rilca," smiled Einar. His voice seemed richer, deeper, here in his own house. "Svein tells me that you've come to ask questions of Bjorn, but sit and have a cup with us while you do so, eh? Tell us your news, and when you wish to leave, Svein can see you homewards, I'm sure."

A few people who sat opposite Einar shuffled to

either side, making space for her and Svein. Cups were placed on the table before them; over the fire, steam rose from the big iron pot, full of tempting, meaty odours. Rilca sat: suddenly, it seemed as if she had little strength for anything else.

CHAPTER FORTY-ONE

After she had sipped a little of the ale in her cup, Rilca's knotted muscles began to relax a bit. The bench was too wide for her to be able to lean back against the wall, and the people to either side were sat too closely together to permit much in the way of getting comfortable. It was very different to the stools clustered around her own home-fire, even to the shape of the room. So she concentrated on regaining her composure.

"What happens now?" she whispered to Svein, who seemed to be enjoying the sensation of being squashed in close beside her.

"You get warm, you have a drink, you listen to what's going on and what everyone else is saying, and when you're ready, you catch the old man's eye and he'll shut 'em all up in order to listen to you."

"And is there a polite sort of time to all of this?"

He shrugged. "Not that I'm aware of. If it were something urgent, then obviously you'd be wanting to talk already, yes? Mawgan's strange habits will be considered important enough, I'd've thought, but if we're talking about searching for him, it'll have to wait until morning anyway."

She shook her head. "I need to be home before then."

"Oh, I know that! Have another swig or two, and

then we can make space for you to speak. How's that?"

"Good enough for a first visit, I'm thinking." She raised the cup to her lips again. It was just ale, different in its taste but otherwise just the same as her own folk brewed, and her fears about being in this place gradually dissolved. She leaned forwards a little again, resting her forearms on the table, her head held high. Einar was turned away from her, talking to someone at his side. When he eventually twisted back to face her, Rilca met his eye. A faint smile reached into the old man's eyes, and he banged his cup on the post beside him.

"Come then Rilca, let's hear what brings you to us tonight."

The level of general noise fell around her, although people still spoke and cups were still raised to mouths. But it was quiet enough to be heard over.

"I actually came this way, sir, to ask your younger son if he had seen much of my cousin Morgan recently. Since his...since Drosten died, he has been acting strangely: going off on his own for much of the time, speaking very little, growing thin and pale. I'm worried about him: we've grown up together and he's like a brother to me. I know that he and Bjorn used to go about together until recently: I had hoped that he might have some idea of where Morgan could be going when he's away from us all." She ran a hand through her hair, brushing it back from her face. "We've all been so wrapped up in ourselves over recent events, I think he's sort-of not been noticed much," she concluded apologetically. "Has anyone here seen aught of him lately?"

Heads turned to murmur together, although Rilca suspected that might be as much to translate her words as to discuss their content. Overall, though, the tone did not sound encouraging. She turned to Svein, questions in her own eyes.

"It's not sounding promising," he confirmed. "But wait here: I'll go in to Mothir and see if Bjorn's with her."

He pushed to his feet and threaded an awkward way out of the room. Some woman peered into both his and Rilca's cups and on seeing them empty, took them away to be filled again. Einar was listening intently to those at either side of him, but his eyes stayed fixed on Rilca. She attempted to smile a question.

"It would seem that none of my people who are out in the fields most days can remember seeing him," he said slowly. "I noticed Svein going out: I'm assuming he went to find his brother and ask the question direct?"

"Aye, sir."

"Well, if Bjorn's not seen him either, here's what we can do. Now that we have the harvest in and safe, it's easier to spare a few pairs of eyes. Come tomorrow, if you like, I can send a handful of my folk over to help you look. I recall a man who lived not so far away from my own fathir, many years ago now, who mislaid a child... not a lot left by the time he was found, what with the frost and the water and the wolves. So we'll lend help to look for Mawgan, and gladly, too. I daresay Svein will be wanting to join in – ah, and here he is! Well, lad, what news from your little brother?"

"He's no idea, fathir: hasn't seen him in some months, I think, although it's hard to be sure. But he said he'd come and show us the places where the two of them explored in the summer."

"Then there's your work for the next day, and hopefully that'll be all that's needed. Come the morning, pick out a handful of sharp eyes and take 'em along." He grinned across the fire. "It might not be the ship-mastery that you've dreamed of, lad, but it's a serious command of men all the same. Rilca, can you make this acceptable to your aunt and her people by morning?"

"Gladly sir, and I'll thank you for your offer of help. But I should head back, I think, before the night gets much further on."

"I'll take a lamp and go with her," added Svein.

Einar looked at the little soapstone bowl that sat on the table before him. Its rush wick and mutton-fat fuel did nothing to inspire much confidence. "You'd better hope it's a moonlit night, boy, and watch your footing. One missing person is enough to search for."

Rilca picked her way past the members of Einar's household who still sat around her seat. On reaching clear floorspace she turned, and bowed gravely to Einar. He grinned again, and inclined his head in return, before picking up his own cup and turning back to his benchmates. Svein's hand on her elbow took her gently back into the cooler, darker hallway.

"Is that door the one that goes to your mother's place?" she asked while she steadied herself after so much heat in the main room. "Why doesn't she come and join your father by the fireside?"

"Sometimes she does. Sometimes she doesn't because she's angry with him again over something or other, but other times it's because she's in the middle of something that can't be left very easily. You and your aunt must weave and spin, surely? You know how sometimes it just can't be stopped, then."

He pulled open the outer door. The wind had lessened a bit, at least in this spot, but the sky remained full of dark, shadowy clouds that let little light through. Svein picked up another of the little rushlights and used the one next to it to provide a flame.

"We'd better take it slowly, I think: there's not much light to be had, and the moment a breeze hits this thing it'll be gone." He grimaced. "It's going to be a long night's walk..."

Rilca leaned in close to him. "I don't care how long it takes, Svein. Truly I don't." She lifted her mouth to his as the door banged shut behind them.

CHAPTER FORTY-TWO

Einar casually watched his older son from the corner of one eye as he escorted the Orcca-girl out of the hall. He discussed where to best keep the sheep out of the rain with Gisli and old Ottar for a short while, and wondered about how best to get their share of the grain-harvest over to where his own people could thresh it without causing any disturbances to his neighbours – although in the end, he and Skapti agreed, it probably wouldn't make any difference where it was done, and it might be easier to divide the spoils once it had been separated out and sorted through.

"There's flax been growing in our part too, remember," he added thoughtfully. "We don't want 'em throwing that out!" He glanced again at the doorway into the passageway. "Do something for me, Skapti: get one of the women to go and ask Ragna to attend me here when she's able?"

"It's alright sir: I'll go. Signy's in there with her anyway, and it'd be good to share a cup with my own wife before we sleep!"

"What's up?" asked Havard.

"Nothing at all: I just want to let her know what I've offered to do for our neighbours, and see how she feels about it." He shifted and stretched comfortably in his seat. "It's as good a way as any of judging her mood these days."

"If you're agreeable, I'll go with Svein tomorrow and lend my own eyes to the searching. I was going to go and look after the grain anyway..."

"By all means – but if you want an opinion, I'd rather you stayed with the grain. Let Svein do this other thing and impress the girl: who knows where it might lead, hmm? Especially now with Drosten out of the way."

Havard smiled easily. "That's fine. I remember being that age, too. These things become important beyond all reason, sometimes."

"That they do, brother-in-law, that they do. But I'm willing to bet that the stakes this time are higher than you or I ever got to play for." He looked closely at the other man for a moment. "From what I've seen and heard you're getting quite a reputation over the way, too, and if there's a job that needs our lads mixing in with theirs, I find that I'd rather have you in with it. Things seem to work more smoothly when that can be arranged."

Havard shrugged and returned to the original topic. "So do we really care whether we find Mawgan or not?"

"Not really; if he *is* dead, it removes problems for both Ragna and Svein... and for me, in a way, I suppose. But as I told her, I still remember how old Thorlief was over his own boy, and I wouldn't want that for anyone. Olwen's not my enemy: she's just... I don't know, she's a surprise at this point in life, and no mistake! I'd forgotten about her entirely... but if I sit by and do nothing to help find her only living child, I'd become her foe, even more than I probably am already, and I don't see any need for that to happen. I'm willing to put silver on the future of this place – all of it – sitting with Svein and Rilca, and *that* will be an easier matter if we help keep the girl happy and friendly towards us. So, for the moment, that means helping her look for her little cousin, and giving her the time and room to make her own arrangements with Svein."

"Well spoken," commented Ragna from his other side, as she settled herself beside him. "What else is there of importance, husband?" Einar realised that she had resumed her proper place between the High-Seat pillars, but thought better of saying anything about it just yet.

"Mawgan's run off somewhere," he said instead, "been doing it quite a bit lately, I hear. The girl, Rilca, is worried enough that she came to ask our help in looking for him. So Svein and a couple of the lads are heading over that way come morning. He's walking her back right now."

Ragna smiled. "And are we expecting our son back in his own bed once he's done all this?"

Einar shrugged. "That's up to him – and to her. But I suggested he take her back to her aunt for the night, just to keep things peaceful."

Ragna nodded. "Astoundingly far-sighted of you, husband. It's a good plan, even if it does involve Mawgan's well-being."

"I can't see what harm it does to be helpful, Ragna. If we find him alive, we have Rilca's gratitude, not to mention the boy's mothir's. If he's dead we still come out of it well, since he's not died at our hands and we still helped find him! Show me where we lose anything in this!"

"It's only me that has to suffer that constant reminder of things gone by," she replied quietly.

"And would you take that so far as to cause the

death of a child no older than our own Bjorn?"

Ragna was silent amid the noise of the hall for long moments before she finally answered, "No."

Einar nodded slowly and reached out for her hand. "Svein is happy to lead the gang," he said gently, "you and I need do nothing. It's all taken care of, and however it turns out, we gain from it. Svein in particular ought to get quite a bit from his taking part if I'm any judge."

"Really? That's good news, then, news to lift spirits and bring us a bit of hope for the future. I think they'd do well together."

"Aye, it's a relief to see them getting closer in some ways. There's little else around here for either of them, after all, and it's hardly the season to go visiting Ottar down the coast."

"Not that such visits would do much for Rilca if she were inclined more towards her own folk."

"My point exactly, the one I've been making ever since we got here. It still holds good: they're on the wane, these Orccans, and we're the stronger power now. It's only my own attitude that needed changing, and that's getting easier and easier."

"Especially now Drosten's gone?" asked Havard suddenly.

Einar smiled and nodded. "Especially now he's gone."

CHAPTER FORTY-THREE

Rilca ducked her head through the curtain that hung between the door and the warmth of the central space of her aunt's house. The dividing hangings were still up, still swaying gently in the air currents swirling up from the fire, but the cluster of stools sat largely empty, as if waiting for the return of better, more happy days. Where had all the people gone, she wondered idly: once, not so long ago, crowds of their farmhands and similar people had pushed their way in here every night, to share the meal and talk things over. She recalled just such a time only last spring, soon after Einar had first come ashore. What had changed? Although she could see no way in which the blame could be fairly laid at his door, it seemed to her as if Einar's coming had driven wedges between all her folk... or perhaps he had just been a method of exposing the cracks that had already been there.

Olwen sat by the flames, her bowl on her lap and her cup set on the sandy floor beside her. She looked up as Rilca entered; a smile creased her features.

"I was wondering where you had gone, child!"

"Have you not noticed that Morgan's spending so much time on his own lately?" Rilca responded gently. "I've not seen him in days. I went over to the other house to ask if anyone there had."

Olwen frowned in thought. "I... well, now that you say it, I wouldn't know for certain where he goes during the days. But I know where he is now: he's in here with me. He headed for his bed not so long ago."

Rilca breathed a sigh of relief. "Einar – well, Svein as well – offered to come and search for him if he wasn't to be found," she explained. "I realised all this only today, and since then I've got more and more worried over him... is he asleep yet? I ought to go and look him over..."

Olwen laid a hand on her arm. "Hush child: you can do that in the morning." She peered more closely at her neice. "Did you not get my message earlier?"

Rilca squirmed slightly. "I thought finding Morgan might be more important."

"Usually, yes, I'd agree. But your searching for him took you over to Einar's house, and at that point, my own worries rise even higher." Olwen regarded the girl with serious eyes. "There has been much that has happened around here that I've not had a liking for lately. Some of it I've had a chance to alter; other parts have been beyond my power to change. But I might be able to change this, and save us all a lot of heartache."

"You're talking about Svein and I?"

"Yes I am. He spends a lot of time with you: some might say that he does so even to the neglect of his own work around the place."

"He's the... what's their word? The holder's son, or something: their equivalent of Morgan and I. The child of the landowner. What work he gets is largely up to him, as a lot of mine is to me, aunt. We're well-matched in that respect..."

"I'm aware of his place in his people's clan, just as I'm aware that *that* isn't the right word for it either. I'm more worried about what future you and he see in it – if you see any, in fact, or perhaps more importantly, whether he does."

Rilca was about to respond, but stopped. "You're thinking back to how Morgan came to be," she said eventually.

Olwen nodded. "A great deal of our trouble here, since Einar came, has been because of how he came to be. You needn't worry," she added in answer to Rilca's troubled look over to the little boy's bedchamber. "He's been asleep for a while, and I looked in on him more recently. He won't hear what we say if we keep our voices low."

Rilca fumbled for words again. "Svein's not the same as his father," she managed eventually. It sounded feeble even to her own ears.

"It might not be a matter of fathers and sons," said Olwen. "What if that's how they're *raised* to be? What if such attitudes are part of who they are? What do we really know about them, about how they think and act, hmm?"

"That sounds more like Drosten than you, aunt."

"Perhaps he's left me his sense now he's dead, then; perhaps now I can see more of what he always saw. Perhaps in some small way, part of him lives on in me."

"But does it have to be the suspicious part?" complained Rilca. "He was so much more than just those difficult last months made of him..."

Olwen's eyes softened. "Aye, there's truth in that," she smiled wistfully. "But however true that might be, it's also right that he had plenty to be wary of."

"I don't think you can blame your part in any of this last years' business for his death, aunt, I really don't. He chose to think the worst of everyone; he could've managed it differently if he'd wanted to. And I don't think he ever stopped thinking of Morgan as his own son."

"And yet I'm pretty sure that if Einar hadn't arrived among us, he'd be alive still," said Olwen. "And it's not me I wanted to talk about, or Drosten come to that – it's you. I know there's nobody else around here of your own age: Svein has the field to himself, and I know from my own early years how lonely a place can feel when there's nobody else to be with, nobody of your own age to talk to, to understand, to sympathise... I was luckier in one way, I suppose, in that we still had neighbours around us then, other families who we could visit and trade with. That's changed, too; there seem to be fewer of our own folk these days, and it's not that long ago that I was a girl. We see nothing of the king now, when once he came around twice a year – or so I was told." She shook herself suddenly. "I'm rambling again, Rilca: forgive me. I feel so old and tired these days; it's harder and harder to keep my mind on things, on what's important."

Rilca took Olwen's hands in hers. "It's alright, aunt. I'm not planning on going anywhere. Not even Svein could take me away from your side, and I don't honestly think he'd try."

"It's not his taking you away that worries me," Olwen replied. "It's the chance of his leaving you here with another like Morgan on the way."

"Ah." Rilca sat back and regarded the older woman carefully. "I've seen nothing in him that suggests he would do that, really I haven't. And things are different from when you met Einar. For a start, they've made a proper home here: their house is hot and it keeps the wind out. He brought his entire household over with him this time: it's not just a camp of tents put up for the summer. He can't just sail away this time! And Svein has said that he's never been out on the ship before this trip anyway, so there's another difference. And he's *better* than his father, aunt: I don't know how I can show you that, but he is. There's none of the harsh edges that Einar has, although he was kind and gentle to me tonight when I went into his house, so maybe even those edges are softening. I *like* Svein: he's thoughtful and always happier to see me than not. We sit for long times, just talking and getting to know how we both think and feel. And he's never even suggested a tumble in the grass..."

Olwen sighed. "I'm not doubting that you know him far better than I do, and I would like to think that you're right in everything you say about him. But I only have my own memories to go by, and those won't let me think well of him, no matter how it goes between you. Einar has blighted so much of my life with what happened that summer..."

"And yet, had he not come ashore here, that might not be true," Rilca reminded her gently. "You've said so yourself before now. Everything might have gone on as before, and his memory might have gone on sleeping inside your head for ever. Morgan might have grown into manhood with Drosten being his father, and been none the wiser. You might never have felt any need to say about his real beginnings, and who would have suffered for that? Perhaps it's time to try and see what happened in its proper place and time, and stop trying to shape our whole present and future around it. Morgan still thinks of Drosten as his father, since nobody appears to have taken him aside and explained the real truth of it to him. Now that father is dead, but Einar is still his neighbour, you are still his mother and I'm still his cousin. How much has really changed, aunt? And if we say that nothing much has actually altered, my seeing Svein is just another happening that need have no strings to what went before between you and Einar. Neither you nor Einar seem to have noticed, but Svein and I are building the footings for what could be a good, strong marriage. I know as well as you do how our people pass their property on when we die: is it that you're worried about my having a son with Svein and not giving Morgan a chance at getting all of this?"

"That's not how we think; it never has been. If I'd been bothered about that, why would I have looked after you so well all these years, hmm? Sending you away would've solved any such problem far easier, surely? But there is no problem, Rilca. There's just my worry for you, and my own guilt at what I did with Einar, and what that has led to since his arrival. I just think of how different it all might have been. I don't want you to find the same regrets and troubles in later years, and it doesn't matter what you say, those fears will always be there. I'm trying not to let this influence what I say towards you Rilca, but I fear that it will nonetheless. I'm worried for you, and what might happen however much you believe it won't. Svein's not of our people; we don't know what these northern men think about marriages, about children, about any number of other things. We only have what they say to our faces when they want something, and my fading memories to guide us."

Rilca stood up with a sad expression on her face. "Then there's little left to say. I won't stop seeing Svein just to ease your worries, aunt: you have to find me a better reason than that. He's a good and a kind lad, fast growing into his manhood: he's taken more interest in me than anyone over this side of the stone ever has, and that interest shows no signs of fading. Einar's men will be over in the morning, and since Morgan's come home safely this time, I want to be awake enough when they arrive that I can speak with them – and him – with a clear head. So I'm going to go and sleep."

She skirted the fire and disappeared behind her own little curtain. Olwen stayed by the fire, feeling another thread in the fabric of her existence snapping even as she looked unblinkingly into the flames.

CHAPTER FORTY-FOUR

Rilca awoke to faint sounds of voices somewhere outside. As she lay huddled in her blankets rubbing the sleep from her eyes she tried to identify the tones, even the accents, that might give a clue as to who was speaking. But it was not to be: she couldn't hear enough to be sure. With a sigh, she crawled out of the stone-edged bed and pulled on her overdress and shawl before venturing any further.

Olwen sat at the hearth again, although not at the same place as before, which gave Rilca some hope that her aunt had actually gone to bed at some point. There was no sign of Morgan: she padded round to his little alcove and poked her head in. He slept on, seemingly oblivious to the worry he had caused last night. She smiled grimly. That wouldn't last.

"Were those some of Einar's folk I could hear outside?" she asked, seeing no other suitable opening for conversation.

"I haven't looked, but it does sound like their sort of talking, doesn't it? It must be early: I've not seen Gwen or Danna yet, either."

Rilca wrapped her shawl tighter around her and looked half-heartedly for her shoes. "I'll go and see who's come, then," she said eventually.

Once outside, she found Svein and two others, who he introduced as Thorstein and Halvgrim.

She smiled. "You've had a wasted trip: I got home last night to find Morgan already here. He hasn't woken up yet, but I plan on having strong words with him about this sort of behaviour."

"Not to worry: Havard came over with us, as did a couple of the other lads, to lend a hand with the grain, so we'd be coming this way anyway." He grinned back at her. "Want to come over for the day-meal? Mothir seems happier about it since last night."

Halvgrim coughed and nudged his companion.

"We'll see you in the shed, lad. Take your time..."

Rilca watched them go open-mouthed. "Svein, what've you said about us, that we're suddenly so bloody obvious? Now we've got your mother and father beaming approval about it where once we thought there'd only ever be harsh words and trouble, and as for those two..."

Svein ran his hands through his hair. "Nothing that I've said or done, I swear it! Maybe it's just the right time, or the right place, or... meant to be?" He added the last comment hesitantly, as if expecting a rebuke for it. But Rilca only smiled wryly.

"We're not out of the mire yet: I've got my aunt worrying over us now."

"Why?"

"I don't want to say, Svein. You won't like it."

He regarded her steadily. "That tells me pretty much all of it: she's concerned that I'll turn out like my fathir, put a bairn in you and then sail away?"

She nodded mutely. He smiled into her eyes.

"Well I'm not. Not like he was – because I don't honestly think he's ever made a habit of that sort of thing – I'm not about to put a child in you until you tell me you're ready for it, and I've only ever sailed on the ship this once on the way here, like I've told you before. Besides which, there's nowhere for me to go from here: this is home, like Einar said. I couldn't go back to the old country: it was getting too hard to stay before, which is why we came away." He looked around at the windswept fields, the gentle slope of the land, the high, tattered clouds that let shafts of scattered sunlight through all across the land and then out over grey, heaving ocean. "We should call this place the home of leaping men: men who jumped here when things got too tight for them somewhere else. That's how it will be now, in More. This is home; even if I do go away on the ship when summer comes back, it's here I'll be coming home to." He winked. "You should ask Mothir about that."

"Think she'd praise it? The going-away and the long days until the homecoming, wondering where you are and what you're doing?"

"If I'm being honest, I don't think she minded it a bit until she found out about Mawgan! But fathir still swears by all he holds dear that your aunt was the only other woman he ever bedded, on all his trips away. If it worries you, we can marry: I'll even go to the kirk with you and take a baptism in order to wed you. And then we're tied together, aren't we? Me to you and you to me, with no others to come between?" He looked at her upturned face fervently, honsestly. "I'd do it in an instant: just say the word."

"I wouldn't hold you to that, Svein, or at least not yet. And anyway, it's not so easy these days. We've not heard from king or priest in over a year."

"So what *do* you want to do?"

She laughed. "Is it needful to do anything? We're here, we're together, and everyone, or nearly everyone, is slowly coming round to the idea. If my aunt isn't happy about us being together, then from what you say we could go and find space in your father's household until we have the chance of making a place of our own. I'd be happy with that; and if it comes to it, I'd just as easily wed you in your people's way as you would in ours. D'you think there'd be any problem in doing both, at some point?"

"Can't see any worries over it from my side. It would make a lot of sense, in a lot of ways."

He gathered her into his arms: she nestled against his chest, and reached up to kiss his lips before pulling gently away again. "Good though it is to be with you Svein, you and I both have work to do, and that takes us in separate ways."

He grinned. "Sure I can't persuade you to stay?"

"Only too sure that you could! But it would only catch up with us later. Morgan came home last night: I need to take some time with him before doing anything else. You have grain to thresh and your own men to sort out – quite the chieftan you're becoming these days. And you have both my thanks, and my aunt's, although she's not in the mood for speaking it, for coming over just to find Morgan, had we needed to." She leaned in closer again. "And I'll come and find ways to thank you properly later on, when all the work's done..." A hand drifted down to stroke his crotch.

"Later, then?" he asked, pulling away slowly and reluctantly.

Rilca beamed her most dazzling smile and tossed her hair in the wind. "Later, Svein: and that's a promise."

CHAPTER FORTY-FIVE

"Good of you to join us!" laughed Havard as Svein entered the small shed where the bere had been stored since the traumatic days of the harvest. Unlike most of the other buildings, this one had a raised wooden floor that sat over the pit dug into the soil, giving a dry platform largely free of vermin. Nevertheless, traces of rats could be found here and there, and so the race was now on to get the precious grain separated out and put into linen bags before the rodents had too much of it. There was also an unspoken but all-pervading contest against the weather as it darkened and worsened into winter. Every hand that could be squeezed into the little shed, therefore, had urgent work to do, and part of Havard's mind wanted to give Svein a good thrashing for his tardiness. But then, another part accepted that the lad was of an age where such beatings weren't appropriate any more – moreover, Svein was big enough now to fight back and stand his own ground. The days for punching compliance into him were gone; now he had to be asked and persuaded, and if need be bribed, just like any other man. He was truly his fathir's son, Havard reflected; and so, rather than giving out harsh words, he chuckled and accepted the unspoken reason for Svein's late appearance.

"And how is your lady love today? Still as handsome and desirable as ever?"

Svein smiled awkwardly as he reached for his threshing-stick. "She sends her thanks, and those of her aunt, for our willingness to go and search for little Mawgan, but it's not needed since he made his own way back last night. But Rilca says she's going to have words with him about his behaviour, so I'm happy to be somewhere else while she does it..."

Halvgrim chuckled. "How many nights d'you think before the little shit can sit down again?"

"Oh, I'm not going to put wagers on that sort of thing. I might be young in years, but I'm not that stupid!"

He swung the stick: the leather thong creaked, sending the other end of the wood whacking down onto the dried and spread husks of bere. After the threshing there would be winnowing, but Olwen's women had accepted that task so it wasn't his problem. The exercise felt good in his muscles; snatches of song and moments of idle chat between strokes sped the day along. Soon the air in the shed got thick with dust and the bits of flying husk as more and more was beaten off. Somewhere in here there should be a broom to keep the threshing-floor clear. He would have to have a look for it the next time his shoulders began to ache more than he could bear.

"Did anyone bring ale?" asked Havard suddenly. Svein looked up. "Not I: I was expecting to be out and about, looking for Mawgan."

"Or tumbling in the grass with his cousin!" chortled Eyjolf. That brought louder laughter all round, but there was a tinge of admiration and understanding in it which Svein found more comfortable.

"You're going to get teased about it lad," confirmed Havard with a smile. "Best to take it in the spirit it's meant, as you are. Those of us without a pair of loving arms to go to are only envious."

"But there must be other women somewhere around these lands," said Svein uncertainly. Havard shrugged.

"Ottar down the coast didn't mention any on his farm, but then again perhaps that was only prudence on his part. I'd've agreed with you Svein, if I'd had more chance to look; but it hasn't worked out that way so far. I daresay there's time yet." He looked around. "Is nobody going to go and ask for ale, or must I do it myself?"

"It'd be one way of meeting the girls," observed Skapti, but he said it as he stood up and headed for the door.

"You feeling the need then, uncle?" continued Svein as he pulled out a brush from a corner of the hut and began sweeping the threshed grain into separate pile.

Havard shrugged. "It's been a while, I'll not deny that, and your fathir hasn't always been the easiest of *hauldar* to work under – but not a word of that in his hearing, if you please. No, Svein, it's not the best place to find wives and such just now, but in a summer or two more, that ought to change. And I wonder if perhaps I'm starting to look for more than just a bed-companion these days..."

"There are some among us who'd settle for less!" grinned Thorolf. "Aren't there *any* available girls in this place? Or do we have to brave the waves and the winds again to go off and find some?"

"You've bloody got one, you bastard!" retorted Havard. "You stay out of it! Or shall I tell Hildegard that she's in danger of losing your affections? I would imagine there'd be a line of willing replacements for you in very short order."

"Don't you dare do anything of the sort: I was trying to help your own problem to some sort of solution! Helping you think, I was, and scant thanks I get for it!" He looked around, and then at the door. "Think any of the local lads are coming to join us today?"

"I've no idea," said Havard, "but they might follow Skapti if he's bringing a jug back I suppose. Think there's room for any more of us in here?"

"Possibly not, but it would be useful to have someone scooping this stuff we've done into its bags before it spreads out and mixes again," suggested Svein.

"Hmm: we need shovels, then."

"Ah: not seen any of those. Thorolf? Halvgrim? Anyone seen any shovels?"

"There must be some, somewhere..." said Eyjolf. "Should I go and look?"

Havard chuckled again. "Better you go than Svein; he'd only get distracted."

"I would not! Well, not very much..."

"Ah lad, you ought to be safer at this time of the day: Rilca must be at her own work by now, surely? Safe under her aunt's careful eye?"

"Like as not, uncle, aye. But I'll stay here and lend my young strength to this work, at least until the jug arrives!"

Svein took up his tool again, and the air thickened once more with dust and chaff. Havard stood and swept the threshed grain aside, and wondered about shovels. He also wondered about his own place in this new world of his brother-in-law's making, and what he in turn ought to be making of it.

CHAPTER FORTY-SIX

Skapti returned with a clay jug filled with the tangy, heather-flavoured brew favoured by the Orcca-folk: but none of the men from Olwen's steading came with him. Havard wondered why, and he wondered aloud.

Skapti just shrugged. "They seemed to have enough on their hands as it was, or so the women in the house suggested."

"And who exactly did you ask?" Havard asked more closely.

"The lady's housemaids: Danna, is it, and Gwen?"

"So you didn't go and talk to any of the lads at all?"

"You sent me for ale! Ale is in the lady's house," complained Skapti, "you know that as well as any of us! What was the point in going out chasing other men in the fields when there's throats getting dry in here? Oh, she sends her greetings by the way."

"Who does?"

"The lady herself, no less." Skapti grinned. "Said

to be sure and tell you that your work for her people was noticed, and appreciated." He handed the jug to Svein, who filled the one cup and drained it without pausing.

"Well," said Havard wryly, "if the lady knows we're here and about, we'd better be getting on, hadn't we?" He looked around at his workmates. "We still need shovels, and there's no sign of Eyjolf coming back with any... here Svein, you're the son of our *hauldr*: take over for a bit and see how well you can get this unruly crew organised. I'm going for a walk to see what I can find."

"If you head for the lady's house I'm betting there'd be ale in it for you!" called Skapti as he shut the door behind him. From beyond the wooden boards he heard playful laughter. He smiled to himself. They weren't bad lads: it had been a hard year so far, one way and another, but they were taking it all better than he might have hoped. But Havard was also aware that much of what they had achieved had been down to him, at times far more so than his brother-in-law.

He shook the thought away and looked around. The Orccans had put up lots of these little square huts, seemingly all at the same time, as if trying to make a whole new settlement where nothing had existed before. But instead of spreading them out they had clustered them together so that there was barely room to walk between some of them. Perhaps it kept the grass down, but Havard didn't care for the idea: he preferred open spaces with the houses placed further apart.

Shovels: where would he find such things? From one side he could hear the noises of Conyn hammering away at something: the smith might be a good place to start. For all that he had seemed to spend a good deal of his time with these people lately, especially since Drosten had dropped dead at Einar's feet so suddenly, Havard realised that he had no real idea of how they lived. He thought that some of these houses might be living-space, but how they used their rooms was a complete mystery to him. He wasn't even certain where to go and ask about borrowing a shovel...

He had to take a few turns around other walls before he was headed in the direction of the smith's workshop. It at least stood a little way apart from all the other buildings, as if holding itself aloof and somehow special. Havard grunted skeptically at such notions. He could hammer iron as well as the next man, and even had a vague idea of how it was got out of the ground. He had made nails for the ship, and had shaped arrow-heads; Conyn held no special mystique for him. But he was a certain point from which information could be had, at a time in the day when everyone else appeared to be out with the animals or clearing the last of the grain from the fields before burning began.

There was little point in knocking on the door; Havard just pushed it open and went in. Inside, the place was dark, with only the glow of the hearth providing any light; the smith's large frame could be seen hunched over his work, hammer poised for another strike.

"Conyn?" called Havard before the hammer fell. The smith straightened and looked around.

"Havard, is that you?"

"Aye. I won't trouble you any longer than to ask where I can get a shovel for using on the grain."

"Hmm; if you don't know one place from another, you'd never find the ones that Urien keeps clean. Most of the others are in with the pigs: if you give them a good brushing they ought to be alright, I suppose. Will that do for an answer?" The hammer had never moved; only Conyn's head had turned to speak with his visitor.

"I ought to be able to find pigs easier than people," smiled Havard. "My thanks, Conyn."

"Easier to give help to you than to your own lord, friend," murmured Conyn in return, but Havard was already heading out of the door again.

There still seemed to be nobody about: what were they all finding to do at this time of year? Not even the women appeared to be in their houses: Havard could hear nothing of idle gossip, children playing, wood being cut or any other domestic sounds. It suddenly felt as if the whole place were deserted, as if Drosten's ghost had come stalking out of his grave and gathered up his people, denying Havard their company and their assistance. He looked around wildly, his brows drawn low, and a hand on his knife, before he took a deep breath and steadied himself. Even if the old lord were out of his little hole in the ground, he could be put back in it: there were charms for such things. And if he were abroad and his strength greater than ever before, Havard reckoned he could still wrestle the dead man to the ground if he had to. But not in broad daylight, surely? Such things only ever happened after dark, from what he'd heard. He grinned suddenly. He'd put up an even better fight if he had a shovel in his hand!

He looked around more calmly, and headed towards what he thought were the sorts of noises pigs might make. He had wasted enough time on this nonsense already: that jug would be empty by now. Perhaps there was some merit in the Skapti's suggestion of stopping by Olwen's own house after all. He could always beg another measure of ale while he was there.

CHAPTER FORTY-SEVEN

"Was that Einar's men?" asked Olwen mildly as Rilca came shuffling back into the house. "Were they annoyed at your not needing them after all, at the thought that maybe we are capable of doing a few things for ourselves?"

"That's unfair, aunt," replied the girl in a surprised tone. "It's unlike you to be so nasty, even to our neighbours. But yes, it was Svein and a couple of the other lads: they're off to help with the threshing, so it's not been a wasted journey."

Olwen's mouth settled into the familiar lines of disapproval. "Makes you wonder how we ever managed for all those generations before us, the amount of effort these newcomers take off our shoulders." She looked slyly up at Rilca. "So how is Svein today? Eager as ever to take you away from us?"

Inside her, Rilca could feel something snapping. "I won't stand idle if all you're going to say is bad words and complaints, aunt," she responded icily. "Svein's done nothing that any other lad his age, whether from our folk or his, wouldn't be doing or saying, having known me as long as he has. I'll not grow old and alone just because you didn't have either the sense or the strength to say no to his father. He's a good man, and getting better every day. You show me where else I'll find a husband with such promise and I might listen to you; but until you can, just be quiet about Svein and I. He's not his father, and I'm not you."

"Strong words from someone who still sleeps under my roof, my girl. You'd better rethink them if you want to keep on doing so."

Rilca stared hard at her aunt. "So has it come to you making threats now, to get what you want? That's not something you've ever done before."

"Perhaps things were never so desperate before. Perhaps you were a bit more level-headed before..."

"And perhaps you were never quite so scared and alone before?" interrupted Rilca. "If it would suit you better, I'll make arrangements with Svein to move over into his house. I'm told that I'm welcome there, something I'm evidently not in this place anymore!"

"And who told you that?" sneered Olwen, "Svein? Another trick to get what he wants, that's all."

Rilca flashed a triumphant smile. "Actually, aunt, it was from his father's mouth. I'm getting kinder words and better treatment from that household than I do from you, these days. Svein is kind to me: he's considerate, caring... and who else is there, aunt? Who else is there?" She frowned at Olwen: she could feel anger building inside her at the unfairness of the old woman's attitude. "I can't remember you ever being this way before," she continued. "We've been together for a good few years now: we've always had each other, often when there was nobody else for either of us to turn to. Are you so determined now to have it your own way that you'd let all that go? And is it really out of concern for me, or out of this pity you've been growing for yourself ever since Einar failed to know you when he first came ashore?"

She clearly heard Olwen's intake of breath in the ringing silence that followed.

"In all those years we were together," Olwen said eventually, quietly, "you would never have spoken thus to me. I suppose it's just another sign of the changing way of things, when you feel you have so little regard for me."

"I've helped Danna and Gwen hold this place

together all summer, aunt, while you just sat by the fire and shed tears!" flamed Rilca. "That's the regard I have for you – that we all have, even now. But it can't go on like this forever: I'm coming into my womanhood, you've said so yourself. And Morgan wanders around as he will, with nobody to look out for him these days... part of that's down to me I know, but I'm his cousin, not his mother. And you know what else, aunt? Every time there's been a problem, every time I've felt a need to talk things over, Svein has been there. Just as you used to be – but you're not there any more. You sit here, wrapped in your own thoughts; you don't speak to those around you, you take no part in the life and needs of this place..." she threw her hands up in frustration. "What am I supposed to do, aunt? What is it that you really want of me?"

"You're my last link to how things used to be," answered Olwen. "Part of me says that if you go, then it all ends. Everything is over, then. And what place is there for me in such a world? Haven't I lost enough already this year, without losing you as well?"

"That's already happened."

"Well in that case, go ahead and leave us to whatever the Lord has in store. Run to your new life over the way, and I hope you choke on their newness and their strange ways. Better still," continued the older woman bitterly, "choke them as well, and the lot of you be damned."

"Well, there it is then," stated Rilca. "So it ends, in harsh words and bad blood between us. If that's what you really want, then that's what you'll get." She looked around the little house, but saw nothing of herself in it any more. "I'll talk to Morgan now," she said more quietly, "and then I'll talk with Svein."

She vanished into her alcove, leaving Olwen just

as she was before, beside her fire, alone.

WINTER, 902 A.D.

CHAPTER FORTY-EIGHT

"Fancy a walk, lad?"

Svein looked up at his uncle. "Anywhere in particular? And any special reason for it?"

Havard grinned. "The somewhere would be the farm across the way, where Olwen still lives, and the reason would be that it must be heading for the bloodmonth and I want to see how they do things over there."

From his place across the fire, Einar sniffed. "Are you sure they're doing anything, Havard? Do they have anyone to rally behind these days? I seem to recall your spending a great deal of your time over there only recently; maybe they're looking to you for leadership now that Drosten is gone from them." He leaned back with a thoughtful expression on his face. "Now there would be a thing: our two steadings, not exactly united, but not exactly apart any longer, either." He looked over at the other two. "Fancy it, Havard? I'd not object if you did: you spend enough effort on 'em, it'd only be a fair reward." He nodded towards Svein. "Be useful for you as well, what with Rilca being beside you pretty much as a done thing. Olwen's not going to live forever, and although Rilca's not showing any signs of childbearing yet, I'm willing to bet it ain't for want of trying, hmm? When you do finally get it right, you have to start thinking about claiming your lad's inheritance as soon as you're able. It would be as well to know how the place works; so if your uncle here is going across the stone, taking you along is a good idea. I'm sure Rilca will be happy in with Ragna for a day..."

"They do seem to have taken to each other since you brought her across," chuckled Thorstein.

"Thick as thieves, almost – in the best possible way," added Gisli.

"Well, since it's long past the time when men like you ought to have been out and working already, you'd better come along as well," replied Svein with a merciless smile. "We'll see what's about, fathir; I take it you've no objection if we offer any spare help we have, should it be needed?"

"None at all: just remember that I'm going out to look at our own animals and that it's bloodmonth for us as well, so don't go taking everyone over with you." He rubbed his beard idly, and looked forlornly at the empty cup that sat before him. "It was always such a race back in the old place: rush to get the sheep down from the shielings before the days darkened and the weather turned; then rush to get the killing done while there was still light to see by, and before the last of the hay and grass was gone. It's not so urgent a matter here, which makes me think it was worth coming just for that aspect."

"Not to mention the warmer air and the long, flat lie of the land - where we can actually grow stuff," added Skapti. "I think, sir, that if you were to ask any of us we'd say much the same thing. It was a good move, a bold move, to come westwards as we did. Even allowing for the, er, shall we say, unforseen difficulties along the way."

"Such fine words won't get you out of whatever Havard has planned for you," laughed Einar. "Come on, it's time we were all up and about. These animals won't sort themselves out, and I'm pretty sure you'll all want meat over the coming moons, hmm?"

Svein rose from his own place at the table. "I'll go and let Rilca – and mothir – know what's about."

"Think she might want to come along?" asked Havard.

Svein frowned. "Given the terms on which she and her aunt parted when she came here, I doubt it. But if you've no objection, I'll ask."

CHAPTER FORTY-NINE

Outside, the ground was still thick with frost. Mist lay heavily over the ground in the dim winter's light, turning the whole landscape into a white-wreathed, unfamiliar world, where only the clusters of houses stood blackly above the solid-looking fog. Here and there, sheep bleated as if also lost and confused, forgetting that such mists were becoming more and more common in the depths of the winter. There was, however, bright sunlight shining out of an almost cloudless sky – which only served to heighten the sense of strangeness.

Havard's breath steamed from his mouth as he shivered in his cloak and his feet crunched over the frost-hardened soil. "Your fathir don't half talk some bollocks sometimes, you ken, Svein."

"Why d'you say that?"

Havard snorted. "All this talk of putting homesteads together! Nobody over there shows any signs of wanting it, least of all the one person who has the position to make it happen! But it's difficult to argue with him when he gets that sort of mood on: sense and reason go out the door, and no mistake." He smiled wryly. "Nor can I see any of her lads coming over and asking me to be boss over 'em! I'm pretty sure Owain's been doing the job up until now..."

"Aye," agreed Svein slowly, "but he's not got your position in life, has he? He's not a *hauldr's* kinsman: he's just another *bondi*, for all that he acts as if he were more. They've no reason to follow him other than that he's got a bit more sense than many of 'em, and he's that little bit older than most. To my ears, a lot of what fathir said was making a sort of sense. You *would* be a good power over the way, and having you in command there would make things a lot easier in years to come – and for you as well, not just Rilca and I. After all, what is there to tie you to my fathir's house, really?"

Havard laughed. "The ship, which I have a share in, your mothir, who is also my sister, and my oaths to your fathir when he took me in all those summers ago! Which adds up to quite a bit, after all..."

"Yes, I suppose it does." They fell silent as they picked their way through the mists that reached almost to their chests. There was an easy path these days between Olwen's house and their own, but it seemed hard to find when covered in fog. Not that keeping to the track was particularly important: there were no real hazards wherever they chose to walk, but the ground was less even and so the going would be harder.

"I'm sure Einar would strike some sort of deal if you did decide to come over," Svein said at length.

"Eh?"

"I said it was likely that both fathir and mothir would be happy to come to some arrangement if your wyrd did take you over this side of the stone."

Havard grunted. "All very kind and good I'm sure, but it's not really just up to them, is it? This is still

Olwen's land, after all, and for all that we think she's here alone, if we started putting our own people on it who's to say that some unheard-of clan of distant relatives wouldn't suddenly come howling down on us, hmm? And then there's all her own people: for all that they've taken our help when it was needed, I'm not convinced that we're any of us really any more welcome here than we've ever been. Tolerated might be closer to the truth there. Welcome when we're needed." He smiled. "Much as your fathir's treated Olwen and her folk ever since we arrived here; now there's an irony for you."

"So you're not interested even in the idea, then?"

Havard laughed. "Not really, Svein, no! There's little enough solid thought to base an idea on, after all. If things change, then perhaps I might think a bit more seriously: but I'd need assurances from your fathir that he's doing it for my benefit and not just his own, and I'd need assurances from Olwen and her lads that they were in favour of it, and would give me the proper dues and respects, just as they did to old Drosten. Come to that, I'd be wise, I suppose, to be certain there's enough left over here to even feed me as well as your mothir does! It's a lot to expect, though, and that's why I'm not expecting it to ever actually happen. I reckon they'll carry on as before, and just gradually fade away one by one, until there's nobody left but you and Rilca, or perhaps little Mawgan, who won't be so little by then. And there's a good chance that Einar'll be dead by that sort of time as well, so who knows what will happen to it all, eh?"

Svein leaned closer. "All I'm saying, uncle," he said in a low voice, "is don't dismiss it out of hand. Rilca is still hoping to bring her aunt around to accepting our betrothal, and I'm doing my best to be a familiar face over this way, so that if we do come over to run the place before she dies, nobody's going to be especially shocked or worried by it. And I'd be better at such things if I had you by my side, if only for a few seasons. This is where things stand right now, and right now I can see that there would be little to persuade you. But it won't always be so: besides which, I think Olwen's already taken a bit of a shine to you! I doubt there'd be any danger of a marriage proposal – I think fathir's put that idea to the death some years ago – but there might be a better welcome than you're imagining. The lads here need someone to look up to, and Olwen can't command that respect any more. Nor can Owain hope to get it, since he's been one of them for too long." Svein looked earnestly into his uncle's eyes. "The time is right for a strong leader to come in and take this place. My silver's on you being that man. Between us, we can make this place wealthy again, make it a good place to be; and in time, put it together with our own lands and become a real power in these parts."

He took a pace away again, and concentrated on finding his footing. "Just think about it," he continued after a moment. "For now, that's as much as I can ask."

Havard looked more thoughtful than before. "Alright, I can do that for a bit. It doesn't interfere with anything else, after all. But promise me that you'll not be taking this any further without talking to your fathir as well: I'll not go behind his back after all these years."

"Easily done." Svein put out his hand. "So do we understand each other, uncle?"

Havard reached out his own hand. "Aye Svein, I think we do."

CHAPTER FIFTY

There were few people to be seen in Olwen's fields: it was the wrong time of the year for outdoor work and most folk felt that sheep could be left to look after themselves. Cattle were different, however: they were taken indoors and given close attention – at least until killing-time came around.

Svein and Havard tramped on through the rough grass and heather that covered most of the space around the marker-stone between the two farmsteads. They aimed broadly for the northerly cluster of little rectangular huts that included Conyn's forge out to one side and the animal sheds to the other. Here was where Urien kept the pigs for the most part, when they were not out foraging in the open fields beyond, and here was where the small, dark cows of the Orccans came to be milked – and to be slaughtered when the winter's feed stocks could not support them all any more.

There was a great deal of noise from these houses: the sounds of beasts confined in close quarters, eager for food or a return to the pastures. In among the grunts and snorts could be heard voices. Havard looked over at Svein and raised his eyebrows.

"They've got 'em in already: I half-expected to be lending a hand with that."

Svein shrugged. "Evidently someone's decided on doing the kine first, then. The sheep are still out."

"Just like the old home, eh?"

"You see, uncle, you're getting into the habit of this place already!"

"Don't read too much into that, lad. Come on, let's go see who's about today."

The cowshed was larger than some of the other buildings, although still hemmed in by its neighbours. Havard privately considered that by next summer, when the surviving animals were let back out to graze, it would be stinking the whole settlement out. He frowned slightly: it was a problem his fellow-countrymen did not have to worry about this year, but next time would be different. He could see the need for a lot of new building when the weather improved – just at the time when Einar would want most of his own men out aboard the ship once again. Could he pull the same trick twice and get away with it? Havard decided not to share that particular line of thought for now, and directed his efforts to finding the door.

Inside it was warmer, and the increased smell was a fair price to pay for that comfort. Gaps in the walls allowed a little air to circulate and some of the winter's weak sunlight came in with it, but most of the illumination still came from little lamps set on brackets around the roof-pillars. There were no partitions: the floor was trampled earth and the kine wandered about within the shed as they wished. Clustered just inside the door, Owain, Maccus and Rhodri looked around as it opened and let cold air onto their backs.

"Havard? What brings you our way, then? You're welcome enough, but I'm curious as to what brings you..." began Owain.

"I came to see how you deal with things at the bloodmonth. We've no kine to worry over this winter, but some of the sheep will be heading for the knife pretty soon, and then, once more, it's all hands to the work if we're to get the most from it." Havard looked over at the huddled cattle. "These the ones you keep, or the ones you kill?"

"This is all of them," chuckled Maccus. "We've not decided which are which yet."

"It's not something we've had to do before, at least not without some help," said Owain with a touch of worry in his voice. "None of us are too certain what to look for, how the lord ever decided which were kept..."

Havard put a hand on his shoulder. "That's also part of why I came," he said gently.

"We seem to be needing each other more and more these days," added Svein after his uncle quietly nudged him. "We – my uncle and I – are happy to help, just as you're willing to do for us."

"There's no ale here," put in Maccus. "Come over to the house: the beasts can wait a while longer. At least we've got them all in."

Once they were all outside Rhodri and Maccus pulled the wide door shut and lifted a heavy length of timber across to keep it so. Then Owain led the way back to the building they all called home.

"Most of us are out in the fields with the pigs and the sheep, now," explained Maccus, "and Gwen ought to be with the lady, as will Danna." He exhaled heavily as he pushed the inner curtain aside from the only entrance. "They seem to have hard days of it just now, too."

Inside, the house was remarkably different to the one Havard and Svein were used to. There were no benches along the wall; instead, narrow partitions stood from floor to roof-beams, with more curtains to hide what lay behind. The fire was still in the middle of the floor, but around it were clustered small stools, with no tables. Baskets lay around the edges of this central area, filled with the utensils of life: bowls, cups, spoons. Bigger vessels of clay or iron clustered between them, but there seemed to be nothing over the fire just now, not even bread being baked over the cinders. Havard raised a puzzled eyebrow.

"So... who cooks? And when?"

"Oh, there'll be roots and leaves to stew up later on," replied Rhodri easily. "We're a bit short on meat right now, but we have carrots, turnips, cabbage, peas..."

"I'd've thought you'd be out fishing," said Svein carefully. "Plenty to catch out there, I'd've thought."

Owain shrugged. "Never really been sea-folk: for all that we live our lives right beside it, we've always looked to the land for our needs."

"Ah," said Havard sagely. "It's been different for our people since the beginnings of time. We've always fished; even now, even if we don't take the boat out, some of the lads throw lines from the beach there and pull in useful stuff. If you ever want to come over and have a go, it's worth the effort. Fish is good in a stew."

Maccus dipped a jug into the ale-cask in the corner. "Once again, Hevedd, you come over here looking to learn something, and we end up learning more!"

Havard shrugged. "Just the way of things: I'm learning enough to keep me satisfied with the deal."

"I'm just happy to feel my way around," chuckled Svein.

Rhodri looked at him carefully. "Your case is different, young sir. The way things are heading, it's likely we'll have you set over us before very much longer, wouldn't you say?"

Svein shifted uncomfortably on his stool. "And what's the opinion of that, Rhodri?"

Owain shrugged. "So much has changed, it's hard to hold a view on anything these days. Rilca was always a good... foster-daughter, would be the closest to describe her and the lady, I suppose. She was skillful with her hands, quick with her mind, ready to take her turn at whatever work came up..."

Svein grinned. "No wonder she and mothir are getting on so well!"

"That's good to hear in one way," Maccus said, "in that it suggests she's settling into her new life and doing well at it. But it does mean that *our* ways of doing things might not outlive us. God, I suppose in truth they might not even last that long; how will we hold out against such pressure for changes, when our lords and ladies are already embracing them, eh?"

"From what I've seen, there's not that much difference between us," replied Havard. "I wonder if perhaps it's Einar's ways that have coloured your ideas about us, Maccus. Tell me, then, how many others here think as you do? And what is it that you're worried about losing to us?"

"I've no idea what thoughts people have, Havard," said Owain. "It's not as if we could stand up and say "these are our ways, it's how we've always done things", because our ways have changed as the world around us has changed. We've not seen the king or the kirkmen in over a year, now, to give just one example. But it all adds up to feeling alone, and besieged – you know that word?"

"All gathered together in one place and surrounded by enemies," murmured Havard. Svein nodded grimly.

"I'm not calling you our foes," Owain went on, holding up a placatory hand. "You've been decent men and good neighbours to us, pretty much since you arrived here. Can't say that for all of you, of course, but then I'm sure you'd find the same about some of us. But there's no denying that we've lost contact with the rest of our people, who used to be everywhere in these isles." He nodded towards Havard. "Didn't you say once that you found more of your folk along the coast?"

"Aye: Ottar, once of Oslofjord. He's been there a while; longer than we've been here."

"My thought is that he's not the only one. My worry and fear is that, were you to sail further, you'd find more and more of your people, and few if any of ours."

Svein swallowed. "And what d'you think happened to all these Orcca-men?"

Rhodri shrugged. "Either they were pushed off to go somewhere else, or..."

"Or?" prompted Havard.

"Or they had harsher neighbours even than Einar, and nobody with your capacity for holding him back. I'm willing to bet there are places now where the bones of my own people lie in Northmen's fields. Let's face it, you people have known where these lands are for long enough; you've been coming and taking what you wanted for just as long. Like Einar did... it was only natural that eventually it would occur to some of you to bring your households over here, rather than fight your way home every winter. But I think that spelled the end of the Orccans. The energy that sent you over the sea in the first place will send my folk into their graves if we stand too hard against you."

Havard nodded slowly. "If you were ever going to be rid of us, you should've done it on that first day, before we were even off the boat in any numbers. That was even before your lady realised who had washed up on her shores; had we all been speared then, it would have meant nothing to her." he grinned suddenly. "I'm happier that you were stopped from doing it, but you should have. I'm pretty sure that were anyone else to come calling even now, Einar wouldn't make the same mistake."

"And there is another difference between us," observed Maccus bleakly.

"You say that and you seal your own wyrd, surely," Svein answered. "And Rilca shows that there is a way out, even if you might not care for it. I'd've thought it was still better than laying cold in the ground."

"Oh, I think it'll happen: it's more a matter of how and when, rather than if." Maccus leaned forward on his stool, his face ruddy in the firelight. "The time is fast approaching to make terms and strike deals, and here's what I'd want: I'd want you, young sir, and Rilca, to come back over to this side of the stone and take over from our lady when she's ready to make her own peace with your father. Either Morgan will get this place on her death, or your own sons will: and Morgan's too young to do anything useful with it. So what I'd also want, were it up to me, would be to have Hevedd here come over and run the place in Morgan's name, teach him how it's done, until he's of an age to take over. Either way, we end up under your folk's influence: but we have things of value too, such as our skills and our knowledge of the lands here, so if you were to throw in an assurance of our continued well-being, and promises to look after us, you might well find us all willing to support you in such a move."

There was a dumbstruck silence. Havard stared at Rhodri for long, long moments before he could even consider speaking; beside him, Svein's face was a mask of astonishment. Eventually, however, the older man found his voice.

"Well: that's quite a thing to say, Rhodri." He looked around. "Have the rest of you nothing to say on this?"

Owain looked over at him resignedly. "Only that we agree with it all."

"When did this happen?" asked Svein. "When did we – or some of us at least – turn from being enemies into... well, not just friends, but people you're all suddenly willing to work under? That's a huge step, lads. You'll never convince me that it's happened overnight."

"No, you're right enough there. It's been a slow-growing thing, and some of us are further along the road than others. But I'm pretty sure there's not one of us who's not reaching the same conclusions: our lady Olwen isn't fulfiling her obligations to us, Morgan needs a firm hand if he's not to turn out either bad or useless, and Rilca's already made her choices, which took her to your house. Then, Hevedd, along you come, when your own lord gives us nothing but troubles and hardship, and you offer help and comradeship and even your friendship. Our own mistress seems to have lost all interest in us, whilst your lord gives the impression of wanting to see us all killed and the lands taken for his own. But you come in and offer another way: a clear head and a firm hand, that keeps alive a hope for all our futures. Are we such fools that we wouldn't jump at it?"

Havard tugged at his beard as he listened. "This talk is all very well," he said at last, "but it's getting a bit near the knuckle, too. What you're proposing means a betrayal of Olwen by you, and an equal betrayal of Einar by me – and perhaps by Svein as well, if you're wanting Rilca and he to come back to this place." He put his cup down by the fireside. "If there's any meat to these words, then you should get yourselves together and put it to your mistress. If you can get her to agree to it – which I can't see happening under any circumstances – then, and only then, could you approach Einar about it. And that's a long, hard road, I'm betting, but one I can't come with along with you."

"Why not?" asked Maccus.

"Because I stand at the other end of it! If I were to come before Olwen and make a case for coming in and taking over from her, what would be the difference between me and Einar, hmm? No, friends, if you really want this to happen, then you're the ones that have to make it come about. But however it turns out, whatever happens, you have my thanks for thinking so highly of me, and my promise of help in other matters around here, whatever you might need. And besides, I would think that you might be better off trying to mend the relations between Olwen and Rilca. That would throw far more help and unity your way, and make a better road for future days."

"If we were to do all this," said Owain slowly, "would we be able to expect your agreement to it? Or would there be other fences to jump?"

"Were you to get the agreement of Olwen to give up her place as *hauldr* here," answered Havard cautiously, "the next thing would be to persuade Einar to release me. It's different for Svein: he and Rilca could just up and come at any time they chose. But even though I'm brother to Einar's own wife, I'm also bonded to him and in his service. You would have to convince him that his own best interests were served by having me as overseer to you people – which would, in turn, mean your placing yourselves in bond to him. Think you'd all be ready for such a step? It's a big'un."

"It seems to me that what you really need to do next is gather yourselves all together and talk this through," suggested Svein. "You are only three out of twenty-odd, after all, and if you were to approach me with any of this I'd want a bit more proof that it was how all of you were thinking. Otherwise I can see it causing more harm than good all too easily."

"That's well said, Svein: a fair point, too," said Havard. He stood up abruptly. "But we ought to go: we've spent a long time on this business already, and the next part is not for us." He looked over at the three Orcca-men. "If you're sure about taking this further, you need to agree among yourselves to it, as Svein says. Then you need to take your thoughts and opinions to your lady, and get her agreement – if you can. Then, and only then, is the way clear to discussing it with either Svein or his fathir."

"But would we have your support when we get that far?" persisted Rhodri.

"That's not so easy to say: it depends on what you offer me, and what Einar has to say. But if all else is right, then I'd be agreeable, aye."

"That's enough to be going on with." Owain decided. "We have work of our own, too. Come on, lads. Hevedd, is there anything more we can help you with today?"

"I think we've learned enough, don't you, Svein?"

"That," said the younger man wryly, "would be the least of it."

CHAPTER FIFTY-ONE

"You thinking about any of that more seriously now, uncle?" asked Svein as they trudged homewards. The mists had faded with the frost, but overhead the sky had darkened with long, streaky-grey clouds that looked smeared against the whiter background. As they got clear of the huddled buildings of the Orccans, a wind pushed into their faces, making each breath into an effort and each step a battle. Havard gritted his teeth and concentrated on putting one foot in front of the other, and on keeping hold of his spear. When Svein tugged at his sleeve for an answer, he pointed ahead to the shelter of Einar's own house and put his head down into the wind again. So they struggled on.

At last, though, after what seemed like a lifetime, the force of the wind began to drop as they headed into the lee of the house. Once walking and talking were more like their usual levels of effort, Havard drew his companion aside from the path that led to Einar's front door.

"I need you, obviously, not to mention any of this, not even to Rilca," he began. "If it comes out the wrong way, or from the wrong mouth, the damage might be beyond anyone's capacity to mend. We have to keep it to ourselves for now, and let Owain and his cronies try to bring the rest along with them."

"Think they can? Or were they just speaking their own minds, d'you think?"

"Svein, I've no idea, and that's the honest truth. Which is why I've no intention of saying anything about it in this house, and why I did my best to leave the problem on their shoulders. Good work with your own speaking over there, by the way."

Svein cracked a smile. "You gave me a pretty obvious lead to follow! But, if they can do it, if they are talking what most of them are thinking already – would you consider it?"

"What, going to be boss over them? Why not? I've said before that your own fathir's not the easiest of masters, Svein: we've had our fair share of run-ins and rows over the years. But I'll not just run off into the night like some breakaway thrall: that would be a disgraceful thing to do, and the end of any reputation I've built up over the years. But I will say that theirs was a better offer than the one Ottar down the coast made me when I went to see him and buy timber."

Svein looked astounded. "You've never even mentioned such a thing before!"

"What would be the point? It would only anger your fathir, and I turned Ottar down anyway."

"Can I ask why?"

"He offered me only what I already had, with a change of faces. When he found out that the ship wasn't all mine, he cooled a bit anyway."

"No, that's not so encouraging, is it? And is this one any different?"

"Hugely: I'd be my own master, pretty much, and certainly master of the rest of them, even if only until Mawgan grows up – or if your own lad does the same, whenever he arrives. Even if they come to you and Rilca, Svein, could you hold that place together on your own?"

Svein shrugged. "I'd rather do it with you by my side, I'll admit. I've had precious little practice at doing very much of anything, one way and another."

"Not entirely true, lad: you've done lots of things, and usually very well, too. What you've not had, which I have, is experience of leading men, and that's not an easy thing to learn. You have to just do it and learn by the mistakes you make, as often as not."

"So if they come to me and offer me the place, would you come if I asked you?"

"That would depend on your fathir, lad. There's no way around that one, and talking him round would be just as hard as Owain and his mates will find persuading Olwen to be."

CHAPTER FIFTY-TWO

"Have we said too much?" whispered Maccus to Rhodri as the day faded into a grey, gloomy evening where the huddled shapes of beasts, men and houses all merged into the gathering darkness around them. Firesides were the natural place to gather for warmth and light, where food could be had to remove the chill of the winter days, and where ale could take away the chill of bad thoughts and rash decisions. Scant wonder, then, that they and the other farmhands of Olwen's estate hurried homeward so readily.

"Whatever we said earlier today, friend, let Owain do our talking now," advised his companion. "He's the one who's been filling the shoes we put out for Hevedd today: if anyone ought to be deciding how this goes, it's him, surely? He stands to lose quite a bit if the Northman does come over to us: more than we would, at any rate. For us, it's just a change of who tells us where to go each day. For him..."

"And yet he sounds so happy with the idea. Why would that be?"

"Because I'm getting tired," came Owain's voice from behind them. "I'll speak up, never fear. But I'm tired, lads. Come on, though, let's get in before all the best places are taken. I'll say my piece when everyone can hear it."

The main house was already crowded. Keen eyes had evidently seen Havard and Svein earlier in the day, and ears were eager to hear what was said. Owain looked in: there was Tangwen, his own sweet wife, alongside Danna and Gwen. There was the source of news regarding their lady: nobody ever seemed to see her out of doors these days. Owain found he was was forgetting what she even looked like.

"Owain," called Conyn from beside the ale-cask, "are you going to tell us what Havard wanted today, or are you going to wait for Perif and his brood to finish with the sheep before you speak?"

"This is serious enough that I'll wait and have him hear it from my own lips, Conyn. Is the stew ready yet?"

"Aye," replied Branwen after peering into the collection of clay pots stuffed into the edges of the embers. "Fetch bread someone, and bring the bowls over. I'll spoon it out."

"Ah," smiled Rhodri, "if my own wife is serving us, then I'm first in line!"

Where stewpots huddled at one side of the fire, other bowls sat upturned over flat stones to the other end. Bread baked beneath them, the smell seeping out and then filling the place as the bowls were lifted off. Hands eagerly broke it into chunks, while mouths murmured snatches of prayers and graces, thanks for another day done and good food at the end of it. Hot stewed mutton slopped into bowls, with late or dried roots and cooked barley to give it substance. Taste, although splendid, came a poor second to warmth and the ability to fill a belly.

Owain felt as much as saw it when Perif and his family came in: there was a blast of cold air at his side from the opening of the door, and a general movement of those bodies around him to let the latecomers closer to the flames. Little Indeg was still small and young enough to need the fire on her limbs, although she wasn't a baby any more, not by any means. Neued settled in with the other women in their own little huddle at the side of the hearth; for a short while, the main sounds were of eating and drinking. But Owain knew it would not be long before the food was gone and it would be time for him to start talking. He silently prayed that he had read the mood of his workmates right.

Not that it made much difference if he hadn't, he reflected: all that happened then was that his words to Havard would be quietly dropped and forgotten. By his own comments that morning, Havard seemed unlikely to push the matter if nothing more was heard, for which Owain was grateful. But on a deeper level, he remained convinced that things could not go on as they were. And he was reasonably sure of his mate's intelligence and awareness; they would know this, too.

Plates and bowls quickly emptied; the sounds of jaws working became fewer, and quieter. Bread was dipped into the last dregs of gravy, before being savoured on tongues and washed down with bitter, heather-flavoured ale. Talking resumed, the gossip of the day shared among all who had their living on Olwen's lands. But eyes kept returning to Owain.

Eventually, as other talk fell silent or petered out more gradually, it fell to Bran to broach the subject. "So then, Owain," he began, "tell us what was said with Hevedd and the young lad today."

"Well, Maccus and Rhodri were there as well, so they can attest the truth of my words. He came over to see how we did our slaughtering, but I reckon there wasn't much for us to tell that he didn't already know. So we came inside, and we spoke of Drosten a little, and our lady's distance from us, and how one day, not so long away, it might be that Svein and Rilca came back to these lands and took them over from the lady. Or, it might be that Morgan reaches his manhood without ever learning very much from us of what he ought to know, and how, in either case – in fact, even in the situation we're in now – a good, strong headman would be a good thing for us to have."

"And you asked Hevedd to come over and be that man over us all?" asked Urien, amid a general clamour of unease.

"You're as much of a leader as we've ever needed, Owain," protested old Efrawg from the corner. "Why do you talk of such things now?" His words were greeted with a low, murmured chorus of agreement.

"I've only acted as head of us here because somebody needed to," replied Owain. "Next to me, Bran is perhaps the best suited to such a thing, but in truth neither of us would be ideal for it because we're too close to the rest of you. We began here as hired men, and we became part of the place, as it were, just like the rest of you. Drosten was our head man, the one we followed, even into war if we had needed to. He told us our work and knew what was needed to be done, as was only right for someone of his position. But who do we have now? I'm not that man, for all that I've been carrying the lord Drosten's work as well as my own, pretty much since Einar got us to build his house for him and the tale of young Morgan's real parentage came out. It's not been right that I do all that and get nothing for it, is it? I'm just the same as the rest of you: I'm no lord, I don't share the lady's bed or anything like that – and nobody beyond us lot seems to have noticed. So it's time to shed the burden: we need someone to take Drosten's place here, and none of us can dream of reaching that far. We can only look elsewhere, try and get someone to come and be master over us for the good of the place, and of us; and if that means doing away with the lady as our mistress, then so be it. Those are hard words, even to my ears, and I don't say 'em lightly. But it may come to that, for all our unwillingness to think about such a thing. Now that Rilca's taken up with Einar's boy, we have other choices open to us. We ought to be looking at them a bit more closely, 'cos just doing things as they've always been done ain't going to put food in our stomachs next year. The world is changing around us, and if we don't go along with it, we'll wither and die here."

"So you put this to Havard and Svein." asked Conyn in a level voice. "What did they say?"

"Havard said he'd not go behind Einar's back, and he also said that it was up to us to persuade both ourselves and the lady that it was needful to do it at all. He also said that he thought it'd be a hard path to tread..."

"He's not wrong there," murmured Allun. Beside him, Urien nodded agreement.

"What you're saying is that we ought to be uprooting everything we know and do, just to let the Northmen in more easily," said Danna. "How can that be right? What's it going to solve?"

"You spend your days with our lady," answered Rhodri. "How is she? Does she ever remember us out here, working her fields and keeping her beasts well for her? When did we see her last, Danna? When did she last give us our orders for the day, and come to look over the land with us, hmm? Or has she just abandoned us in her own head? Is she so broken by her past misdeeds and the death of her lord that she either can't or won't come and do her own work any more?"

"It's true that this plan allows Havard pretty much to run the place however he sees fit," said Owain more gently, "but if things go on as they are now for much longer, can we really expect Einar not to make a move of his own against us? If we do it this way, there's a good chance of us all living through it, and things going on much as before. If we wait, if we chance our luck against Einar and his ambition, my reckoning is that some, if not all of us, would end up dead or in chains. It's a hard choice, and not an easy one. But it's one we're less and less able to avoid."

"This is all very sudden," declared Allun, "and this is a busy time of the year, what with the killing and all that happens after it. I for one could do with a bit of time to think things over in my own head. I'll not be pushed into deciding right here and now."

"There's time for that, I would hope: Einar and his crew are going to be just as occupied as we are, after all," said Owain. "I'm not wanting to push any of you into anything. I'm just trying to see ahead a bit and trying to make the best deal I can, for the benefit of us all. My own mind is made up: I can't see any future for us here unless the Northmen are involved somehow, since that's where all the power in the land seems to be right now. We've had no word from the king since before they came here: Maelchon went off to bring them, and he's not come back either. So we're on our own, with only Einar's lads for company. We can try and fight them, but these are seasoned sea-fighters: they'd slaughter us just like we kill the animals. Svein and Rilca offer us a chance at a peaceable solution; having Havard in charge offers us another. Since Drosten died we've had more help from them than ever before, and they've had the same from us. I'm only suggesting that we make formal and legal what's beginning to happen already. But you're right: it's a big step for all of us. It's only right that we take some time and be sure about it."

"Did you give any idea of when things might move along?" wondered Bethan from beside Bran. Owain shook his head and spread his hands.

"How could I? There was nothing to base any such thoughts on, after all. These things happen at their own pace, I reckon, and we just travel along with 'em. I don't think Havard's in any hurry, if that's what you mean. If we're talking about getting impatient, I say again that I think Einar would be more of a problem. One possible advantage of talking to both Havard and Svein together, though, is that they might be able to work together in keeping their master from rampaging over us just for the fun of it." He shuddered involuntarily.

"We ought to give ourselves a length of time for thinking and deciding," suggested Conyn as he lowered his big frame back onto his stool. "Once that time is up, we take our answers and requests wherever they need to go: to our lady, if we decide we're for this plan, or to Havard if we're not." He looked around at the lamps and candles that clustered around the floor and hung from cords under the roof-beams. "The easiest way is to choose a number of days and someone cuts a notch somewhere as each day ends. Since we're all here every night, I'd vote for the doorpost over there. But how long do you all want for your thinking?"

"How does three days sound?" suggested Maccus. "One day for deciding, one for arguing and recanting, and a third for sorting through the thing properly before making a final choice. On the third night, we all come in and we speak our minds; if we can find a couple of bits of wood, we can cut marks for counting the ayes and the nays. Then we know where we stand."

"Three days is good," remarked Owain. Slowly,

gradually, others agreed. Conyn got out his knife and slowly, deliberately, cut a deep notch in the timber of the doorpost.

"Three days it is, then," he said gravely.

"Wait, though," said Gwen suddenly. "What to we do if we all agree – and I'm not saying that we will, or that I necessarily want us to – and then, on taking it to the lady, she doesn't? What then? Do we just take her decision and carry on as before, or are we maybe talking about rebelling against her at some point? I've been with her a good many years: I'm not sure I could betray her like that."

"It's a fair point," admitted Arlen. "Owain, do you have any answer to that?"

"Not offhand, no," admitted Owain. "I hadn't thought that far ahead just yet. It's tricky, though: it raises questions of who actually has the power in this place, and the authority. Is it she who inherited it from her family but is no longer running it, or is it us, who don't own it but do keep it producing the things we all need? Mind you, if the king's no longer in a position to lay down the law to us, if he's no longer taking any sort of interest in what goes on around him, it's maybe a bit of a moot point anyway. Maybe authority rests in those who are prepared to use it, when that happens."

"It still not a good feeling to be talking like this against the lady," persisted Gwen.

"Be still," snapped her husband, "it's not like we're going against her this moment, now is it?"

Gwen glared back at Maccus. "I'll have my say like anyone else here," she insisted. "How would you take it if you suddenly found out that the rest of us had been discussing taking you away from your house for three days and not told you? That's not right. We should tell her what's about, and we should do it now. Why shouldn't she have three days to think it over as well?"

Conyn raised his eyebrows. "It's hard to argue against that one," he admitted, looking over towards Owain.

"Would you go and do the talking then, Gwen, or would you rather some of us went along?"

"I don't mind," she replied. "Perhaps if a gang of us went, it might make it look more serious to her. Harder to ignore; you know what I mean. Those who are more senior among us should go along, and be certain of getting the idea across properly."

Owain grinned. "I'm assuming that means me, then, hmm? And Gwen; and who else?"

"I'm happy to go," said Conyn. "Maccus ought to be there, if only to lend Gwen his support. Who else is going to put their hand up, or should we draw lots?"

"Allun or Urien should come, if only because so far, theirs have been the loudest voices against what I'm suggesting. If we take both sides of the argument, the lady can hear it all and make her own mind up, without accusations later of anybody having rigged it in their favour."

"You're being very fair-handed about all this Owain, and I thank you for that," replied Urien.

"It's a big thing we're considering: it could change all our lives, for the rest of our lives. The last thing we need, whatever we decide in the end, is to be divided over how we did it. That would finish us for sure, far more surely than having Havard come in and take over, let alone Einar." He looked around the huddled faces bathed in firelight and shadows. "So, we could go and talk with the lady tomorrow, after our first round of work. Danna, Gwen, would you smooth the way for us with her?"

CHAPTER FIFTY-THREE

Olwen looked frail, thin and old as she sat in her habitual place at the fireside. Around her, the floor was dusty, and the whole house carried an air of neglect, or perhaps disinterest might be closer. As he stood just inside the doorway and looked around, Owain had the strong impression that it was mostly because of Danna and Gwen that any work such as spinning, weaving, or even cooking, got done at all. His lady seemed to have retreated within herself: he realised that he was staring, shocked, at her frail-looking figure. He wondered where Morgan was, and how the lad was coping with all this.

"Is it always like this, these days?" he whispered to Danna as she came over to greet them. She nodded mutely; looking closer, Owain saw red-rimmed eyes and pale, taut skin. The woman was near to collapse, he realised with a start. He took her arm gently.

"Danna, what's wrong? What's going on here that we haven't seen yet?"

"The days are so hard in here now," she whispered back slowly. "All she does is sit: she rarely talks, so Gwen and I have to find our own work. She doesn't join in, doesn't even seem to know we're here much of the time, and the silence is awful when I think back to how it used to be, how we all used to crowd in here and talk, sing, be alive and joyful..."

"Where's Morgan? Will he hear what we say?"

The woman shrugged. "I fed him his porridge and then he went out, as he usually does. Beyond that I've no idea where he goes or what he does. Rilca used to go around with him, but even that's changed now, too." She sighed heavily. "It's all this that starts me wondering if maybe you have the right idea after all, Owain. Maybe we've lost the fights with Einar already, or maybe they're all part of a bigger one that we don't have the measure of just here." She shok her head sadly. "Perhaps it is time to change our ways after all. But you can say such things to her – if she'll listen."

"Right then," said Owain grimly, with a look round at his own companions. "In we go."

Olwen looked up as they approached. Her eyes, once so dark and full of energy, seemed pale and dull, set in a face that had withered and wrinkled and etched frowns around a downturned mouth. Hair formerly a blaze of rich auburn now hung limp and dull, whilst her clothes hung from her limbs as if they had been made for someone else. There was little to be seen of their former lady Olwen at all, and inwardly the visitors all quailed.

"Danna told me people were coming," she said eventually. Even her voice has grown old, Owain thought suddenly, or perhaps tired through lack of use. What has happened here? How did we miss this change?

"Speak then, Owain... Maccus, is it, with Gwen? And who else?"

"We are Conyn, your smith, lady, and Urien."

Something that might have been a smile flickered across the wrinkled features. "Ah yes, of course. What is your business here, then?"

"Lady," began Owain, "since the bad events of the harvesting we have had a lot of help from Havard, Einar's man across the way. He has brought a good few of his people over whenever we have needed the extra hands, and asked little in return. He's a good man, I feel, and it occurred to me – and a few others – that, with our rightful lord gone from us, we would benefit from having somebody in to take those parts of his position that have to do with the running of these lands. We have been talking it over: we still are. But it would not be right of us to even think of such things before bringing our thoughts to you, Lady, to hear what you have to say."

"We are in a difficult place, lady," added Conyn. "Most of us need leadership in our work, and since harvest we've not had much of that – except from Havard."

"Some of us are in a harsher place yet," retorted their mistress with a flash of impatience, "and no more of their making than you claim yours to be. What comfort is there for me in these things you talk of so freely, now your master is gone and your esteem for me has vanished, eh? Well, no matter what you choose to think of my conduct in years gone by, my position in this place has not changed, as far as I am aware. Have we had word from Bridei? Did his messengers come and I missed them? Am I homeless again, a wanderer by royal decree? There's no other authority that I will bow to, Owain, and you are still under your obligation to bow under mine, in case you had forgotten."

"Lady, I had not forgotten that, and no, you have missed no messengers. But if you will permit my saying, neither have we had messages from you about how we should organise ourselves ready for the winter. The cattle are in their shed, lady, but we still await your wisdom regarding how many to kill and which to keep; likewise for the pigs and the sheep. But the grain is all in, and thanks mainly to Einar's men it was a good harvest."

"I would expect nothing more of them than that they would go on working to their own advantage whilst my own husband lay dead among them," said Olwen curtly. "It has been that way ever since they got here, and I curse myself for not having realised it sooner. So tell me then, Owain and you others, how low is the esteem in which I am held over in your little houses?"

"We value you highly, Lady, and it is not our place to judge your actions of long ago," said Maccus. "All we have said is that we feel the need for a master who will guide our work. We have said nothing of wanting you gone, Lady, not here or among ourselves. I don't think any of us would even consider such a thing."

"And yet if you want to put yourselves under Einar's yoke, that might yet have to happen," came the reply. "Any idiotic hope I had of extracting some sort of mercy or consideration from him has long since died. Morgan will remain without a father, and his mother appears less and less able to look after him – or her household. Not even Rilca would stay beside me, and I thought our bond to be strong enough to see us both through such hard times as these. But then, we've done it all once before; perhaps it was too much to expect her to be a frightened little girl again...

"I know I have been sitting here for far too long, and now I find myself either unable or unwilling to move. You have said nothing that is really so extreme, and since it's your own livelihoods that sit at risk as well as my own if we don't get this place running properly again, I can understand why your thoughts have gone they way they have. But I will not stand for just being cast aside in favour of a man who has already done me far too much harm: that would be too much to accept."

"Lady, we are with you in that," said Owain after a moment of awkward silence. "There is, though, perhaps a way to accommodate everything and everyone. How would it be with you if, say, Rilca were to return to this hearth, and Svein along with her? Your place would not change: you could sit at the fire or go about as you always used to, just as you chose. Rilca would be here to help where needed, and to assist in raising Morgan. Svein has no real experience of running his own farm, although he's a handy lad and learns quickly, but if Havard were to come over with him, they would be a formidable pair. And Einar need never come this way: he would think his own family were in charge here, so any threat we once posed has gone." Owain stopped and frowned uncertainly. "How would that be as an answer to everyone's needs?"

"That might depend on how far along in this deal you've gone with Svein and Havard."

"Lady, nothing has been settled, or even offered properly yet. Your people have been talking it over, and we gave ourselves three days to think about it before we came together again and voiced our thoughts. But whether anything can come of it is up to you: if you won't have it, then that's an end to it, although a good many of us think that such a choice might be the end of us all here eventually. Einar and his folk seem strong, while we seem to be getting weaker all the time. It was a desire to try and avoid a takeover at spearpoint that started some of us looking for ways to avoid it."

"You could always just up and go," Olwen pointed out.

"Lady, where is there to go? Here is where we belong, with you as our mistress. None of us have talked of deserting you, Lady. Besides which, there's been no word from any other of our folk for nearly a year now. How can we be certain that there are any others left? Einar washed up on your shores, Lady; perhaps others of his kind have been doing the same in other parts too."

"A cheery prospect. So then: what is it you want of me?"

"Lady, we came to seek your thoughts on this. If you are amenable to Rilca returning, we can take an offer to her and Svein at any time you give us leave to. And we could take it in your name, which lends it some weight that we cannot give. In return, we get support from Svein and hopefully Havard as well, and the chance to have our homes here safe and still feeding us. Yours would be the watchful eye at the fireside, advising where it was needed and watching your children – and their own children, when the time comes – grow and be safe in a place of wealth and security, just as it always was before."

"And who is it that would set the terms of any such deal, hmm? I'll not trust Einar to be fair to us, or perhaps more closely, to me. No matter what lies in our past together."

"Lady," said Gwen, "if it is you who makes the offer, surely you will be the one setting the terms?"

The corners of Olwen's mouth tugged down further. "Only to begin with, I suspect. You would need someone as strong as he to hold up your part in the bargaining, and we have nobody here who could do that any more."

"There is Svein," Owain reminded her. "In this sort of a deal, he and we are together on the same side. Whilst it's true that none of us have the wit or the position to stand against Einar, I'd reckon his own son could – and would, especially if it were to defend Rilca against him."

"You said you had agreed to think on this for three days," Olwen said after a moment's pause. Owain nodded.

"Come back to me at the start of that third day, if

you are all having your say at the end of it. I don't think I will need so long to consider my decision."

CHAPTER FIFTY-FOUR

Three days had never stretched so long, or passed so slowly. It was hard to attend to what needed doing, when all the mind could turn to was whether or not such matters were even worth bothering with. What if their lady turned them down? What if she insisted that it all go on as before? Try as he might, Owain could not make such a thing work in his head. They needed, or had grown used to, the help that seemed to flow so readily from Einar's door these days. But was there actually any extra work to do? No, he decided, that wasn't where the problem lay. The root of it all was that, until his death in the barley-field, Drosten had carried the secrets of who did what, and when, and most importantly why, in his head. It was *that* which they lacked now, and no matter how much faith the others claimed to have in his own ability to carry on in his old lord's place, Owain knew better. He was a weeder and a tender of crops: he knew about watering, and the importance of well-turned soil. He knew when to sow, and when to harvest, and how to get the seeds out of the barley to use next time around – but that was about all he really knew. He had been lucky with the sheep from time to time, and he had paid attention whenever Drosten had spoken about what he looked for when it was lambing-time, or time for the rams to go in, or when it was time to slaughter. It wasn't enough to warrant elevating him into Drosten's position, and he knew of nobody else among his fellow men who had more knowledge than he. They were headless, blind, stumbling forwards as best they could – but sooner or later they would fall. How could anyone, even the lady herself, not see that? How could they possibly convince themselves that everything would be fine if they just went on as before? And so Owain passed the days as best he could, tormented by his own certainty and the dread of what might happen if he hadn't done enough to carry his workmates with him in this matter.

It was hard to judge the passing of the day as well because the clouds closed in, smothering the tops of the gentle hills and flowing gracefully across the lands beneath. The sun was nowhere to be seen and night tended to come suddenly, a faint dimming of the sky and land before plunging their world into darkness for longer and longer each time. At least, he thought ruefully, that would soon change again and longer, drier days might prevail for a a while.

"When are you thinking to go?" asked Bran as they stood in the long rows of roots, looking at forlorn little clumps of leaves that showed where the precious food lay beneath the soil. "It's hard to judge when in the day we've got to."

"Want to come along, then?" asked Owain. "No matter what sort of time it is, I ought to be getting some people together."

"You're likely to be overwhelmed: I'd say that pretty much everyone is going to want to come with you. This is important: they'll all want to hear what the lady says."

Owain looked around, as if expecting to see the whole farmstead walking out towards him. "Would we all fit in the house?" he wondered. "I've no objection to everyone coming if that's what they want, but I do wonder how comfortable or practical it would be."

Bran laid his tools in the dirt. "Let's go ask them, then," he said. "We can collect people on the way over. I don't see that it really makes a lot of difference when you go, Owain: it's past the start of the day and before the end of it. She's either made up her mind or she hasn't."

Owain grinned. "That's what I like to hear: simple optimism and blind faith! Come on then, let's go find everyone."

Bran had been right: every shed and hut they approached yielded more and more of the farm's people, who all followed as they headed, slowly but surely, southwards towards the older, round houses of Olwen's own family. As they travelled, a few cast worried eyes in the direction of Einar's house, barely visible as it loomed through the gathering mist and rain, but no signs of life could be seen. It was suddenly as if they walked through a little world all of their own, on a path from one life to another. It was not a comfortable comparison.

"I'll go in first," offered Bethan, "and tell Danna that we've nearly all come to hear the lady's words. It's not right to all just surge in together without some sort of warning."

"No, it's not like the old times, when we used to gather here every days-end as folk should with their lords," admitted Owain. "It's a good idea, Bethan; Bran, are you going in with her?"

"She spoke with you last time," Bran said thoughtfully, "so you ought to go in with Bethan. One of you can come out to give the word when she's ready to speak with us."

"Fair enough: in we go then. No point in waiting around."

"I heard voices," said Danna worriedly as she met them by the door. "What's going on?"

"Everyone wanted to come and hear what the lady said." explained Owain. "If you let the lady know, and make a bit of space, I'll go back and bring 'em in."

A brief flash of a smile crossed the young woman's face. "Almost like it used to be," she said before turning away again. As Bethan followed her into the house, Owain turned and waved the rest of his companions through the door.

Olwen had evidently made some preparations of her own. Whereas before she had sat on a stool by the fireside, now she awaited her visitors in the one and only chair, that usually spent its time tucked away in an alcove and only came out for special occasions. Her hair was brushed and swept back from her face, which itself looked more alert and less tired than previously. Something approaching liveliness shone out of her dark eyes, and her long, thin fingers drummed on the arm of the chair, as if impatient for all her farmhands to be in and before her. For their part, the assembled bondsmen clustered on the far side of the hearth, their heads bowed respectfully, and waited.

"Owain brought me notice of your thinking on certain matters," she began. "It appears that some at least have thought that we have no future here without the inclusion of the Northmen who appeared at our shore last spring, and who have pushed further and further into our lives ever since. What made matters harder for me was the fact of their chieftan being the true father of my son Morgan. I was foolish enough even in my old age to hope that he might have remembered me, and that I might have used that to make us all a better deal. But it was not to be: he has taken, and I have had to give.

"So if I understood Owain properly, what you have talked about is asking my foster-daughter Rilca to return to this house as its new mistress, along with Einar's son, who she has taken as a sort of husband, although I don't for a moment suppose they have actually married. They will in effect inherit this place, and any children they have will get it in the course of time. Morgan, I suspect, will get nothing of value beyond his life, but had Rilca taken one of our own folk and had a son by him, that would have come to pass anyway. Do I have it right?"

"By and large, lady, aye," Conyn replied.

"The only other thing was that we wondered if Svein's coming might bring Havard with him as overseer," added Owain. "In honesty, it was his experience and clear-thinking that we were looking at more than Svein, but he didn't seem at all interested in moving over by himself."

"The bonds these folk form between each other are not always so different from ours," mused Olwen quietly. "Perhaps it is time to take a fresh look at things." She straightened in her chair and looked levelly at her visitors. "You have my permission to put an offer to Svein and Rilca," she said firmly. "Subject to their agreeing that Morgan and I remain here as a proper part of their household, with full honour and consideration in all things, they may come over and have the running of this place. Havard may come or not as he chooses, but if he does come, he will be welcome here. Since you all made the offers to him in the first place, I leave it to you to make your own terms with him.

"I want all this sworn to in front of myself and Einar, along with his promise that he'll let it all happen without interference, now or in the future. That has to happen before any of them cross the threshold of this house, for whatever reason. If they need to talk matters over beforehand, I'll come outside to them. There: those are my terms. Take them over the way, and bring me the news of how they're received."

CHAPTER FIFTY-FIVE

"We've got a bit of a problem," said Rhodri as he, Owain and Conyn approached Einar's homestead. "How are we proposing to put our news to Havard without tipping Einar off as to what's been going on? If we walk in there and put the lady's terms out, it's going to be bloody obvious that there's been some talking done already. Einar ain't going to like that idea: he could get difficult because of it. Then what do we do?"

"You've got a point," agreed Owain. "I don't fancy the idea of him flying into a rage at us in his own house with all his crew around him either. We'd better ask Havard to step outside in the first place; and we're going to have to find a suitable form of words as well. Sooner or later, we'll have to say something in front of Einar, and we can't exactly take days over it, can we?"

They trudged on through the soggy winter ground, where sand and soil conspired to produce a slushy, liquid mixture that clung to the shoes and sent freezing, damp cold into the feet and the bones. It was not dark yet, but looking at the ragged edges of the clouds where rain fell far away, Rhodri privately wondered if they might yet see the last of the sunlight before this business was done. That might mean staying the night in Einar's company, something none of them except Rilca had ever done before. He decided he would rather do this swiftly and head home again, where the comforts were familiar and the danger far less.

"Any ideas yet?" he asked as they came into the lee of the house and began picking their way along its length towards the door.

"We put all the credit for the idea on to the lady," suggested Conyn, "and for this reason: Einar might take the proposition more readily if it comes from his equivalent in our place. If we present it as our own, he'll laugh us out, but if it comes from Olwen he might just listen to it before saying no – which gives Havard and Svein a chance to get an argument together as to why it ought to happen."

"Aye... but then we're in *their* hands, aren't we?"

Owain shrugged. "Wasn't that always going to be the way of it? We're looking to get a master back, after all; it isn't like we're trying to get rid of our lords and betters and go it alone somehow." He huddled into his cloak before going on, "I can't see that any of us would've stood for that sort of thing."

There was nobody outside as they came within sight of the porch. The three looked at each other.

"Now what?"

Owain grunted irritably. "Well if there's nobody out here, then they must all be inside! So in we go..."

He pushed open the heavy wooden door, noting absently that it was good timber and wondering briefly where it had come from. Beside him, Conyn nodded. "Gives more weight to the idea that Einar's found some friends somewhere nearby, doesn't it? You might yet have saved us all with your mad idea, Owain. How come it's so hot in here? Do they like it like this? I have a struggle some days to get the forge this warm! What in the world are they burning?"

The source of the heat was clear to see, even from the outer passage: the orange glow of a big fire threw light and warmth to the furthest corners of the building. The three visitors stood huddled for a moment, trying to adapt to searing heat after such freezing chill outside. On an impulse, Conyn leaned heavily on the door and shut it with a bang. There was a distrubance in the noises that accompanied the warmth from the main room. "Who's there?" came a voice. Thorolf and Thorstein followed it out into the passage.

"Oh... welcome," said Thorolf after a surprised pause. "This is an unexpected visit, Owain: what's up?"

"We've come with messages from across the way: it's Havard or Svein that the first ones are for, but if your master's in the mood there might be words for him as well afterwards. It's difficult," he frowned in response to puzzled looks from the two Norsemen. "It's a message from our lady, but its delivery is wrapped up in this other matter that Havard's already got knowledge of."

"Ach, secrets and difficulties," replied Thorstein sympathetically. "I'll ask him to step out, then, and we'll get some ale in you while you're here. You know the pace to proceed at; no doubt Havard'll see you in when the time's right."

The two vanished back into the heat, seemingly unaware of it. The three emisarries stood, dripping, and waited. It was not long before Havard appeared; behind him, Gytha came with cups for all of them.

"Well then," said Havard once the woman had retreated, "what's about?"

"Further to our discussions of a few days back, almost all of us are agreed that we need a master over us, and that the way things appear to be going, that master is eventually going to be one of your people whether we like it or not. Even our lady Olwen sees this, and she sent us here with an offer to Svein and Rilca. We can tell you that here, or if you think it better, we can present it to Einar. But we wanted you to know that we were here, and that we are all agreed on what we said last time, before we took it in to the lord of this place. We had no idea of what you had or hadn't told him."

Havard grinned. "I've said nothing, and neither has Svein, not even to Rilca: I wanted to wait and see how it went at your end, since if your lady had said no to it, or if the rest of you people has not wanted us there, then it could've ended quietly and Einar need never have known. But it goes otherwise, eh? Everybody wants it to happen?"

Owain nodded. "Pretty much. The offer is for Svein and Rilca to take over the place, and you are welcome to move over with them. Our lady wants promises of safety and well-being for herself and Morgan... and that's it. That's all she's asking. I think that, like us, she realises where the strength is in these lands just now, and it's not vested in our king, Bridei, any more."

"We noticed the door," smiled Conyn with a nod towards it. "Good wood, that: not from around here. That's enough of a clue as to how things stand, and how they're likely to shape up in the future."

Havard was silent for a few moments, his head bowed in thought. "Well then," he said eventually, "in you must go. Give me a moment to find Svein and Rilca, and I'll send someone out for you."

CHAPTER FIFTY-SIX

The hearth was a searing blaze of orange, almost yellow heat in the centre of the long, square room that made up the majority of Einar's house. The wide benches that ran along its longer walls were as crowded as ever; behind the eager, contented, curious faces, blankets, bags and all the other detrius of everyday life were pushed into heaps and piles of unruly shape. Somewhere among all of that, children slept and those wanting a little privacy or quiet lay against the wood-panelled walls. In the narrow space between the benches where guests might usually have stood to address their host, tables stood instead, heavy boards of wood upon three-legged trestles, two on either side of the fire. Empty bowls and cups stood crowded on their tops; from an iron pot hung above the raging flames, steam rose and took the smells of good cooking with it. Ranged around the edges of the hearth were bowls made from what looked like stone; bread sat flatly on levelled stone slabs, slowly baking. The three Orcca-men stood and stared on the threshold for long moments before Havard caught their eye and waved them in.

"I can't see Svein..." murmured Rhodri nervously.

"Over to the left, beyond Einar and his lady. Now stay calm or you'll be the death of all of this!" Owain hissed back.

Einar was still in his usual workday shirt: although he had removed the green tunic he habitually wore out of doors, his pale blue linen still clung to his chest and arms, the square collar tied tightly around his neck and the cuffs close to the wrists. His face sat stern and ruddy above it, his hair combed low over his forehead and his beard close-cropped around his jaw. His expression was hard to read, but his eyes were firmly fixed on his visitors as they wormed their way around the tables.

"We'll find seats for you when the time comes," he said in acknowledgement of their bow to him once they had drawn level. "In the meantime, tell us what brings you this way in the middle of the day."

"Lord," began Owain uncertainly, "I am sure you're aware of how it has been for us lately. We have done our work as best we can, but we have felt the loss of a master, a leader for our efforts. It was hard enough over this last summer, sir, but since our own lord died, our lady has done little to guide us or look after our interests."

"I appreciate your worries, and I have some sympathy for your troubles," rumbled Einar, "but I don't see how any of this is my problem. Why do you come to me? Why not go to your own lady and ask that she resume her place among you, instead of sitting and wishing things would just go back to how they were?"

"You have keen ears and eyes, sir," smiled Conyn grimly. "But it was our lady's idea that we come to you. She has a proposition to make, but its nature means that you ought to be in on the hearing of it."

"Now I'm intrigued," their host murmured. He turned to whisper something to Ragna sitting next to him. "Tell it, then," he urged.

Conyn nudged Owain to speak again. "Sir, our lady offers her house and lands to her neice, the lady Rilca, and, since they appear as good as married, to your own son Svein as well. This offer is also extended to your liege-man Havard, who has given good friendship to us all in recent months, in order that he can manage affairs while Svein learns whatever he doesn't yet know about organising such things. Her conditions are that both she and her son Morgan are promised safety and security for as long as needful or desired by them: and that is all she asks. I think, sir, that she has come to believe our time is gone in these lands: we have had no word from our king or any others that we know of since before your own arrival, while you are clearly finding friends in these parts, to judge from the quality of your timbers here. I think we of Orcca are all agreed that it would be better to invite a new master in, than have one come anyway and bring his spears with him."

"I notice that she does not bring this offer to Einar himself," said Ragna sharply. "As *hauldr* here, such things should be his concern, and his decision."

"Lady," said Conyn carefully, "we merely bring the message."

"Well you won't get an answer to something like this straight away," observed Einar mildly. "If you're not needed back over the way, you're welcome to stay for the night-meal and the ale while we discuss it. There's quite a bit to think over, I reckon, so we might be some time. But we'd look to having an answer for your lady in a day or two. Is that acceptable to her, would you think?"

"I can see no problem in that, sir," answered Owain. "Nothing about this is particularly urgent, after all, and the important thing is to make the right decision for everyone."

"Come and sit, then," said Ragna in a kinder tone. "We'll gather everyone together and talk it over. Signy, go for the jug, would you? Havard, Svein, Rilca: come closer. Get comfortable: this is going to take some considering."

"I see she's joined in with this crew already," murmured Owain as Ketil, Asbjorn and Thorfinn shuffled aside to make room for them on the bench opposite. "We were right: here is where the future gets shaped."

Conyn looked across to where Rilca and Svein sat side-by-side. Her face and the colour of her bright red hair were the only things that distinguished her from

Ragna; from a distance, she looked like any other well-to-do Norse woman might. Brooches sat on her breasts, with a string of beads hung between them; beneath a pale blue overdress she wore another of almost-white linen, whose sleeves hung to her fingertips and whose shape turned her into a flowing, graceful figure whenever she moved. Gone were the heather-dyed, close-fitting garments her farmhands had always known: she was alien suddenly, different... yet perfectly at home in this new place. She turned her head slightly to listen as Ragna murmured something in her ear; whatever it was brought a smile to her lips.

"Our people are finished," agreed Rhodri in a whisper as he watched, unable to tear his eyes away. "Here is where it ends, and where the new world begins. Our only hope is to go with it, wherever it might lead."

CHAPTER FIFTY-SEVEN

Crowded though the hall always was, Einar knew his deliberations would not be overheard. Well, actually, yes they would: to overhear snatches of talk was unavoidable. But he remained confident that none of his folk would actively eavesdrop on what was being said, and that, perhaps, was the most important thing.

"This is a considerable offer," he said when everyone around him had settled. "Olwen wants to put her lands and powers into your hands, Rilca – that is how it works among your folk, isn't it? She's not able, even if she were willing, to give it to Svein?"

The girl nodded. "It comes to me, well, to any future son really, but Morgan's too young to inherit and I think she must have realised that some time ago. It would be lovely to think that she's finally coming around to how things are, and that she's willing to go along with it."

"Did you hear the conditions she laid on it?"

Rilca smiled and shrugged slightly. "Hardly a difficulty for me, keeping my aunt safe after all she did when my own mother and father died. And I couldn't turn Morgan out, not ever... how does that sit with you?" she asked, turning to Svein.

"I have no argument with either of them, so I can't see that it's a problem. One day, your aunt will die, and if she's looking for peace and happiness again, perhaps we can give her some in this life before she goes searching for it in the next. And Mawgan's alright: he reminds me a bit of Bjorn sometimes, and it would be good to let them get together again, after everything that's been going on." He reached quietly for her hand. "I'd put up with pretty much anything if it kept us together."

Einar rubbed his short beard. "I can't see any difficulties there, either. In many ways, it's far, far better that these lands pass to you two than my trying to take them: I'd say the men over there will be far more willing to work for you then they ever would for me. What of you, Havard? You have a place in this deal as well; got any thoughts?"

"I'll not go behind your back, if that's what you're asking: nor will I desert either you or my sister. But I've spent a lot of time with the men over there, and it's true that they miss Drosten and his ability to steer them in the right direction. They're capable enough, but is it really right that they be responsible for so much, with no reward for it?"

"What of Olwen? Spoken with her at all?"

"Not even seen her. I reckon she spends all her time in her own house, which is probably where all this upheaval stems from..."

"So really we only have the word of our three visitors to go on, that their mistress has even agreed to all this," mused Einar. "What happens if we send Svein and Rilca over there, with whatever retinue we agree on to start them off properly, and she swears that she knows nothing of it?"

"Owain and Conyn – in fact all of them – are good men," replied Rilca earnestly. "They wouldn't do that sort of thing: I don't think they have such baseness in them. Besides, what good would it do? What would they gain? Nothing that I can see, since it's hardly the sort of deal that could be kept quiet for very long."

"Sensible words," smiled Ragna in agreement. "Husband, you're looking for trouble where none exists! I for one have no reason to see treachery in any of this, and even if there have been misunderstandings, I'm sure Rilca is capable of sorting them out without resorting to spears. This looks likely to become a source of good income for our son and his intended: don't you go putting any of it in jeopardy, you hear?"

"Aye, I hear you. So then, we're agreed that Svein and Rilca should take the deal and move back over the way, yes? Havard, if you want to go as well, I'll not stand against it – providing I can still call on you should I need to. I can see, though, that such an arrangement is likely to lead to the two households acting more and more as one..."

"Which was what you wanted ever since we got here," sighed Ragna.

"Funny sometimes how these things come to pass," was Einar's only comment. But the look of satisfaction on his face spoke volumes more.

EPILOGUE: WINTER, 904 A.D.

"How would you fancy coming into our house for a little while in the spring?" Rilca asked of her mother-in-law. They were walking through the winds of early winter, rain lashing towards them over the sea out of a blackened, grey-streaked sky, towards the house that Einar had built. "I reckon ours might leak a bit more, but it's smaller and so the fire keeps it warmer without having to burn so much peat.."

"Einar mentioned that you were saying something about it to him as well," answered Ragna. "With that belly of yours, is Svein really being wise to suggest such things? The bairn'll be with us before winter's done, surely?"

"I'd hope so," groaned the younger woman. "I'm getting fed up of carrying this weight!"

"So what's behind it all?" Ragna persisted as they came into the shelter of the porch. "Come inside, lass, and let's get you sat down. Then we can both warm up and you can tell me everything."

The house was as hot as it had always been, and Rilca felt a sudden pang of worry. What if Svein had it wrong? Did they really need to be doing this just now? Then she walked slowly into the hall, and saw so many faces crowded along the benches – faces from both Einar's following and her own across the way. *That* reassured her.

These days, even Einar himself stood up to greet her whenever she came to his house. Since her pregnancy had become so visibly obvious, he had even been prepared to yield his own High Seat to her, should she require it. But something in her still would not easily sit between those two posts: she wondered in quieter moments whether she would ever be free of their memories. At least her aunt was, now. Her mound still sat, brown and freshly turned, in the old burial-place.

So, rather than take Einar's place – although she fully understood the honour she was being accorded, thanks to her husband's patient explanations – she sat beside the pillar, and let Ragna take her own proper place beside the master here. It was nice, she reflected, to think that the tensions of previous days were gone. Now she knew she was welcome here, and Ragna was a frequent visitor in her home. Their workmen mixed and mingled, and slept in whichever house was closest at the time; Rilca was becoming more and more certain that some of that was due to the attractions of certain ladies of either house. Which, if not allowed to get out-of-hand, was probably also a good thing. They were indeed becoming one household. Svein's ambitions would bring that even closer to reality.

"So how is my brother?" Ragna began as she set cups before them both. "I've not spoken with him in a day or two."

"What with bringing all our beasts and yours together for the killing, he's been out and about. Svein says that all is well, though; Morgan's still following him like a shadow wherever he goes. Mind you, so is Bjorn, as often as not: I think they're all getting quite fond of each other these days."

"Not easy on the lad since his mothir died..."

Rilca sighed. "No, not easy at all, but still easier at his age than if he were younger, I'd say." She grimaced and stretched. "It's getting harder to even sit still just now: I get so stiff and then everywhere aches."

Ragna patted her hand. "Not much longer, though.

Then there'll be a whole new set of troubles!"

"Aye, but at least I'll be able to see my feet again," said Rilca wistfully.

"So what is it that's behind all this talk of us coming over to your houses?" asked Einar. "Svein's not given much away, and while I can see how he might want Ragna close to you when the bairn comes, he might be better thinking to put you with us, rather than the other way around."

Rilca waved a hand airily. "It might yet come to that. Our house is leaking more and more every time it rains, and we don't seem able to fix it."

"Well, then, why bother with it at all? Come back over here: make a home with us."

"Because he and I have made our place *there*... and we couldn't just up and leave Havard to it, for all that he and Danna seem to be getting on pretty well. No, what Svein's got in mind is – or ought to be – better for all of us, if we can be certain of your support in it. Because it will need your support."

"Oh come on," groaned Einar with a grin, "tell us, then! Svein's not here, and you're dropping far too many hints to leave it where you have!"

"Come the spring, he's thinking about building another house, further to the south of this one. A bigger house: he's told me that back in your old home there were houses even three times as big as this one. That's what he's got in mind."

"What, on our side of the old marker? I thought you said that you wouldn't abandon your own lads..."

Rilca leaned forward, enjoying the heat from the burning peats. "The idea is to bring them with us into this new house. And you, if you'll come. With all your own people. One house for all of us: one holding of land.

That's why we need to ask your support before we move on it."

"Well." Einar sat back with a serious expression on his face. "That's a thing to say, and no mistake. But a hard thing to ask, too, especially after the troubles I had when we first came here. This was intended to be my land, my holding, and even getting a finger-hold hasn't been easy. Well, you've been here for it all, so you know how it's been. I'm not sure that I'm so willing to give it up just yet."

"You needn't: we run our two holdings pretty much as one even now, Einar. Our people and yours flit back and forth as they're needed, and nobody's come asking for taxes or anything. But having everyone in the one house would mean less peat to cut, less food to gather and cook each day, and more chances to sit and talk without having to force our way through storms and rain!" She laughed. "It just means that things go on as before, but we're all just that little bit closer in the flesh." She looked down at the brooches adorning her breast, and the strongly-coloured fabric of her clothing. "We're already getting closer in every other way. Did you hear that Neued's bairn is born?"

Ragna nodded with a smile. "A strong and healthy lad, I was told. I'm betting Perif's playing the happy fathir again."

"That he is. They're planning on calling him Svein."

Printed in Great Britain
by Amazon